LOST CLAUSE

ELLE MAE

For those who kept this story alive even when I wanted to give up.
Without you Silvia and Keir may never have the HEA they deserve.

Also by Elle Mae

Short and Smutty:

The Sweetest Sacrifice: An Erotic Demon Romance

Nevermore: A Deal with a Demon

Blood Bound Duology:

Contract Bound: A Lesbian Vampire Romance

Lost Clause (2023)

Winterfell Academy Series:

The Price of Silence: Winterfell Academy Book 1

The Price of Silence: Winterfell Academy Book 2

The Price of Silence: Winterfell Academy Book 3

The Price of Silence: Winterfell Academy Book 4

The Price of Silence: Winterfell Academy Book 5

Other World Series:

An Imposter in Warriors Clothing

A Coward In A Kings Crown

EDEN EMORY (CONTEMP)

Club Pétale:

The Ties that Bind Us

Don't Stop Me

Don't Leave Me

Don't Forget Me (2023)

Other Worlds:

Two of a Kind

This is a work of fiction. Names, characters, places, and incidents either are the product of the author's imagination or are used fictitiously. Any resemblance to actual persons, living or dead, events, or locales is entirely coincidental.

Lost Clause

Copyright © 2023 by Elle Mae

Cover design by SeventhStarArt

www.seventhstarart.com

Edits by Corbeaux Editing

ISBN 978-1-959187-06-6 (paperback)

ISBN 978-1-959187-99-8 (ebook)

www.ellemaebooks.com

 Created with Vellum

NOTE

This is a work of fiction. Names, characters, business, events and incidents are the products of the author's imagination. Any resemblance to actual persons, living or dead, or actual events is purely coincidental. Before moving forward, please note that the themes in this book can be dark and trigger some people. Triggers can include but are not limited to: sexual assault mention, death, gore, mutilation (eggplant cutting), child abuse mention, farming humans for blood (mention), drinking blood of minors (mention), dubious consent, trafficking mention, blood play, biting, starvation, torture mention, violence, knife play.

Or visit https://www.ellemaebooks.com/triggerwarnings to view the TW for my other books as well.

If you need help, please reach out to the resources below.

National Suicide Prevention Lifeline

899

https://suicidepreventionlifeline.org/

National Domestic Violence Hotline

1-800-799-7233

https://www.thehotline.org/

LOST
CLAUSE

ELLE MAE

7333560

██████████████████Gathering Report

████████████████████████
████████████████████████████
████████████████████████████
████████████████████████████
████████████████████
███████████████████████pleaded for life
████████████████████████████
████████████████████████████
████████████ recommend keeping████████████
alive for longevity of experiments
███████████████████
████████████████████████████
little reaction while ████████████████
bed ridden for three days deserunt
████████████████████.

Will continue to monitor.

PROLOGUE

Everything hurt.

Everything from the blood rushing through my veins, to the pulsing of my all-but-dead heart in my chest and the wind whipping against my skin.

All of it was making it harder and harder to push through, but I had no choice. If I faltered just once, my life would be over.

Vampires were closing in on all sides.

I could hear their feet pounding against the soft earth behind me, matching the rhythm of my heart. There were at least twenty of them. The scent of my own blood caked on me clouded my senses, but I could smell them through the filth.

It was Keir's clan. They all had the same smokey scent to them.

Even against my wishes they had come for me. It was a painful reminder that, no matter what happened, I would never be free.

I ran through the forest surrounding the compound, not knowing at all where I was going. The scent of an oncoming rain permeated the dark forest. I had to wait for it. If I could just hang on a bit longer, I could give them the slip.

My throat burned. My body begged for blood. A disgusting revelation that was almost enough to deter me.

Shouts echoed behind me, and before I could dive out of the way, vampire hands were already grabbing at me. One tangled through my hair and sent me flying backward.

I growled, kicked, and screamed at the perpetrator. He was a young vampire who I had never seen before, but he was wearing the standard guard uniform I'd seen often in Keir's compound, so I put two and two together.

He tried to wrestle me to the ground, but I used the newfound strength in my legs to kick him right in the chest. My hands dug into the damp soil, and I pushed myself up on shaking legs.

I made the mistake of looking back at him.

He pushed himself to his feet and readied himself to lunge at me, but just as he launched himself, an arrow lodged in his forehead. His head flew back but he stayed unsteadily on his feet. It was like his body hadn't caught up with his injury and was still trying to persist. He took one, shaky step forward, his eyes wide and his mouth open, before falling to the ground in a heap.

I recognized that arrow. It was one that I'd seen often in my last few years as a vampire hunter, and even held in my hands at one point. Hope threatened to tear through my chest at the sight.

My head snapped to the direction it came from. I strained to hear the slow footsteps that were coming from all around. They were different from the vampires that were slowly gaining traction on us. They had to have been lying in wait until the perfect moment presented themselves. They were calculated as they pushed through the forest. I could make out the small whispers of the humans that commanded the small army. Then just as I hoped, they appeared.

Humans in all-black Order uniforms materialized from behind the trees. Each had their weapons drawn. Blood coursed under their skin and called to the hunger that was tearing apart my entire being.

A burst of relief filled me even as my brain sounded the alarms, telling me to run. The familiarity of them was enough to put my instincts at ease.

The hunters stopped when the vampires got close enough to show themselves. There was a pause from the other side. I didn't have to look back to know that they were staring at their dead comrade and the now handful of hunters who were poised to kill them all.

One of the hunters stood out from the rest as he continued to walk toward me. His footsteps were careful and calculated. His weapon was drawn, but as he came closer, I realized that it wasn't the vampires behind me that he was aiming at.

. . . it was me.

Just as lightning flashed above I got a glimpse of familiar dark hair and hazel eyes.

Damon.

The person who had been with me through school. The same one who had been there to help fight off the fake rebels. The same person who had spilled what I had done with Keir to the Order.

And now, in the final act of betrayal, he had a weapon pointed at my head.

It hurt more than I could rationalize in that moment. All of what happened before seemed miniscule in comparison. I was willing to forgive it all, if only he would but the weapon down.

The desperation another aspect of my own foolishness.

"Damon," I whispered. My voice cracked and my throat threatened to close. "Stop, you know me. I am one of you."

His gaze hardened, and he pulled the arrow back. There was no familiarity in his stare. It was like everything we had been through in the Order was out the window and I was no different than any other rogue vampire we were sent after.

"I signed a contract," he said in a dead tone.

His words tore at my chest. Growls surrounded us.

Desperation clawed at my insides. I didn't want this to end. Not here. Not by *him.*

"Please," I begged and inched closer to him. "You know this isn't right. I am a hunter, just like you. Your *friend.*"

He swallowed thickly before shaking his head. "You're not the only one who was offered a contract they could not refuse," he said.

"You can't. Damon—"

"I didn't know about the blood in your system before, but I guess the second time's a charm," he murmured.

The sound of arrows being shot filled the air around us. Some vampire wailed as the arrows hit them while others lunged at the hunters around us. My fight-or-flight instincts kicked in, and I rolled out of the way before planting my feet on the ground and using it as leverage to lunge at Damon.

Please give up. Please, I begged him in my mind.

But of course he wouldn't. We were hunters after all, and he was facing his number one enemy. A vampire.

His bow and arrow were knocked to the side. His arms twisted around my head, but with my strength it was but a moment before I snapped his arm.

His guttural cry echoed through the forest.

I used his stunned state to climb on top of him while pinning his arms to his sides.

"Calm!"

He jerked against my hold. This was nothing like when we were sparring. We were both fighting for our lives. All of the Order's training went out the window, and we were left with only our instincts and strength.

But he wasn't giving up even as the battle around us turned in favor of the vampires. He continued to struggle under me.

I didn't want to fight him. I didn't want to fight anyone from the Order. They were like me. Taken advantage of and thrust into a world that only used them for their skills.

Why would they do this to us?

I wanted to believe the Order would come for me, would help me. But this. . .?

I didn't realize he'd grabbed the arrow until it was lodged in my shoulder.

Pain burst across my senses, but it wasn't a normal wound. It started to burn. My entire bloodstream lit on fire, and I became paralyzed by the pain.

I fell into him. His free arm wrapped around my back and held me to him.

"I'm sorry," he whispered.

I couldn't move as the elixir worked its way through me. My mind was screaming at me to move. To sink my fangs into his flesh. His blood, it smelled so sweet, so mouthwatering. I could almost taste it on my tongue.

"Please don't make me," I whispered more to myself than anyone else.

I didn't want to be the monster they made me into. Even as my body begged for it, I was all too aware of what I was about to do. And I couldn't stomach it.

"Shh," Damon whispered. His hand stoked my knotted hair. "I'll be here to the end. You're one of us. It's the least I can do."

Rain pelted us from above and washed the sticky blood from my body. The stark coldness of it against my heated skin was the only thing to lift the cloud of pain over my mind.

Survive. I needed to *survive.* I wasn't ready to go. I had so much to see. So much to make up for. I couldn't let it end here.

Jane's face flashed through my mind, and slowly, I opened my mouth. My fangs pulsed as they trailed his skin. The rain only made his scent that much more potent.

"I'll be quick," I whispered. Guilt ate at me but it was nothing compared to the pain tearing through me. I would have time to play this time in my head over and over until it made me sick, but in that moment I could only do one thing.

"Silvia—"

I clamped my hand over his mouth and sank my fangs into his skin. They cut through it like a knife to butter.

Hot, sweet blood filled my mouth. I moaned as the taste of it burst across my taste buds and chased away the burning in my throat. Warmth exploded inside me and mixed with the blood as it traveled through my body.

Blood was like unlike anything I had ever tasted before. It was strong, spicy yet sweet, thick enough to coat my tongue and throat but moved like water through my body. It caused my entire body to vibrate.

The only comparable human flavor would have been something along the lines of a sweet berry with a spicy tang at the end but it was so much more potent. It was the world's most powerful drug, so intoxicating and downright addictive.

He tried, and failed, to stop me from sucking the life out of him. His tears mixed with the rain and pooled in my mouth. I'd planned to stop once I regained my strength, but it became impossible to pull away. Each gulp of blood warmed my body in a way I had never experienced before.

It washed away the pain. The feeling of helplessness. I

could feel it strengthening my muscles and feeding me energy. And then there was nothing.

I pulled away to see Damon's wide-eyed, empty stare.

I hadn't even heard his last breath.

There was a rustling behind me. I stopped and turned to face the newest enemy. Another guard, but this one was injured in the battle. He was clutching the arrow that was stuck in his stomach. His face was contorted in pain and his breath came out in pants.

I needed to run. Even now, among the bodies of hunters and vampires, I knew it would be moments before I was surrounded again.

Against every thought in my head, I pulled the arrow out of my arm and threw it to the ground before stepping toward him. He stared at me but did not move to grab me.

"Give Keir this message," I said and gripped the arrow still lodged in him.

He let out a pained moaned.

"If she comes after me again, I will personally see the downfall of her clan."

With that I pulled out the arrow. His mouth opened to scream but no sound came out. I threw the arrow to the ground next to mine and turned to leave.

I cast a single glance back to Damon's body. Shame, disgust, and hurt washed through me all at once. It wasn't supposed to be like this. *I* wasn't supposed to be like this.

I leaned down to close his eyes.

"I will kill them all," I vowed.

The Order. The captain. Everyone who helped to put me in the dungeon. Everyone who had ruined my life until now and stolen every possibility of happiness I *almost* had.

Another set of footsteps came to my right, and I let out a sigh. A vampire ran past me in a blur. My gaze snapped to them, and I was met with the image of a vampire I had never seen before tearing the guard's head off his shoulders without so much as a second thought.

So much for my message.

"Hunter turned vampire," a familiar airy voice called just barely above the sound of the rain. "I never tend to trust Order intel, but I guess sometimes they can surprise you."

I looked to the new intruder and my heart dropped into my stomach.

A man I had only seen once stood with two vampires by his side. Both dressed in casual clothes, one held an umbrella for the man, but they themselves stayed out in the rain.

The man in the middle had stark white hair that stood up at all ends. His black eyes were starting to turn red, and there was a smirk spreading across his scarred face.

Tobias.

Just like before there was an aura around him, and even though I was a vampire now, the difference between us was palpable. He stood there with his shoulders hunched over and an easy-going expression, but just below the surface lingered something dangerous. And it was *watching* me.

He waved the vampires away from his side and stepped out into the rain. He walked until he was right in front of me and held out a gangly, pale hand.

"If you're here to kill me I won't go easy," I growled.

His eyes narrowed, and the smirk on his face only grew wider.

"If I wanted to kill you, you'd be dead by now," he mumbled. "I come to offer my support."

He pushed his hand closer to me. I eyed it with suspicion.

"I can keep you safe," he said. "In the Underground. No one would know you're there. Not the Order. Not Keir. You could be *free* from their burdens."

I looked toward the vampire behind me. He was eyeing me warily and just waiting for his master to give him the command to off me.

"And what do you get out of it?" I asked as I turned back to him.

His eyes lit up at that. "Your services," he said. "We could use a hunter in our midst. Come work for me, and I promise you shelter and safety. It's as simple as that."

Nothing is as simple as that. But nonetheless, his offer intrigued me. We both knew at this point I had no one to turn to. I was on the run from the two most powerful organizations in this area, and I would last but a few days until they found me.

It didn't matter how good of a hunter I once was.

They would send hundreds after me. The Order had already proven as much, and if they didn't blink at blowing up a building full of humans for a single vampire, there was no telling what they would do to get me out of the picture.

Slowly I placed my hand in his. The coldness of his skin shocked me so much that I tried to jerk my hand away, but his long fingers gripped my hand, stopping me. I stood up on shaky legs, taking in a calming breath as his powerful aura washed over me.

"I work for you, you provide me safety," I breathed. "Nothing else."

His smile was so wide even my cheeks began to ache.

"I am an immortal of my words, Silvia," he purred and turned to lead me out of the forest. "Let me take your new home. While the others *clean up.*"

He pulled through the trees as the sound of more hunters began to fill the forest.

I looked back to see the three vampires getting ready.

"They will be slaughtered," I said.

Tobias let out a soft chuckle.

"They may surprise you yet, Silvia," he said and sent me a look. "Maybe you can learn a thing or two from them while you are under my care."

I let out a scoff that was drowned out by the clashing of the vampires behind us.

"Come," he whispered. "To your new life."

I didn't realize then how lucky I had been to get on Tobias's good side. Over the years I would come to understand that the hand that held mine so gently was the same that ordered the murder of thousands without so much as a falter.

But it was also the same hand that molded me into what I needed to be. *Who* I needed to be.

The Silvia that was once would cease to exist as soon as I entered the tunnels underground, but until then I allowed myself one last moment in the rain, imagining all the ways I could get back at those who hurt me.

CHAPTER 1
SILVIA
TWO YEARS LATER

From the outside, I looked like a hunter.

I kept a similar uniform. A turtleneck with tight black pants, though these ones had many more pockets that those cheap Order-approved leggings. I kept the diamond-encrusted dagger on my thigh and layered on a harness that went around my shoulders and torso.

It was the perfect battle-ready outfit.

I didn't fully understand why I gravitated toward a hunter uniform. Maybe it was because I was secretly missing my work at the Order, or maybe it was because being a hunter was the only other thing I could cling to.

I didn't have a family. I didn't have a lover. And Tobias wasn't exactly what you would call a friend. I had no hobbies, no place of my own. . . I really was just floating along until I got to this *very* moment.

The one where I would get back at all those who'd fucked me over.

It had been a long time coming. Night after sleepless night I ran through this moment in my mind until it was numb.

I didn't try to sneak across the property. Instead, I jumped right over the back wall of the compound and walked toward the large manor without a worry in the world.

The Kazimir clan's compound was not much different from Keir's. I remembered seeing the building that was reserved for the event, with all the hunters lining the perimeter, and thinking that it was too overboard.

Their manor was even worse.

While it was in the same New England style as Keir's, it spanned far wider than hers. The main house was big enough to fit hundreds while the surrounding properties were stacked tall, all with their own sprawling yards and hedges. It was its very own world and separated from the outside by just a poorly kept wall.

Night had fallen long ago, and the small cool breeze that would have once felt unbearable to my human form, felt nice against my reinforced skin. There were only a few lights that littered the property, giving me the perfect cover in the shadows. Luckily, I had memorized the layout from the years of planning and followed a forgotten path that led through the garden and into the basement.

The old door that divided the manor from the garden was weak enough that I easily broke off the handle and pushed my way in, the only thing giving me away was the small creak of the metal echoing throughout the empty hall. I paused, listening for anyone coming my way, but there was not even a whisper as I shut the door behind me.

The manor was silent as I walked the halls. Even the vampires seemed to retire for the night. I could hear some of them on the floors above, drinking from their various feeders, others just existing, maybe reading or something else. . .but none of them minded me.

Walking through the halls, I passed room after room until I got to the main staircase.

I could hear the moans of a feeder coming from the floor above, and I smiled when I heard Vance's groan. It was the same one that was permanently etched into my brain along with the feeling of his fangs slicing through my soft human skin.

Perfect.

I stalked up the stairs, careful to not call too much attention to myself. As I got closer to where Vance was, I could tell that he wouldn't even pay me any mind. He was fucking the feeder.

I guessed he was in one of the various feeding rooms that were littered around the house, which was not where he normally had been. After all my research, I had only heard of him being in his room and his study for these sessions.

Shaking off my suspicion, I carefully snuck up on the door.

"That's it, baby," Vance cooed from beyond.

The feeder let out a loud moan. Her breathing was ragged and I could smell the mixing of their scents. The sound of slapping skin disgusted me, but regardless, I took a deep breath and opened the door. Vance didn't even pause in his thrusts as I entered.

"Harder," the feeder gasped. "Yes, *Vance.*"

The room was about the size of a bedroom, with only a few loveseats available, and instead of fucking the feeder in the chair, Vance had her on her knees, her face on the ground, and he pounded into her from behind.

Unfortunately, his bare ass was the first thing I saw as I walked in.

"Wait your turn," he grunted. "I'll be finished soon."

I let out a light laugh. The sound caused him to freeze and slowly his shocked face turned to lock eyes with mine.

A thrill ran through me.

How many times had I daydreamed of this? Too many to count but nothing even compared to seeing the panic flush through him. In a single moment I could see every insignificant memory flash cross his mind as his brain worked out what to do.

"Hi, Vance," I said in the sweetest tone I could muster.

He let out a shriek and pushed the human away from him. His abrupt actions forced him to the ground as he lost balance.

"Silvia? Is that you—"

"Yes," I answered and pulled out my dagger. His eyes dropped to it as it sparkled in the dim light. His face contorted, and he scrambled into a kneeling position, forcing his face to the dirty ground. He was still half-clothed, and the whole thing was just so humiliating.

The action angered me. I didn't want to see a vampire bow to me again. I was not royalty, no matter what my killing of the previous king did, and I never wanted to be.

"Please forgive me, my lady." He shuddered. The title caused my mouth to sour. "I have had time to reflect on my—"

"Leave us," I commanded the human who lay in a heap on the ground. She blinked rapidly before slowly standing. She didn't bother to try and find her garments as she left.

When the door clicked behind her, I rushed at Vance. He jumped up, flailing his arms around as he tried to find his balance, and tried to run away.

But I was faster.

I tangled my hand in his hair and forced his head back. The anger that had been festering inside me for all these years had come boiling up to the surface.

I wanted so badly to slit his throat. . . but that would be far too easy. He needed to suffer. He needed to feel what it felt like to be at the hands of someone far more powerful than him while he could do nothing but squirm.

"You're gonna regret you ever touched me," I growled and with quick movements I placed the tip of my dagger against his still-erect dick. I let out a laugh when it twitched. "Oh no, don't tell me you're a masochist?"

"Please, Silvia," he begged. "I promise I can make it—"

His scream filled the air as I sliced his pathetic dick off. That was it. The moment I had been waiting for. I had salivated over the idea of making him pay in a way that would guarantee he would suffer. I thought that this moment would bring me all the closure I was hoping for.

I basked in his screams and waited for the euphoria to hit me. . . but it never did. Seconds if not minutes ticked by and instead of the rush I was expecting, I was left with a sinking feeling.

I was...disgusted.

I hated this vampire. Hated him with my entire being, yet I still felt like there was something *missing*.

Throwing his writhing body away in disgust, I stood and readied my weapon. I would let him suffer for a few minutes before ending his life. I froze as three sets of footsteps sounded outside the door.

They were quick and light which only meant one thing. . . they were trained.

I cursed under my breath.

There was only one way out of this room and no place to hide. I would need to fight my way out.

I held my breath as the door was pushed open, my hand grasping my dagger so hard my fingers began to ache.

My entire world froze when I saw a tall messy-black-haired man enter the room, with a strikingly obvious golden emblem in the middle of his Order uniform. Hunters, but not just any hunters. *Enforcers.* The ones who kept the hunters in line. The ones who threw me in the Dark Room at my time in the Order. They didn't care about hunters, they only cared about enforcing the rules.

They were the worst of the worst.

But these weren't any enforcers. I knew them.

Behind him trailed the black-haired witch, and Jase, the vampire enforcer, after him.

Keep a look out for hunters. . .

That *bastard*!

Tobias had to have set me up.

I let out a growl and crouched as Isaac stepped forward. He was the leader of this so-called faction. He raised his hands, and I noted that none of them had weapons. I eyed the witch carefully.

"Silvia," Isaac said. "We mean you no harm."

I let out another growl.

"Fuck *off*," I hissed. "I don't want anything to do with the—"

"We need your help." The witch spoke up. I don't remember him speaking last time, and the raw emotion in his voice made me pause.

They need my help?

I stood slowly, but kept my dagger in my hand.

"Where are the others?" I asked and tried to listen for more heartbeats. There were two missing. "I expect they are waiting to ambush me when I walk out of here?"

The witch's face dropped.

"They are gone," Isaac said. "His brother and Chase. . . they went missing. Just like the rest. Just like what I *told* you would happen."

The anger in his voice took me by surprise.

They had mentioned this, back when we were a part of the

Order. Hunters had been going missing for years. Many of their teammates and the people who had the highest ranking in the Order. They were highly trained, and deadly, yet there was something amiss.

Each of them somehow turned up dead while on missions or just never returned at all.

And now it had hit too close to home.

I looked over Knox, the black-haired witch, with a heavy sense of grief in my chest. It made me uncomfortable to realize just how much I had come to care about the people and the organization that tried to kill me.

But I too had felt what it was like to lose family. To lose a sibling. It was like the other part of you had been ripped away and you were nothing but half of a soul.

I couldn't let this sway me. I had a job to do and anything that would make me doubt myself, and my actions, had no room in my life.

Jase's hand squeezed his shoulder, and he took a hesitant step forward.

"We need your help, Silvia," Jase said. "Our hunters are still dying, and we cannot stop it. We had hoped that you could help but. . ."

"I died," I finished for him.

Sighing, I shifted on my feet and stared at Vance. He was holding back tears as his dick healed itself. Unfortunately, this wouldn't kill him. . . but at least he would think twice before biting someone like me again.

"You won't let me go, will you?" I asked and turned back to look at Isaac.

Isaac stepped to the side and motioned toward the door.

"Go ahead," he said.

My slow beating heart stopped, and the breath was stolen out of my lungs. *I could. . . go?*

"Just. . ." The witch's voice trailed off, and he looked up at me with a sorrowful expression. "Ash. . . he—they took my brother, and we just thought that you—"

"I don't understand what you want from me," I said and walked toward them, ready to take the exit they provided.

I knew what he was trying to do. I wouldn't fall for it.

"How much did you know about your parents' role in the Order?" Jase asked and stepped in front of me, blocking my exit.

"Not much," I said with a shrug. "Just knew they were good at what they did."

There was a pause as Jase looked to Isaac.

"Seven three three three five six zero," Isaac said, his eyes drilling into mine. "Do you recognize that number?"

Images of Raphael and his guards forcing blood into my system flashed through my mind. They too had tried to prod me for these numbers while torturing me.

What the hell did my mom have to do with all of these people?

"Why?" I asked through clenched teeth.

Jase let out a sigh.

"Come with us and we will explain," he said. "Not to the Order. Not to Keir's. Not to wherever you have been staying. . . come *home* with us, and we'll walk you through what we know."

Trap. Alarm bells went off in my head. I had been running for *two years*, them reaching out to me now was suspicious, no matter what stories they spewed.

I would have liked to trust them, especially given the expression on Knox's face when he talked about his brother, but my survival was key.

I let out a growl and pushed Isaac to the side.

"Don't look for me again," I warned.

A hand shot out to grasp my shoulder, but I was too quick

18

for them. I was out of the door and running down the hallway before they could even yell. Footsteps chased after me, and Vance's cries echoed down the hallway.

Sirens ran through the silent night, and a twisted smirk played at my lips.

This was the thrill I had been waiting for.

Fuck the vampires. Fuck the Order. I would bend to no one.

Not anymore.

CHAPTER 2
KEIR

T threw my blood-filled goblet at the vampires sitting across from me.

In an instant everyone was standing up, and loud growls rumbled from their chest.

The head and staff from the Waita clan had shown up on our doorstep at two in the morning without an invitation, and now they dare insult me like this?

They were a smaller clan based in Oregon but had a reputation similar to my father's reign. They had built their place through blood and violence. An ally on most occasions, but now they had shown their *true* colors.

The dining room was dim save for a few lit candles. The air was tense, and the once calm quiet had turned to something more volatile. There were only three of them. We could fight them if push came to shove. Gil was at my side in a flash, and I could hear the footsteps and slow beating hearts of our guards waiting outside the door.

The white tablecloth was stained with blood, some of our last bit of supply. I cursed my own foolishness, but it was quickly burned up in the anger that flashed through my veins.

The king, Anthony, waved off his right hand. His fair hair shimmered in the light, and his bright red eyes cut through the darkness. The vampire beside him, looked much like a mini version of the king. He was most likely his son. The only difference between the two was the hint of impulsiveness that wavered behind the younger's glowing red eyes.

I could see right through his thoughts. After all, I had been just like him once. Ruled by my anger and wanting to destroy anything in my path.

Then I was forced to rule while the real clan head hid out, refusing to show her face. It had changed my whole outlook on the position I was born into. Though that didn't mean I liked it any more than I once had.

There was a time where the title had looked shiny and enticing, especially when Father was still holding it. But the truth was hidden in moments like this. The politics of it all was enough to drive me insane, and no matter how innocent my cause had seemed, the world seemed stacked against me.

Wanting to protect your clan was not enough. It never was.

"You dare insult me?" I asked. "In my home?"

Gil shifted besides me as the guards filed through the door.

"You are weakening," Anthony spat. His narrowed gaze shot to mine. "If it is not I to come warn you about what is to come then it would be your own people who try to see you fall. I am offering a way out."

"A way out?" I asked with a bitter laugh. "You want to *take*. You think that *I* am unable to provide for my clan. That I am not fit to run—"

"Because you are not!" the younger one jumped in. "You are not fit to rule because you *are not* the ruler."

His words hit me square in the chest. I gripped the side of

21

the table and took a deep, calming breath, but it did nothing to clear the red that had covered my vision. The table splintered in my grip.

I may not be the true leader but that did not mean that I hadn't been here for *two years* running this clan as if I were. But no one saw it. No one saw just how much I had put into making sure the people here were taken care of.

With another deep breath, I stood and straightened my dress shirt before turning to the guard. No matter how much I wanted to lunge at them, I had better things to do than to entertain their absurd "offer."

"See them out," I ordered, then turned back to Anthony. "And if they are ever caught on these grounds again, uninvited, I want them executed on sight."

The guards came to their sides to grab them, but Anthony shooed them away.

"This is a warning, Keir." His tone was dark, and his posture had straightened. "Your people will leave. You have no blood. You cannot renew your Order contracts. You will lose everything. You are a clan without a king."

"Thank you for the warning." Gil spoke for me before the small thread that was holding me back broke completely. "Though our clan's business is just that. Our own. Now leave, before Keir changes her mind."

They shifted before turning and leaving the dining room. Their eyes were on me, but I couldn't tear mine away from the blood staining the tablecloth.

It had been like this for *two years*.

And the worst part was that Anthony was not too far off with his guesses about what was happening to the clan.

The people were waiting for their leader who had yet to show. News had traveled fast, and the gossip started quickly after it. The halls were filled with whispers about Silvia and I.

About how I was too much of a coward to take the throne and how demeaning it had been to have it be stolen by a *hunter* of all people.

They were leaving us in droves. What was once a bustling compound was now reduced to half its size. Money was never a problem, but we were lacking power.

Kings were not just for ruling over the compound and its various businesses.

They were a key role in negotiations with other clans and the Order. Without the proper head, the Order would not let us renew our contract, and therefore, our blood supply was being slowly cut off.

It was a miracle that they had let us continue for so long without shutting off our supply. But my guess was that they got a sick satisfaction in seeing the slow ruin of my clan.

Soon, we would be starving. Soon, the vampires who once belonged to the most powerful clan in the world would have to hunt for their food on the streets.

Making them the perfect victims for the hunters. It was just another excuse they needed to start killing us off.

"Keir. . ." Gil's voice trailed off. His hand squeezed my shoulder, forcing a sigh out of me.

I looked out the window and out to the compound. Just in time to see Anthony's limo leaving from the gates, but he wasn't alone. Two more cars followed, and I had no doubt it was two other families packing their bags and leaving.

Maybe Anthony had even been kind enough to offer them a spot in his clan.

"Have we heard *anything*?" I snapped.

I didn't mean for it to come out so harsh. Gil didn't need that. He had stuck by me through everything. The least he deserved was a little compassion.

I turned to look at him. A knot had slowly risen in my

23

throat, and when I met his gleaming blue eyes, it swelled. His light hair was dim in the candlelit room, and there were bags under his eyes.

He was half-human, so the late nights were horrible to him, but at least he would never have to worry about starving from the lack of blood.

He had been the right hand to my father, but even without a clan head, he stayed and acted as my right hand instead. Something I could never repay him for.

"She has been quiet," he answered. "All the free guards are out looking for her, but they haven't caught sight. Keir, I know you don't want to—"

He was cut off by the sound of someone running down the hallway. A vampire. I could tell by how fast he was moving. The vampire burst through the doors, heaving. I recognized him as one of the ones we had put in charge of trying to find our clan head. Him and his team had been working with me for the last two years, though we had been unsuccessful in finding her.

I had an inkling that she had been taken in, but had no idea who would have been stupid enough to do it.

"Kazimir estate!" he gasped through breaths. "She's at the estate!"

I was out the door before he could stand upright.

"The car will take us twenty minutes if we speed," I said as I rushed down the hallway.

"It will be too long," Gil added on as he followed closely behind.

A lean figure with glowing red eyes in the hallway cleared its throat. In the moonlight, I could just make out the smirk spreading across her face.

Emery. Her long golden hair that was pulled into a low ponytail at the nape of her neck shone in the dim lighting. Tan skin peeked out from her skintight vest. Beneath it was a white button-up that was stained with blood. She lifted her gloved hand, the sound of keys clanking in the tense silence of the hallway.

I'd realized quickly that Gil and I wouldn't be enough to run this clan. We needed someone who wouldn't hesitate to bring the hammer down. One who didn't hesitate to kill even the most innocent-looking vampires.

I thought once that I was capable of doing anything for my clan, for Silvia. . . but I was nothing compared to the monster in front of me. A title that she wore with pride.

What she wanted in return was minuscule compared to what she offered us.

"Five minutes by helicopter," she said and fell into step beside me as we rushed through the house.

"We don't have a helicopter," I grumbled, but a part of me was bubbling with excitement at the notion of what she had done to get it.

"Now we do," she said, the smile in her voice clear.

"Keir," Gil warned from behind us.

"Out in the courtyard, my queen," Emery said as we came to the double front doors.

I reached out to grasp the keys from her hand, but she was too quick. In an instant she was slipping out the door, keys still in her hand, with a smile.

"Shotgun." Gil cut through and ran after her.

With a curse I followed after them.

Sirens cut through the sounds of the helicopter blades and the extra-cushioned headphones we were provided.

I leaned as close as possible to the window to look at the Kazimir estate.

Vampires and hunters alike were swarming the place. They all paused to look up at us as we descended. Many of them looked panicked and ready to fight. There was a light-purple magical shield that parted for us as we entered the air space. It was a shaky landing, but I had to hand it to her, she didn't kill us on the way over.

I cursed as a group of familiar hunters waited near the entrance for us.

"We're too late," I said through our connected headphones. Emery turned off the helicopter and opened her mouth to say something, but I threw my headphones somewhere in the helicopter and was out and running across the field before it had even stilled.

My heart dropped into my stomach as I came to a stop in front of the three hunters that I had worked closely with the last few years. Something I would have never thought I would do, but we had a common goal. We all needed Silvia.

Isaac's dark eyes bore into me. At his side was Knox. The black-haired witch with piercing gray eyes looked to the ground. Jase, the vampire, met me head on with his gaze. He had grown his hair out long enough that it needed to be secured at the base of his neck.

But if they were here first, it meant that they had betrayed the rules we had set in place for a moment just like this.

"Why didn't you warn me—"

"It was a setup," Isaac interrupted. He looked down at me with that blank expression that caused irritation to prick at my senses. "We weren't sure she'd come at all."

"If she'd smelled you, she would have bolted even faster," Jase added on.

I let out a growl and looked at the sprawling land around us.

It was a *fucking* mess. Vampires were waiting for orders, their eyes trained on me, and the hunters were ready with their weapons. I only now noted that *all* of them were enforcers. The gold emblems in the middle of their chests were like beacons.

"She went after Vance," Gil noted from behind me. I didn't even hear him come up. "Where is he?"

"Trying to reattach his dick before his wound heals over," Jase said.

My gaze snapped over to him. There was a small smile playing at his lips.

"His dick?" I asked, my own smile pulling at my lips. "I thought she was after his head."

"Wrong head," Jase muttered.

Isaac glared at him in warning before turning back to me.

"She's on the grounds still," he said. "Knox helped us put up a perimeter, and no one will be allowed in or out unless we say so. We didn't want to call the rest of the hunters for fear the captain would be on to us, but we know we won't be able to catch her on our own."

A tenseness rose between us. The one point of contention between us reared its ugly head.

A sort of possessiveness washed over me and my hackles raised.

"We are taking her back," I growled. "The Order can go fuck themselves."

Isaac's facial expression did not so much as twitch, but the two behind him shifted uncomfortably.

"She is our clan head," I continued. "Two years we have been without her. We *need* her."

"Your clan will be fine," Isaac said. "My teammates won't be."

My entire body went on edge. Isaac's hand shot to the weapon on his hip while the two behind him tensed.

"Keir," Gil warned. "We don't even know if we can successfully—"

"I don't care," I spat and looked the hunter up and down. "We spoke about this. Nothing has changed. My clan comes first—"

"Priorities change," Isaac said. "You can have her after we are done."

The growl that ripped through my chest was inhuman.

I was ready to lunge at him when Emery ran past me in a blur, her excited chuckle spilling from her lips. Panic flashed through me when I assumed she was going to attack the hunters, but she ran right past them.

The entire group straightened, and I leaned to the side and watched her run across the courtyard and to the far side of the manor.

Then I saw the flash of red.

Silvia.

She was running toward us. The image of her in hunter-like clothes hit me square in the chest and knocked my breath out of my lungs. Her eyes were bright red, the same red as her curly hair that was now tied up in a high ponytail.

Blood was smeared across her face, neck, and hands. Just like *that* night, I was taken aback by how beautiful she looked. Vampirism was made for Silvia. She looked just like she had all those years ago, but there was a sharpness to her features, and whatever hesitation she had as a human seemed to up and disappear with her turn.

She was stronger, a hell of a lot faster, and positively deadly.

And coming right toward us.

Emery lunged toward her, but Silvia was a millisecond faster and pivoted, causing Emery to tumble to the ground.

I rushed forward with Jase at my heels. Silvia's eyes widened when she saw me, and she dug her heels into the ground. I lunged forward to grab ahold of her ankle, but she hightailed it right back the way she came.

She was fast. *Too* fucking fast. She had appeared like a vision in front of me after years, and she was just about to slip out of my grasp.

I couldn't let it end like this. I needed her back. For the clan. For our blood supply. For *me*.

"Jase!" I growled.

"Fucking on it!" he yelled back and took my place behind Silvia.

A crazed smile flitted across her face, and she turned to slam her fist straight into Jase's nose. A sickening crush echoed across the courtyard.

It was the thing that caused the various hunters and vampires around us to burst into action.

"No!"

"Stand down!"

Isaac and I spoke at the same time, but unlike him, I had no power among the vampires. They were poised to attack, but not Silvia. There was only one person who had power over the vampires in this courtyard, and it was the person who wanted it the least.

The vampires began attacking the hunters. All they saw was a fellow clan head, regardless of what she had done to their heir apparent, in danger. They were allied with us and would stop at nothing to protect a fellow clan head.

It was *us* against the hunters. *Always.*

"Stand down!" I growled at them.

None of them heeded my words.

Emery was back up and running toward Silvia before I could stop her.

Silvia froze as she caught sight of Emery. Then slowly she stood and let out a crazed laugh. The sound sank deep into my skin, and burst of fear hit me in the face like a slap.

"Get the witch!"

It was like a switch. Every red-eyed vampire looked toward Knox.

"Gil!" I yelled. "The helicopter!"

He was already rushing the two hunters toward the helicopter without a second to waste. I didn't like the Order, nor any of the hunters.

They were a selfish organization that fed on people's trauma and roped them into a debt that they would only be able to pay off through death. They took advantage of the clans, and when one didn't want to comply, they made getting blood hard and would do anything they could to eradicate the remaining vampires who hadn't been killed off by starvation.

But the enforcers, we had something in common. Not only did they hate the Order as much as we did, but they wanted answers, they wanted out.

And the only way for us to do that was with Silvia.

With a growl I ran toward Jase who was still lying on the ground as his face tried to heal itself. I grabbed him by his shoulder and threw him over my back. He was fucking heavy.

I shot a glance over to Emery and Silvia, who were in close combat.

They were faster than even my eyes could keep up with.

A part of me worried for Silvia's safety, but the other part realized how badly I needed our clan head back.

"End this!" I yelled. "We are retreating."

Emery let out a noise. "I'm trying!"

The barrier around the compound flickered in and out until

it disappeared entirely, leaving the only cage we had for Silvia wide open. There wasn't so much as a pause before our clan head realized and bolted.

The world slowed and I was forced to watch as my nightmare came true *again*.

We had worked so hard to get her back. We needed her. Our people were going to die if this lasted any longer. There were already people who had begun to show signs of malnutrition. Even I had reduced my consumption to a tenth of what it used to be to protect the little bit of excess we'd saved.

Bright blue ropes shot past me and attempted to wrap around Silvia's body, but just as they were about to enclose her, they disappeared.

I shot a look back toward the helicopter to see Knox turning his focus to the vampires who were trying to board the helicopter as it shakily lifted from the ground.

I cursed under my breath.

Emery was by my side in a second, her breath coming in pants.

"Keir, we need to—"

"I know." I sighed and looked back to the place where Silvia once was. The only evidence that she was actually here was the torn-up yard and the bloodstain on the grass. And just like that, she was a ghost again. The only thing keeping her alive were my memories.

Two years I had been chasing her. She haunted me every waking moment, and I knew that if I could dream she'd be there too.

I was tired. So *so* tired.

I had thought when it was all said and done that I would finally have a chance to be *free*. I didn't know what that meant anymore, just that I didn't want to do this any longer. I loved my clan, my people, but I didn't want to be in charge anymore. I didn't know how to continue on.

Over and over again I had proven to them that I was a *failure*. Not only did I give my title away to a hunter, but she had run away from it, leaving my clan in a cycle of constantly having to pray that they would get blood every month.

They were leaving the clan, and *me*, because of this failure.

I knew I was being selfish by pushing all this onto Silvia in hopes that I wouldn't have to deal with it. . . but honestly I just wanted her *here*. All these mountains of issues would seem much smaller if she was by my side.

The last few years had been a wake-up call.

I wasn't the immature vampire I once was. I didn't spend my days partying or trying to run away from the future that loomed before me.

No.

No matter how much of a failure I was, I wouldn't turn my back on my clan or the future waiting for us. I would try, again and again, until I could safely say that we were thriving.

But there was one unrealistic image that kept popping into my mind when I thought of the future.

It was Silvia. Waiting for me with open arms. Something she would never do but made me yearn for the future nonetheless.

"Enough!" I growled as anger boiled my blood.

How many times would we have to sit through this? How many times would I be forced to come face-to-face with the fact that even though I had been brought up to rule, I continued to fall short?

A silence fell over the area, and the Kazimir clan's guards slowly retreated. Now that the true leader was gone, I was next in line for them to look to.

It was annoying, that I would always come second, but I

would bear it. For her. I would use the hurt and anger to push forward. Because there was one thing I was certain of.

No matter how far she ran, or how much she hated me. . . I would be getting her back and to her rightful place.

As queen, ruling by my side, for all eternity.

CHAPTER 3
SILVIA

T he vampires residing in the underground tunnel must have felt my anger because as soon as I descended the stairs a quiet fell over the rooms.

The tunnels spanned far under the city, and each room was assigned to a vampire and their family, so even through the silence, I could hear their slow heartbeats behind the doors and the hushed whispers of them gossiping. The concrete didn't do much to hide their words.

Maybe this time she will actually be exiled.

She's going to get killed.

Did you hear? She cut the heir's dick off!

My lips twitched at the last comment. Word travels fast, though I'd hoped it would. I wouldn't be surprised if there were already articles and blog posts being published about it.

At bare minimum I hoped that it would push the various news outlets to take a look at what Vance was doing in the shadows. If not, I would be there to finish what I started.

But there was something bigger I needed to take care of. My mind was buzzing with thoughts about the Order, about

Keir. . . but first I needed to know why the hell Tobias thought it would be okay to sell me out like he had.

I didn't even bother waiting at Tobias's door and instead just pushed it open. He was sitting where I left him last, a small smile spreading across his face.

"Quite the show," he said. The amusement was obvious in his tone.

I slammed the door behind me and stalked toward his desk. I didn't stop until my boots hit the wood of the desk, and I shot my hand forward to tangle in the back of his messy hair. I pulled his head back harshly and leaned toward his face.

He didn't so much as flinch as I snarled, "You sold me out."

The smile only spread across his face further. "They merely wanted to speak with you," he said. His hand circled around my wrist, and without even blinking, he squeezed so hard I was forced to pull away from him entirely.

I clutched my hand to my chest, pain running through my body, but it wasn't just because of what he did to my wrist.

"I trusted you," I whispered. "What could you have possibly gotten out of that?"

His smile faltered. "What did they tell you?"

I swallowed thickly. "They knew my mother's number," I said. "And they asked for my help. The enforcers. . . their numbers have been dwindling."

He nodded and leaned back in his chair with a sigh.

"The Order has been looking into us," Tobias said after a pause. "They were warning us of a planned visit from some of their hunters."

Fear froze the blood in my veins.

A *visit* from the Order. The Underground wasn't something they should know about, or if they did they have never publicly stated anything. Even as a hunter I had no idea this place existed until I came here with Keir.

"They're coming for me," I whispered. My eyes fell to the bloodied floor. This place would never stand a chance. They would come here and tear the place apart. The vampires who hid behind the concrete walls would be killed if the Order found them in violation of our rules.

I never thought I cared much about the vampires, even after I had changed. . . but knowing the cruelty of the Order, I suspected that this would become a bloodbath like no one had ever seen.

"There is no hiding it," he murmured. "They offered to take you in. To hide you. It was I who asked for them to give you a fighting chance."

My eyes drifted back up to his. A bittersweet feeling washed over me. He wanted to save me in a way that would make me feel horrible about what was going to happen to them. It was a guilt trip. One that I fell for too easily.

"How long?" I asked. "We can evacuate down the tunnels—"

"No time," he said with a soft smile. "And don't you worry. My people are working to clean up everything as we speak. We will be fine."

I shifted on my feet.

"But the feeders—"

"We will be *fine*," he reiterated and stood slowly. He placed a hand on the desk while the other brushed across the dagger still strapped to my thigh. The one now stained with Vance's blood. "As long as you are not here."

I couldn't stop the flinch. Just like that, after two years, I would be out on my own again. A fresh wave of hurt flashed through, me but I clamped down on the feeling hard.

"I'll pack my stuff and leave within the hour," I said and took a step back, but his hand caught me.

The serious look on his face caught me by surprise.

"There is a way that you can guarantee your own survival," he said.

I gritted my teeth and tried to pull away, but his grip was strong. "Why are you so concerned with my survival?" I asked. "I am nothing to you."

His lips twitched. "I see myself in you," he said softly. "Centuries ago, after my own family was murdered in front of my eyes, I did everything to ensure that I would survive. My perception has changed over the years, but can still remember how it felt to be a newly changed vampire and feeling like the world has turned its back on you."

I swallowed my emotions. I couldn't hear this right now. Not when he was pushing me out. He had been one of the only constants in my life for the past two years. The only person who had never tried to mold me into something I wasn't.

"You don't know anything about me," I spat.

He raised a brow. "I know far too much about you, Silvia," he murmured. "But mostly because I *was* you. That's why I know your survival should be at the forefront of your mind. Your plans for revenge and to get back at the Order will be short-lived if you do not take advantage of the opportunities that have shown themselves to you. No matter how unwanted they may be."

"No," I growled.

I didn't want the title. I didn't want anything that this shitty universe had given me. Keir's face flashed through my mind, and it took all my strength not to flinch at the hurt look that had spread across her face as I ran.

"Why are you so afraid of power?" he asked. "You could have everything you ever wanted. Money, safety. . . revenge. All you have to do is *take it*."

His tone was grave, and it caused the hair on the back of my neck to stand up. The tension in the room was stifling, and the feeling of his power brushing across mine caused my skin to tingle.

"I'm not afraid," I lied. "I just don't want it."

"Don't want the title. . . or don't want Keir?"

His words were like an arrow straight to the heart.

"You get nothing out of me taking the throne," I said. "I don't understand why you—"

"Of course I expect repayment of everything I provided over the last two years," he said, a smile tugging the sides of his mouth. "You think your half-assed work killing my feeders would gain you any favors?"

When I stayed silent, he loosened his grip on me and allowed me to take a step back.

"But either way," he said and cleared his throat. His eyes trailed the room before landing back on mine. "I wish you safety, and right now that is not with me, and I doubt the enforcers will last long given that two of their own were already taken."

My mouth went dry. *Of course he already knew.* I shouldn't have tried to hide anything in the first place.

"Think about it," he said. "But you will need to leave, and it is your choice where you end up. If I were you I'd take advantage of the warm bed and compound full of waitstaff, but to each his own."

I nodded and turned to leave. "Thank you," I said with more difficulty than I expected. "For the last two years. I know I wasn't the best worker, but I couldn't have made it this far without you."

He let out a small chuckle.

"I know." He said it like he knew how it grated on my nerves. "To make the deal even sweeter. . ." I turned back to him. His hand was covering the bottom half of his face but the crazed smile was evident. "If you do find yourself taking over the throne, I will hand deliver Captain Moore's head to your feet."

I froze. My entire body went haywire, and every single thought in my head disappeared and left only the burning image of the captain's cold gaze in my mind. Anger burned through my veins.

Take it.

Kill him.

"If you can hand him to me alive, I may consider it," I said before I could even think through the implications of taking the throne.

For years I had tried to get close to the Order, but every single time I had failed. Even as their numbers had dwindled, the hunters they sent after me had gotten much better in the last few years, and there were many times where I had barely escaped with my life.

Getting Captain Moore was no easy feat.

But I wanted—*needed*—to get my revenge. I needed to see what it looked like when he was so in pain he couldn't speak. I wanted to put him through every single painful thing Raphael had done to me. It was the least he deserved for leaving me there and then sending my own classmate to come kill me.

And he was the only one who knew my parents who was still alive. He was the only one who had an inkling about why my entire family was murdered.

"The day after the power transfer I will seek you out," he said. "It's a promise."

"*If* I go through with it."

"You will," he said in a smug tone. "Now leave before I am forced to throw you out."

I left his office feeling even more conflicted than when I arrived.

Wallowing in my own self-pity inside of Nat's tiny apartment was not what I had in my plan for that day, but nonetheless, that was where I found myself.

Nat, my ex-girlfriend before I joined the Order, had been a constant in my life the last two years and the only person from my past who I stayed in contact with.

"I think you should do it," she said as she sipped her cup of blood. It was in a glass container that did nothing to hide what was inside. The still-human part of my brain wanted to grimace, but the vampire part shut up and enjoyed her own glass of blood.

I let out a noise as I took a healthy gulp from the glass.

I had left the Underground six hours earlier, and between cutting Vance's dick off and running from Keir, I was exhausted. But because of vampirism I was unable to rest fully, so I had to settle for the only thing that would help me regain my strength.

Blood.

"You only say that because *you* don't have to," I murmured and looked around her apartment.

It was the same one I used to visit when we were dating, and it hadn't changed much. The orange couch stood out against the white rug underneath it. The walls were exposed brick, and she had a few plants and paintings hanging from them.

The place was open, and her kitchen flowed into her living room where we were currently sitting. The small table was something we'd picked up from a thrift store back in the day, and I was surprised she hadn't gotten rid of it.

Or much of anything else.

Though I did smell a distinct floral perfume slowing turning stale in the air.

"You literally cannot lose anything, Silvia," she grumbled. "You're being stubborn."

"I don't *want* to run a clan," I huffed. "Isn't that good enough?"

She let out a sigh and put her glass down on the table. "Can you just stop lying to yourself and admit that it's not the clan that you're worried about?" she asked. "You have a group of people there with hundreds of years of experience who can help you. You need to do what? Sign some papers and make small talk?"

I gave her a look. She rolled her eyes.

"*Look* just go there, do your thing, and then when all is said and done and you torture the captain to hell and back—*just leave*. You don't have to stay if you don't want, but if you *don't* take advantage of this than you'll never get closure."

Just leave.

Could it be that simple?

Keir's forlorn face flashed through my mind. Now not only would I come face-to-face with her again, but I would then have to figure out a way to escape her for the third time.

I cleared my throat. The emotions of Keir's betrayal hit me hard, like they always did. I had fallen for her before I even realized what happened. I had hidden behind my hate for so long that I didn't realize how much I wanted to be with her until she stood on the other side of my cage, helping the man who had hurt me.

A part of me missed the hell out of her, but I refused to admit it to myself.

Anger flashed inside me, renewing the watered-down emotion I thought I'd lost long ago. Keir, the spoiled vampire child, was still trying to shirk the responsibility of the clan head. I was an outsider. A *turned* vampire. And yet she was still willing to put it all in my hands.

"The enforcers know something about my parents as well," I murmured.

"But why go to them when you can go to the source?" she asked. "What will they know that you can't get from your previous captain?"

When I hesitated, she sat back in her chair with a frown.

"You're avoiding Keir."

I bristled at her comment. "Her father tortured me," I said.

"And you killed him for it," she noted with a raised brow.

"She lied to me as well," I fought.

"And you haven't lied to her, *ever*?"

I hate you.

The words were still on the tip of my tongue. I could hear them circling around my head in my own voice over and over again. Yes, I lied. . . but never like she had. I never lied to the point where I made her think that she was nothing more than a toy to be played with and then thrown away after.

I stood abruptly, placing my half-full glass on the table.

"I will talk to them first," I said, then hesitated. "If I don't see you again, you can safely assume that I have been captured."

She left out a huff.

"Don't be so dramatic," she said. "I'll see you at the ceremony. If you still decide to have one that is."

I let out a warning growl.

"All right," she said with a laugh, and raising her hands in surrender. "I won't push you anymore."

I grabbed my stuff, but before I made my exit, I paused, taking in the additional blanket that lay on the couch. She was moving on with her life. It was a good thing. Or at least that was what I tried to tell myself as a bitterness filled me.

"I'm happy for you, Nat," I said and turned to her with a smile. "I won't visit you after this. Thank you, for everything."

Her eyes widened. "Wait, Silvia—"

I didn't let her finish and was escaping down the emergency exit before the door clicked behind me.

It was better this way.

CHAPTER 4
KEIR

I walked down the long decorative hallway with Gil and Emery by my side.

I should feel better that I was visiting Xin, but I was nervous about what lay ahead.

This was not the first time that I had met with all the clan heads in the last two years, but with what Silvia had just tried to do. . . things were going to get messy.

There were two ways that we could go with this.

One, I could stand by my clan head. I could state that Vance had done her wrong and it was within her rights to do this. Ian may or may not stand with me on this. He knew his son had fucked up, but would he allow this?

Last I heard, Vance was meeting with the witches to see what could be done to save his member.

This was the option I wanted the most. . . but it put the clan at risk. With Silvia already refusing to take part in the clan and run it, she looked like a loose cannon.

We would then have to sit through whatever punishment

they decided for us. It could even be death if the other clan heads pushed hard enough.

Second, the one that would save the clan. We could rebel.

It wouldn't look great, but it would set the standard that the clan was not to blame, and might possibly save us from the consequences that Ian's clan may want to impose.

But it would be like stabbing Silvia in the back, and there was no way to make it hurt any less. She had earned her right to the clan, and this would be me pulling the rug out from under her feet. I would have to go against her in all senses. I would have to tell every powerful vampire in the room that she was nothing more than a menace. One who didn't belong in her position.

I know Silvia didn't want this, she had made it perfectly clear... but I couldn't give up the hope that she would see this through. And I owed it to her to stand by her.

"Have you decided?" Emery asked. She had been clear about which option she liked the best.

"Not completely," I admitted.

A familiar head of straight black hair and a kind smile poked out from the room at the end of the corridor. *Xin.* Over the last few years our clans had become close. We were both running low on blood and would share our reserves when we had them.

She was able to work with clans here and across the border to get more in, but I was stuck with what we had. I was not their clan head, so I could not renegotiate contracts to fit our growing clan. Regardless of how many people were leaving, the strain on the resources never seemed to give. Those loyal clan members who wanted to live their lives here while building a family of their own would continue to be at a disadvantage.

I may have been forced into this role, but I would make

damn sure that I tried my hardest to provide for our clan members.

"Keir," she said in a strained voice. There was a bit of relief to it, but it was woven with the stress I knew all too well.

The others had already started arguing. I couldn't hear it as we walked up, surely due to the insulation of this place, but as soon as she opened the door and peeked out, I could hear a few voices in there that I had become far too familiar with during my time as interim leader.

Here goes nothing.

"Xin," I greeted and walked toward her with open arms. She let out a sigh and returned my hug but was quick to hurry us into the main room.

Inside was a large round glass table with each of the heads occupying a seat. Their right hands stood behind them, and I was surprised to realize that I was not the only person to bring two with me. Another surprise was that Vance stood behind Ian, looking far paler than I had ever seen him. A smirk pulled at my lips, but I quickly concealed it when he shifted to look at us.

The temperature dropped in the room as a hushed silence fell over the crowd. Xin led me to the front where we sat next to each other. There was another empty seat on the far side of the table.

"All right, now that we have most everyone let—"

Xin was cut off by multiple voices speaking up at once. I singled out a few of the other clan heads, noting that they were ones who would constantly suck up to my father.

"What that rogue vampire has done is an insult to all us clan heads!"

"We should capture her and send her to the Order for punishment!"

"Give her to the Kazimir clan as penance!"

"Strip her of her title!"

Over and over again the same voices spoke up, reacting to the same thing, but when they veered into slightly more violent territory, I slammed my open palm against the table, the sound of it reverberating throughout the room.

The vampires' yells halted to a still silence. Ian's eyes were digging into mine, and when I met his gaze, he nodded.

I knew it would be easier to agree with them. It would get them on my side and guarantee that we would get more blood in the negotiations... but I couldn't.

The way they were talking about Silvia made my chest clench and my blood boil. No one, and I mean *no one*, would threaten her like they had. Not ever again.

"Your words are enough to call an end to this meeting *and* our ties," I warned. "What our clan head decides to do is none of the business of any other clan head."

"She broke into a compound! Sh-she mutilated an heir!" A vampire with thin black hair and sickly-looking skin spoke out. He was showing signs of starvation. I almost felt for him. *Almost.*

"She was right to," Ian said, surprising me. I didn't know how open he would be to having this conversation, but I would be forever grateful for him. "Not only was she right to, but I had invited her into the compound myself years ago." He turned back to Vance and nudged him. "Tell them what you've done. It was enough to cause an outright war."

There was no hiding how pleased I was with this turn of events. Ian continued to surprise me when Vance shifted behind him and Ian sent him a look. Vance lifted his face, his eyes trailing to mine.

I smiled at him and waved just to rub it in.

"Go on, Vance," I said. "Tell them how I walked in on you assaulting our clan head."

A heavy silence passed through the room.

"I have nothing more to add to this conversation," he said. His voice was grainy and did nothing to hide his displeasure.

"That doesn't change the fact that she removed the bloodline's chance to procre—"

"He has been absolved of his duties as my heir," Ian said. "So regardless of whether Vance can have children or not, he will never take over my title. This is what I wished to announce at this meeting. I have a few that I can choose from, but none of that concerns anyone here."

There was an awkward silence that spread over the table. Vance was glaring at me, and I just knew that in his mind he was thinking of all the ways he could murder me. But I was doing the same, and at least I knew that I would have his father's approval.

A wave of relief washed over me. Our clan was safe. *For now.*

"If that is all—" Xin started again, but she was cut off by the door slamming open.

I barely held in my groan as Victor walked through. His blue eyes were alight with amusement, and his unruly black hair was pushed out of his face. He wore casual clothes, a hoodie, and sweats with sneakers, making him look like a normal teenager, but everyone in this room could feel the pure power radiating off of him.

This meeting was about to turn into something much worse.

"Why so silent?" he joked as he took the only open seat. He didn't even bring someone else with him, that how much he trusted in his own strength. He looked toward Vance and made a noise. "Oh! You're alive! I thought for sure that hunter—*sorry* clan head—would have taken your head with her."

"She was interrupted," I interjected.

Victor's gaze flitted toward mine and his smile only widened.

"Keir," he breathed. "Here on behalf of her, *again?*"

I turned toward Xin and motioned for her to start again, but as soon as she readied to speak, Victor held his hand in the air to silence her. The act caused a growl to rip from my chest.

Gil's hand rushed across my arm, and Emery stepped closer to me. They were like two angels on my shoulders. Gil preferred to keep things peaceful, regardless of what his clan had done to him. While Emery wanted revenge for the same horrors Gil had faced.

Two of them, both hurt by the same man who was hurling insults at us. Any action I took would hurt the both of them.

"We are all struggling," Ian said. I gave him credit for how even his voice was. "We came to talk about blood, not clan heads."

"Or lack thereof," one of the men who was just moaning about Silvia said.

Victor pouted. "Listen, Keir, I *really* like you, but we need someone who actually has the authority to speak about your clan," he said. "And it's no small matter. Just go get your clan head and we can—"

"One more word, Victor," I warned. "One more word and I tell everyone here about where you and my father planned to get blood."

Xin and Ian already knew from our small alliance, but it would be news to the others, and I knew many of them would be just as horrified as we all were. There were a handful that I thought may just agree with him, but they were small in comparison to the clans that would shun him for this.

Victor leaned back in his chair and placed his elbow on the armrest before sighing and placing his head in his palm. His whole act screamed that he was already bored. He had come here to play, but there was no one here willing to indulge him.

"Why bring up the past, Keir?" he asked, then his smile dropped. "I will play by your rules for now, but I warn you, if your clan head doesn't come home soon I may just take the throne myself. After all, without her here, who can really stop me?"

I grabbed Emery's arm just as she was about to lunge across the table. Victor's eyes followed my actions.

"I know you," he breathed, then his eyes shifted to Gil. "Taking all my rejects, aren't you? Maybe that's why you were so against the orphans."

Both Gil and Emery were people who'd defected from his clan. I didn't ask them about their past or judge them for it. I knew what kind of ruler Victor was and even being here in the same room with him was much more than I would have ever asked of them.

He never came to these, didn't need to.

If his clan didn't have blood, they would steal it. If the Order gave them trouble, they would kill their hunters. There was nothing that Victor wouldn't do to get his way.

"Enough of this," I growled. "We have come here for a reason, not to goad each other into brawls."

Xin stood and cleared her throat before launching into her speech.

I didn't listen to a single word of it. My focus the entire time was on Victor, and he returned it. But instead of a matching glare, there was a smug smile pulling at his lips. He had come to undermine me. There was no doubt about that.

He had no stakes in this game anymore. My father was long gone, and whatever crazed plan they had made to blackmail the Order into accepting his awful demands had disappeared into thin air.

So why is he still pushing me?

I would have liked to chalk it up to the fact that he was nothing more than a child who had his plaything stolen from him, but the way his eyes narrowed dangerously at me made me think that there was more to this than met the eyes.

I hoped I was wrong.

CHAPTER 5
SILVIA

How hard is it to get ahold of the fucking enforcers?

It had been three days since I'd left the Underground, and there were no signs of them. The hunter's crawling around the Order seemed to have doubled in number in the last few days, and with one wrong move I would no doubt be taken in for *questioning*.

Or maybe for the hell of it they would send me to the Dark Room for punishment.

I was tempted to just walk through the doors and pretend like I was one of them, but I quickly ruled that out. For my survival.

Tobias's words still swirled around my head. As much as I hated to admit it, he was smart. It was the only reason he was able to live in the Underground for so long.

I knew that if I just caved and went to Keir that I would've had a better chance to find them, but I wanted to exhaust all my options before taking on a responsibility that big. There were many things that I could achieve if I just handed myself over. . . but I couldn't give up my freedom so easily.

If I wanted to find out more about what my parents and sister were doing with the Order, then I wanted to find it myself. If I wanted to get revenge on the captain for all the shit he had put me though, I wanted to be the one to bring him to his knees.

And as far as Keir went. . . I didn't know what I wanted from her yet.

Nat was right, to an extent.

I wasn't afraid of the role. I didn't want it, but I wasn't afraid. It was Keir I didn't want to face. Keir's eyes were the ones that hunted my memories. The feeling of her lips against mine and the way she made my chest warm.

I hated that even after everything, she still had total control over my body and mind.

The worst part was I didn't know what I would do when I saw her next.

When I saw her outside the Kazimir clan's compound I had been taken off guard. I thought that I would want to lunge for her. To get her back for forcing me into this life as a monster. . . but I couldn't.

Instead my entire body froze and my throat tightened. I didn't want to hurt her, not like I had in the past. Before everything happened and before I ran to Tobias's protection, I loathed her for what she'd done. Maybe I still did. But so many years had passed that it made it hard for me to remember how much I hated her as the longing for her only strengthened the longer we were apart.

It was far too easy to get lost in everything I felt for her, but there was always that lingering hurt.

I stood straight when I saw a familiar messy head of black hair leaving the Order. From my vantage point on the roof of a building a few blocks away, I couldn't make out much, but I knew that man anywhere.

Isaac looked at the hunters lining the Order. There could have been some words exchanged, but I was so far away that it was hard to even make out his facial expressions. Normally the Order's hunters patrolled for miles, but because I'd been watching them, I was able to secure the closet blind spot. It sucked that it was a fucking roof and not an alleyway right around the corner, but beggars couldn't be choosers.

His head snapped toward me, and I could have sworn we made eye contact, but he looked away just a second later, and I shook that stupid thought out of my head. Even a vampire would have had trouble seeing me from there if they didn't know what they were looking for.

I may have been stripped of my hunter title, but that didn't mean all training went out the window.

Less than a minute later he climbed into an SUV and was headed in the opposite direction of Keir's compound.

I was relieved and annoyed at the same time.

Relieved that I wouldn't have to see Keir but annoyed that I would have to hurry to catch up to him before his car disappeared. With a curse I turned, ready to run after the car, but I stopped dead in my tracks. Jase was standing right behind me. His red eyes narrowed, and a low growl burst forth from his chest. I hadn't even heard him come up, but to be fair, it had been a few days since I last had any blood, and that combined with constantly being on the run meant I was getting worn out. And fast.

"Jesus Christ," I muttered. "I was looking for you guys. Do you know how hard it is to—"

His hand shot out and grabbed the fabric of my black turtleneck. He forced me close to him, his lips twisting into a snarl. I had half a mind to push him off, but I wasn't here to start a fight. I was here to get help.

"You are in the Order's territory," he growled. "If Isaac

hadn't seen you, you would have been taken in. Was the arrow to the head not warning enough for you?"

So we did make eyes contact. *Fucking enforcers.* I brushed his hands off and let out a huff.

"Don't act so concerned," I said. "I can take care of myself, you know."

"No more," he growled, his eyes shooting around the empty roof. "We talk at the compound."

Compound. Keir's compound. I knew they were working together, but I didn't realize how much until now.

It had been two years, what on earth did they still need each other for now?

He turned to exit toward the stairs, but he paused when he realized I was not following after him.

"I am not going to the compound." My hand fell to the dagger that was strapped to my thigh, the last reminder of Tobias's help.

His eyes followed the action and he let out a small sigh. "Home then," he said simply and turned toward the exit.

I stood up straight and slowly followed him. *It was that easy?*

"I though you and Keir had some sort of deal," I said.

He grunted but didn't turn. "I don't want to fight you. Especially after you rammed your fist into my face last time," he said. "And our ask of you is more important than hers, so I am willing to take the chance of bringing you home."

A warmth spread throughout my chest. *Home.* He was taking me *home.*

"Are you fucking kidding me?" Isaac growled as he opened the door to their apartment and saw me and Jase playing cards on the kitchen table.

Apparently his leader didn't share the same sentiment.

I had to stifle my laugh as Jase's lips pulled up at the sides. Had I ever heard their stoic leader cuss before?

"Nice place you got here," I said and placed a pair of jacks down.

The enforcer salary must have been nice for them to afford a five-bedroom apartment on the twentieth floor of a building near the center of downtown. It was far enough away from the Order to give them privacy, but not far enough that it would be hard to get to work if needed.

When I was in the Order, I dreamed of one day having a place like this, even if I shared with Jade and Cain. The memories of them hit me like a truck, and it took a minute of steeling myself before the pain of leaving them dissipated.

I'd never wanted to leave them, and I worried about them constantly. In all the time I'd spent staking out the Order's headquarters I had never seen them. It made me think the worst, but there was always a small light of hope that was buried deep inside me.

They were witches, and proficient ones at that, they didn't need me to look out for them.

Knox pushed past him and took a seat at the end of the table. There was a hot coffee in his hand. A pang of envy went through me when I realized how much I had missed simple things like coffee. The smell of it spread through the apartment, and I took a moment to savor it. It was dark with a hint of nuttiness to it. I would give anything to taste it again.

Gil's smiling face cut through my mind, and I had to blink a few times to dislodge the heavy sadness that settled in my chest. There were so many things that I wished were different. So many people I wished I could see again.

If only things were different.

"So you've come around," Knox said, his eyes twinkling under the kitchen light. "Just in time. The Order raided the Underground tunnels just a few nights ago."

I let the smile spread across my face.

"Thanks to a certain tip. Though I am not happy about being used as a bargaining chip," I said with a hum. I wasn't all that mad about it anymore. The enforcers were the only group that hadn't yet done anything to me.

Well. . . at least not *this* group of enforcers. The ones I encountered in my academy days were still on my shit list.

I jumped at the sound of Isaac slamming the door shut.

"We are not here for fun and games," Isaac warned. "If you weren't careful the Order could have spotted you and all our work could have gone to waste."

"I'm not here for that. I am here to see how I can help and to find out more about my parents," I said. "My turn."

Jase pouted before giving me a nod. I made a show of trying to pick a card from his hand.

"It's not like you, to come to us for this," Isaac noted.

"She's running," Knox said.

I faltered, picking the card way at the end. Jase smiled. I cursed under my breath. I now held the joker.

I placed all my cards down on the table and looked toward the leader.

"So you want to tell me why two years later enforcers are still being taken?" I asked. "Weren't you and your team trying to figure out a way to stop this?"

His jaw clenched. "It's not like we have nothing," Isaac hissed.

I raised my brow at him, urging him to give it up.

"Enforcers all come from hunter parents," Knox said for him. "Every one of them was killed by vampires, usually outside of the line of duty while their children are taken or killed during missions."

"It's connected," Isaac said.

He shot a glance toward the shut door before stalking over to the table. Knox merely took a sip of his coffee, not caring that his leader was currently glaring down at him.

"That's a no-brainer," I scoffed. "Now my mother's number—"

Jase let out a sigh and stood. We watched in silence as he grabbed a handful of things from the fridge.

The scent of sweet blood hit my sense. It had a hint of—*oh*.

It was alcohol infused, like the kind Keir used to drink. He poured two glasses for us, then grabbed some beers for the other two. I greedily accepted mine. My mouth was already watering before I took the first sip.

I used to hate the idea of drinking blood. It used to remind me of the monster I had become, but lately. . . I found it easier. Maybe it was because I had more pressing things to worry about. Jase gave me a look as he took a long sip. Knox had already traded his coffee for a beer, but Isaac waved Jase away when he tried to give him one.

"It was hard to find," Knox said. "Almost every bit of paperwork with our parents' numbers on them have been destroyed. But we did find somethings that gave us a look into the final missions that any of them ever did."

"On top of that some of our parents shared missions," Isaac said and motioned for Jase to get up. Without hesitation he got up and disappeared into the next room only to come back later with a box full of documents and pictures. He poured them onto the table.

Isaac leaned forward and dug through the pile before flipping one of the pictures over to me. It was a group of people all gathered in a room with the walls and floors completely white. There were about ten of them all surrounding a single table. Many of their hands were full of papers, and they all wore hunter uniforms. He pointed to a couple toward the middle. A girl with hair as dark as his, though her eyes were much lighter. The man next to her had light hair and eyes, but the cold look he gave the camera was unmistakable.

"My mother and father," he said and took another photo from the pile. This one was outside at the park. A few hunters in uniform smiled at each other as magic danced around them. It was one of the only happier ones. "Knox and Ash's parents."

I swallowed thickly and nodded.

"Mine," Jase said. He handed me a picture, but this one was the most worn of all and looked to have been crushed. I had to squint to make out the image of his parents. Two men were in the middle of what looked like an empty warehouse, they were smiling at each other and holding hands.

"And mine?" I asked.

Isaac shifted through the box until he handed me a picture that caused my breath to catch in my throat.

The familiar fiery-red hair of my mother was the first thing I saw, then the same soft smile my father wore. But the most damning thing was that my sister stood right beside them. . . in her hunter uniform.

They were smiling at the camera, and the scoreboard was behind them. If I squinted I could make out Mother's number, but I was too starstruck by the smiles on their faces. *Real* smiles. Ones that had become blurry in my mind.

I reached out to touch the photo but pulled back at the last second for fear I might ruin it.

"What does this have to do with the hunters going missing?" I asked and looked up to Isaac.

He swallowed before looking down at the pile.

"We think they were up to something," he said. "These pictures, the files. . . they came from Captain Moore's safe. He was hoarding them. There is no indication of what they were doing but. . . I *feel* it."

I could help but let out a bitter laugh.

"You *feel* it?" I was being condescending. I knew that. But his words also scared me. I too was someone who relied on their gut, especially though the last few years. . . and my gut was telling me he was on to something.

"My brother. . ." Knox trailed off. My eyes snapped toward him, but I had to look away as soon as I met his pained gaze.

I knew it far too well. It was the same one that probably twisted my face when I looked at the picture of Jane.

"Him and Chase were on a mission when we lost contact." Isaac spoke up for him. "But it wasn't an Order mission."

"You were following a hunch," I said and finally got the courage to grab the photo of my family.

"To the Order it looked like we were staking out an area with high rebellion activity," Knox said. "But they were there because we found the last living relative of an enforcer."

My gaze snapped to his.

"You said they were all dead," I accused.

"We said the parents were dead," Jase said, cutting in.

Isaac cleared his throat. "Chase has an aunt," he said. "One who was hard to track down and we only found thanks to digging in these files. This is after a mission where his mom almost died and was rushed to the Order hospital. Chase doesn't remember her, but we think she may know something."

Knox pushed one in front of me and pointed to a part that they'd highlighted with a yellow marker.

Patient suffered from hallucinations and called out to a woman named Krista. Patient claims it is her sister, but birth records indicate no sign of any blood siblings.

"So we looked," Isaac said. "We went through hospital record after hospital record, and sure enough, we found someone. Their name has changed, and there are no pictures of her, but we were sure they were connected. But when they went to go scope it out. . ."

"What does Captain Moore say about their disappearance?" I asked.

"Nothing," Isaac said with a frown. "Just like every other enforcer who has gone missing. They push it under the rug and expect us to get over it."

I sat there shocked and still not quiet understanding what this had to do with me. I wanted answers but going after someone's long-lost aunt? And for what? What would she be able to tell us?

"You want me to go after her, don't you?" I asked.

Their silence was all the answer I needed.

I let out a sigh.

"You don't even know what this lady can do for us. Who's to say she even knows anything? What if you have the wrong person?"

"They disappeared looking for her," Knox said with a hard voice. "Now that either tells us that she has kidnapped them *or*. . . the Order found out and doesn't want us looking into her."

"But you are outside the Order," Isaac said. "So if you go—"

"I can get kidnapped as well?" I asked with a laugh. "Are

61

you serious? You send *two* enforcers after her—one of them a witch—and you think I can just waltz in there with no problem at all?"

Another pause. For enforcers they were starting to look real stupid.

"Keir can help," Jase murmured.

I leaned back with a sigh.

"So this is what your plan was?" I asked. "What is Keir offering you that you would suggest that? I thought this was *more important* than me taking the title."

I stood with a sigh. Knox's cold hand shot out to grasp my wrist. I couldn't look at him. I knew that if I did I would cave.

"*Please*, Silvia," he begged. "I know you know how it feels to lose your sister. Please, my brother could still be out there. No one is asking you to take over the title. If you want to go by yourself you can, but *please* just go."

I swallowed thickly.

My hands were tied. A part of me wanted to go myself, but I knew it would be a bad idea. I may have been a good hunter back when I was still human, but my life as a vampire had taught me that I was mediocre at best.

It was a harsh reality, but there was nothing I could do about it. And I was going to ensure my survival because if I didn't I would never get back at the people who put me in this monstrous cage.

"Raphael had my mother's number," I said in a low voice. "He had hunter numbers and case numbers. Do you know why?"

Jase shifted through the papers and brought out not one, not two, but *five* contracts all related to the vampire clan, though when I looked through them there was no indication of what the contracts were about. There were parts that looked like they'd been crossed out with a black marker while the remaining gave us no information on who or what was involved.

Even the hunter number was crossed out.

Another dead end.

How many would there be before we found an answer? Would it take months? Years maybe until we knew what happened?

But at the end of the day, there was only a few people who held the answer. One was Chase's aunt. . . and the other was the captain. He may be harder to get, but there was one thing for certain.

He was hiding something.

"You're pushing your luck," I said. "The Order is going to find out what you're doing. If Tobias hadn't killed all the hunters that night, they would have reported you back to the captain."

There was a silence that fell around us. It was thick and weighed heavily on my shoulders.

They knew of the risk. We knew all too well what they were capable of now.

And there was only one option.

"I was going to take the title anyway," I said and straightened my shoulders. "I am being hunted by the Order, and I doubt Keir will let up until I take the throne. The only way for me to guarantee my survival would be to take a position in which no one can harm me."

I don't know what part of our conversation had caused me to solidify my decision, but it was becoming clearer by the minute that they were in just as much trouble as I was. They'd lived with the threat of their own deaths looming over their heads for years. To them, it was only a matter of time.

But I wouldn't be like that. I wouldn't waste my time and let the Order get ahold of me.

Isaac shifted on his feet. He looked like whatever he was about to say was causing him great difficulty.

"The captain is not happy with you," he said. "You may become the clan head, but that doesn't change that you have killed multiple hunters in your time on the run."

I shrugged. "Then that is something he can take up with me." I pulled my wrist from Knox's grasp, grabbed my stuff, and readied to leave. "I'll help you, Knox. . . but only because you guys have been the only ones trying to help me. I know your motives are not pure, but I appreciate it nonetheless."

I clutched the doorknob but was stopped by Jase's hand darting in front of me. He was holding the picture of my family.

My chest began to ache.

"For them too," he whispered from behind me. "It's not just for Knox."

I grabbed it from him and pushed out the door.

"I'm not too sure about that anymore," I murmured and set off to the place I never wanted to see again.

Hunter Rules

rule 10 sec 1

There are no funerals for
Hunters.
Please follow section 5 for
process on Hunter deaths.

CHAPTER 6
KEIR

"Say the word," Emery whispered by my side. "Say it and they're gone."

Her words were. . . enticing to say the least.

I sat in a large chair at the end of a long table in one of our meeting rooms. This was usually reserved for clan meetings, but in front of me were no clan heads. Instead, it was all my own bloodline.

Distant relatives, cousins, and the like all complaining —*very loudly*—about the lack of oversight.

They had already noticed the blood shortage. They could deal with people leaving, but God forbid they stop being gluttons for mere days.

Just like my father, they went through feeder after feeder without a care in the world. And now that those feeders had up and left, after I gave them permission to do so, and they noticed the lack of fresh blood. . . they began to complain.

"Your father has been dead for years," my cousin's husband yelled from across the table. "Yet there is *still* no sign of the true clan head."

"We need a leader!" another yelled.

"Our blood is running low!"

"If you don't put an end to this, we will have no choice but to leave!"

All of their words buzzed insistently around my skull. A dull ache bloomed from the back of my eyes and spread all over my head.

How many hours have we been at this? Aren't they tired?

It was every day now that I had to deal with these issues. The first year, not many people bothered me. They were living their lives and trying to adjust to my father's passing. But at the start of this year, they began to get restless. Clan heads, my own clan, the Order, every single one of them had been trying to butt their way into how *I* ruled the clan.

And it was all Silvia's fault.

How many hours had I spent looking for her? How many times had I gotten close enough to see a flash of red hair but never the woman herself?

The last time I saw her at the Kazimir clan's compound had been the first time that I got a good glimpse of her since she left. And it wrecked me to my core.

"That's enough!"

This time it came from Gil and was accompanied by his fists hitting the table. Loud enough to silence the angry crowd but not hard enough to break the table. The entire room fell silent, and I took it as my cue to stand.

"We are working with the Order to redo our contracts, but my decision still stands. No feeders will be here unless they agree to it. None of them will enter under contracts with the clan. If you want one, you have to work out your own consensual contract, and you better bet that I will be there to check on them," I said. "I appreciate your patience during this time. I will answer any questions you may have when I have more answers as well, but right now I do not have them."

I turned to leave, and as soon as the others realized what I was doing, they tried to run for me.

"Emery."

She was there instantly, blocking them from coming any closer. I escaped out the doors with Gil and a few guards following us.

"Thank you," I muttered as soon as we were far away enough that the voices died down.

"They were out of line." Gil huffed and pushed his glasses up, but I saw the pride hiding in his face.

I waved the guards off as we reached the hallway of my room. I hadn't changed it in the last two years even though the clan headquarters remained empty. It felt. . . wrong.

It was the only area in this place that was still *mine*. And hers if I was being honest. Sometimes I would lie in bed and inhale deeply, trying to find the last remnants of her scent. But right now I couldn't even think of doing that or finding comfort in my own space.

I was too angry at everything that had unfolded in the last week.

"Take some rest," I said, noticing his eye bags. They had gotten worse over the last few weeks, and I knew I was the one to blame.

We were stretched thin between him, myself, and Emery.

He let out a sigh, his shoulders sinking as he did so.

"It's just. . . been a lot," he admitted. He ran his hand through his hair and winced as he pulled through some knots. "I thought that at some point she might come back. . . but I am afraid she never will."

I shifted, an uncomfortable feeling building up inside me.

"I have faith," I said. "And even if she doesn't want to, she can't stay away forever. I will be here waiting as long as possible, and every time there is even a whiff of her, I'll do my best to bring her back. I promise, Gil."

He reached out and squeezed my shoulder with a sad smile.

"You have grown into a fine leader, Keir," he said. "I know it's not easy, but contracts aside, you have made changes to this clan that your father never had the gall to make."

"Thank you," I muttered, feeling my throat tighten. After feeling like such a failure for so long, it was nice to get his praise.

"I miss her," Gil admitted. "Seeing her at the Kazimir compound hurt. I know we messed up, but I would have liked to think that after so long—"

"Maybe she wouldn't hate us anymore?" I supplied for him.

He gave me a tense smile in response.

"Something like that," he said and removed his hand. "Maybe one day we will be back together again."

I nodded but had nothing else to say. I wished for it, truly. . . but there was nothing I could do.

Silvia wouldn't come until she was given no other option. It didn't matter if we were literally starving. None of it mattered to her.

It was a trait I both hated and envied her for.

"Call me if you need me?" he asked.

"Of course," I lied with a smile.

His eyes crinkled as if he was going to call me out on it, but he didn't say anything. Instead he just nodded and turned on his heels.

I waited a moment until I heard him disappear before setting off to my room. As I walked that way, I caught glimpses of the extended family being ushered out by a disgruntled Emery.

I owed her my life for helping with them.

Growing up, there were times I wished for them to accept me. To act like a real family and not just one that wanted me for my title.

But that never happened.

I let out a huff of a laugh when I realized that may have been why I fell so easily for Silvia.

I was so exhausted that I almost didn't hear the creak of wood and nearly silent vampire heartbeat. But I caught it just as my hand brushed across the doorknob.

It was low, almost mistakable, but it was there.

I burst into my room, my eyes scanning the dark space. The sun had set not long ago, and the only light was from the moon shining through the window. Everything looked undisturbed. From the couches in the middle of the room to the book shelf to my left. Everything *except* my desk.

A figure was there, sitting on top of it with her feet hanging off the edge.

The light from the hallway filtered in, giving me a glance at the intruder, but even without it I would have known her from anywhere.

Silvia. Eyes glowing and mouth twisted into a scowl. She was wearing her all-black uniform that hugged her body. Her long hair was pulled back into a high ponytail, the curls cascading down her back.

If I didn't know any better, I would've said that we'd turned back time and all the nightmares that we'd experienced up until now never happened in the first place. That she was *here*, back in my room, because she had come back for me.

But the dissatisfaction in her face told me differently. I closed the door behind me and locked it. The tension between us thickened, and I was aware of every acute detail. The way her breath hitched. The smell of blood on her breath. The way her nails dug into my desk. The way her heart sped up.

My surprise quickly wore off to relief, then excitement. *She's here.* I didn't register when she crossed the room. I stood still as she came to a stop in front of me.

"I had this image of how I would react when you were this close to me," she whispered. "What I would do to get back at you for everything that you did to me."

Her eyes trailed my form. I swallowed thickly, and before I could stop myself, the words were out of my mouth.

"Anything," I replied in a hoarse breath. "Whatever will make you stay. I will accept it. Silvia—"

Her hand connected with my cheek.

Shock ran through me, and I tried to steady myself on one of the couches nearest to me, but Silvia crowded me in a second.

I almost regretted telling her to do anything she wanted, but I sucked it up.

"You turned me into a monster," she said in a harsh whisper. "*And* stood there doing nothing while your father *tortured* me."

"Again," I commanded.

She faltered and even took a step back.

"What?" I asked. "Didn't you come here to get revenge? That's all you got?"

The words were bitter as they left my mouth. The anger from the last few days combined with the hurt of her leaving was threatening to overtake me.

"Do not push me," she warned.

But that was *all* I wanted to do. I wanted to see her angrier. I wanted her to get back at me for everything I had done. I needed *some* reprieve. And maybe after, she would finally stay by my side.

"Again," I repeated and grabbed her wrist. She snapped her hand back before pushing my chest.

She didn't like it. That much was obvious on her face. Her eyebrows were pulled together, and her lips were twisted into a frown.

I couldn't conceal my anger and hurt. It was taking over my body, and all I wanted to do was force her to me.

"Fight me," I said and grabbed at her shirt. "Do it. If it'll make up for everything back then, *do it*."

When she pushed me again, I lost all control.

Grabbing her wrists, I turned us, pushing her onto the couch and hovering above her. I gripped her wrists in one hand and held them above her head. My free hand gripped her chin and forced her to look at me.

She bucked underneath me wildly. Her strength was far greater than as a human, but I could hold on. I had to or I would lose this chance with her.

"Silvia," I called.

She growled and tried to headbutt me, but my grip on her chin was too strong.

"Let go of me, Keir. If you don't, I'm going to fuckin—"

"Do it," I hissed, cutting her off. "I'm giving you your chance, Silvia. Take it or leave it because after this there is no way I am letting you go again. I don't care what you do to me, but know that all this running stops here."

She stilled under me, her red eyes flickering to give me a sneak peek of the icy ones beneath. She was breathing hard and all the memories of us in the same exact position years ago flooded my memories.

She was so close it was intoxicating. Her smell was comforting and put me on edge at the same time. The feeling of her soft skin against mine was enough to cause my chest to ache and my belly to warm.

I'd known I needed her, but I hadn't realized just how much until that moment.

"You can't command me to do anything—"

"Evidently not," I growled. "You have been running for two years, Silvia, aren't you tired of it?"

Her eyes shifted to the side. "I didn't come here to submit to you, Keir," she said, her voice still holding that bit of anger in it. "You can't make me do anything. Whether that be hit you or anything else. It won't make me forget the past."

"Is that a challenge, little hunter?" I asked and leaned closer. This wasn't how I wanted this first meeting to go. I had thought through it many times. Some of the times I knew that I would become so angry that I would have trouble controlling myself, but I hadn't expected her to be *like this*.

To resemble her once-fiery self. I had missed it.

Missed her.

Every day I imagined her walking into my compound. Every day I wished she would contact me somehow. I waited for her for *two years*. I knew she was angry, she had the right to be. . . but she had to realize that she belonged here.

With me.

I had learned it long ago. . . so why couldn't she?

Did she not feel as empty as I did without her? Did she not play our every interaction over and over again until her mind went numb?

I yearned to close the space between us. To show her why she had been wrong to leave. I wanted her so thoroughly lost in me that the only thing she would ever think of again was how much she loved me.

I needed to consume her every thought and entire being, after all, it was only fair after she had burrowed herself so deeply inside me. There was not a waking moment where I did not think of this wild, fiery creature below me.

I wanted to marvel at the softness of her skin. Get lost in the way her soft locks felt in my fist. I wanted to learn more about her. How had she survived the past few years? Did she miss this? Miss me?

"I am not a hunter anymore," she said, though now her voice was much weaker than it had been.

"I'm angry," I admitted. "Angry that you left me. I hurt you, but you hurt me as well."

"You think you're angry?" She scoffed. "The only reason I am back—"

I didn't let her finish that damned sentence for fear that I would lose everything again. I didn't want to hear whatever she was going to say to ruin this moment.

"If you're good," I whispered and cupped her cheek, "I will forgive you for leaving and dooming my clan. I can show you how much I missed you. Show you what I have wanted to do to you these past three years. Silvia, I have never once—"

"I'm not here to reminisce, Keir," she said, her tone cool.

My chest tightened and my stomach felt like it was filled with lead. "You can't admit that you missed me?" I asked, trying to keep cool on the outside, but on the inside, I felt like a part of me had just crumbled and died.

Her eyes shifted to the right. "Get off me, Keir," she growled.

Against everything my mind screamed at me to do, I slowly pulled away from her and sat up on the couch.

She stood, putting some space between us. "I have come to make a bargain."

Swallowing everything I wanted to say, I nodded. "I will do anything I can," I said, then paused. When she didn't say anything I continued. "If you become clan head. . . for real."

She stood her ground. Her eyes were burning into me, but she said nothing.

"Still?" I asked with a scoff. "I offered you *anything* and you still won't step up?"

I waited for her to say something—*anything*—but even as her mouth opened to speak there were no words that came out.

It only angered me further.

"Well you have no choice," I growled and stood up. I stalked toward her. "You *killed* Father, and now you have to pay the price. And if you think about running again *don't* because now that you are finally in *my* territory, I won't let you go that easily."

She rolled her eyes and crossed her arms over her chest.

"You're telling me you didn't want him dead?" she asked with a raised brow.

I gripped at the harness she had on her shoulders and pulled her face close to mine.

"I wanted him dead since the moment he murdered my mother," I hissed. Her eyes widened. "But *you* were the one who killed him, so by *clan law* you must be the one to rule over this clan. I have taken over for your lack of responsibility for the last two goddamn years, Silvia. It's time that you pay the price."

Her mouth fell open, but no words came out. She just stared at me in astonishment. "Did you just say I was irresponsible?" she asked.

I leaned closer to her so that our lips were mere centimeters away. "Irresponsible. Hotheaded. A *coward*. You're the only person who I ever met who would work their ass off for an organization that literally tried to *kill* them rather than take over a clan of your own. It's like you don't even care about the people here." I took a deep breath. "They accepted you, Silvia. *I* accepted you."

"You accepted me because you didn't want the responsibility," she growled.

All I could see was red as I backed her up into the bookcase. I could admit my faults. . . but she was taking this too far.

"I have taken responsibility for it my whole life!" I yelled. "I had been preparing for this since day one, and even as you were gone, I took over and ran the clan for you. You should be *thanking me.*"

She let out a laugh and threw her head back. Her hand looped around my neck and tangled in my hair before pulling on it. Pain pricked at my scalp like small needles.

She leaned closer, a smirk pulling at her lips.

"You weren't *preparing*, Keir," she said in a hushed tone. "You were *running*. You went out drinking and partying all the time just so you wouldn't have to face what awaited you at home. You made *excuses* for yourself as a vampire, and when push came to shove, you couldn't even stand up for yourself."

Silence settled around us as her words sank in. I didn't notice until now how close we were or how heavily we were breathing. I could feel her breath waft across my face, and at some point my hands had left her shirt and one had wrapped around her waist. Her free hand had settled on my chest while the other still pulled at my hair.

As if also just noticing, her eyes drifted down my form. I didn't know how much time had passed or who had started what, but in a flash our mouths collided.

I didn't even know if you could call what we did a kiss. It was a battle between us, our teeth gnashed together and our tongues fought for dominance. It was the single most hate-filled and deprived kiss I had ever had. . .

And I *fucking* loved it.

Her fangs sank into my bottom lip, pulling a growl from my chest.

I bent to grip onto her thighs and force them around my waist. Her arms circled around my neck, and she continued to devour me, even after I slammed her into the bookshelf. Books fell around us, but I couldn't bring myself to care.

There was a low growl in her chest and before I knew it, her hands were ripping apart my shirt. I wasn't about to lose though. I ripped her shirt and harness off in one go. An outraged cry tore itself from her lips, and in return, her hands threaded through to my hair and tugged on it enough to hurt.

I didn't even bother taking off her entire bra. Instead I just pulled it down so I could free her breast before disconnecting my mouth from hers. I trailed kisses down her throat, her chest, and finally I was able to capture her perfectly pert nipple in my mouth. Her hands left my hair to grab onto the bookshelf behind her to help her arch into my mouth.

When I bit down on her nipple, she let out a cry and the bookshelf splintered in her hand. I grabbed her by the waist and pulled her away from it, carrying her to the other room.

For the first time, I was going to fuck her in my bed.

Her lips covered mine again, and I barely made it to the bed without tripping the both of us.

As soon as I pushed her to the bed, I slipped my hand into her pants and ran my fingers across her wet underwear.

"Liar," I whispered against her mouth. "I knew you missed me."

She didn't answer me. Instead she just quickly tried to unbutton her pants, but I couldn't wait. I had waited two years. I refused to wait any longer.

I slipped my hand into her underwear and began circling her clit. She moaned into my mouth and tried to kick off her shoes as I trailed my fingers to her entrance.

"Fuck," she groaned when I pushed two fingers inside of

her. She successfully kicked her shoe off and slipped out of her pant leg so she could open her legs wider for me.

"Such a good, little hunter," I cooed and thrust my fingers into her once more, then circled her clit with my thumb.

I wanted to make her beg for it. Wanted to hear her scream my name.

"Don't call me that," she growled and pushed me over so that she could straddle me.

I reached up to grab her neck and connected her mouth with mine, but her hand on my chest stopped me.

She looked down and me with hooded eyes as her free hand came to reposition my hand that was still inside her. Then, while her gaze was locked onto mine, she began fucking herself on my hand.

"God," I moaned as I watched her on top of me.

Silvia being in control was. . . something else. She was magnificent as she rode my hand. She threw her head back and moaned loudly as she took her pleasure from me. I wanted to take her in here to show her how much she'd missed me. To prove to her that there was something unforgettable between us.

I wanted her to be so full of me she forgot her own name.

. . . but here she was doing the same thing to me.

I watched her in awe, and I was sure that I had never seen a woman as beautiful as her. It didn't matter whether she was a human or a vampire, *this* was the girl that I would stand by for the rest of my existence. *This* was the queen I would serve.

And *this* was the girl I would love for as long as she would have me.

Just as I felt her squeeze around me, I hooked my arm around her neck and forced her to the bed. She didn't have time to complain as I began pounding into her faster than she had been riding me.

She tried to cover her mouth to muffle her screams, but I quickly pulled her hand away and forced her to look at me.

"You can't deny us, Silvia," I said against her open mouth. "You may try to hide, but you can't. Not from me."

"Keir," she cried.

The way she said my name ignited shocks through me.

"Come for me, love," I said. "Show me how much you missed me."

With one last cry she came on my hand while throwing her arms around my shoulders.

"*Fuck, Keir,*" she groaned, and I continued to assault her clit. "No more, no more."

"You aren't leaving here until I get enough of you," I growled and bit the side of her neck, right where you could see the faint marks of my bite. She shuddered in my arms, and I felt her clench around me.

She still likes my bites.

"I hate you so much," she whispered.

I chuckled into her neck.

"*Liar.*"

CHAPTER 7
SILVIA

"I came here to take over anyway," I mumbled and crossed my arms over my chest.

Keir looked at me with an expression of disbelief. It was almost enough to cause a smile to pull at my lips.

Almost.

I had to admit, I hadn't known what would happen when I came back to let them know that I would be taking over the title, but fucking Keir had not been on my list.

As soon as I saw her again, instead of being frozen, an intense rage filled me, and that rage spilled into something fiery that could only be extinguished by her lips on mine.

I didn't forgive her though, not one bit, and a few measly orgasms wouldn't fix that. But I was here for something bigger than this. I had a plan, one that I needed to stick to.

"Then why didn't you tell me?" she asked.

I shrugged.

"Your face annoyed me," I said and let the smirk show on my lips. "I thought you may need a bit of humbling."

Gillard stifled a laugh next to me by trying to pass it off as a cough.

The door opened without a knock, and the same woman who had tried to capture me peeked her head through. My eyes narrowed at her, and when she saw me, an annoying smile made its way across her face.

"I thought it was a lie that the famed clan head finally made an appearance," she teased. "So when is the ceremony? I assume now that we have her here we want to get this started right away?"

I let out a sigh and stared down at the stack of papers on the wood desk in front of me.

Just take the title, Tobias had said. *Take the title, and the captain will be hand delivered to you.*

Easier said than fucking done. I leaned back in Keir's chair and looked at the newest intruder. She made her way to Keir's side but made sure to stay just a step behind her. The movement didn't get past me and neither did the way that she looked down on me.

The tanned women crossed her arms over her chest and gave me a smirk. I looked up and down at her outfit. Tight-fitting pants and a loose long-sleeve blouse, the neck plunging deep. Her hair was in a low pony with the golden locks thrown over her shoulder.

"Who are you anyway?" I asked with a raised brow.

Gil, who was still standing by my side, as he should have been, shifted. I glanced toward him to catch the slight quirk of his lips before his face went stone-cold. His glasses shone in the light and obstructed my view of his eyes. His hair had gotten longer as well, and he had ditched the low pony to let it fall loose around his shoulders. He wore a typical button-up and slacks.

It was only Keir and I who donned something somewhat casual, though I wouldn't call my faux-hunter uniform *casual*.

"Emery, my lady," she said but did not bow.

"She's been helping run this place with me in your absence," Keir said. "Took her in from Victor's clan. Without her I am not sure I would've been able to hold off the clans that came to take advantage of us with our clan head gone."

When my gaze shifted over to her, she kept the connection. It was a challenge and warning all at once.

As clan head, I could thank her. I thought that was the etiquette of a clan head, though to be completely honest, I had no idea how I was supposed to act as clan head.

Or maybe even better, I could use my newfound powers to dismiss her. But by the look in Emery's eye, it was clear that she didn't give two shits about what I said.

She reminded me a lot of Keir back when we first met, though there was an air to her that felt far more menacing than Keir ever did.

But I didn't want to do that. Because I never wanted this fucking title.

"As soon as possible," I said and crossed my arms over my chest. "And in return you three will accompany me on a mission."

Silence. My entire body heated under their stares as embarrassment hit me like a slap to the face.

"A week from now," Gillard said. Giving no indication that he heard the second part of my sentence. "Gives you enough time to meet with everyone and get people on your side but fast enough to sign a contract with the Order."

I bristled at his comment and the way Emery's smile widened.

"There are things bigger than this that require my attention. We need this—"

"Your people running out of blood should be your only priority," Keir said. "Contract, then ceremony, then we will help you with the mission."

My jaw clenched and the sound of my teeth grinding against each other could be heard through the silent room.

It was a mistake, fucking her last night. Not only had she caught me off guard, but I had wholeheartedly reciprocated. It was different now that I was a vampire like her. There was no need for her to be gentle, and for the first time I was able to see what it *really* looked like when she lost control.

And it made this whole thing much harder.

I didn't want to admit what type of emotions being with her last night had brought forth. Nor did I want to admit how right it had felt to be in her arms once more.

It also brought along a series of uncomfortable thoughts that I hadn't ever had to think before.

I never hated her. I was hurt, yes. *Betrayed*. But one touch from her and I had melted in her hands.

But it wouldn't happen, not again. It couldn't. And if I was head now, there was no way I would let her continue to push me around.

"And if I refuse?" I asked.

"You can't," Emery butted in, then quickly added, "my lady."

As if Keir and the others could feel my anger rising, they shared a look.

"After the ceremony, I promise. This is not us trying to rope you into something. I will keep my word," Keir said quickly. "In the meantime, we can sign the contract with the Order, get blood for our people, and then do whatever it is you need us to."

I sat still, digesting her words.

There was so much I was getting out of this. The perfect

way to get revenge. . . but I still hated every moment of it. Even just sitting here in this chair felt wrong.

How on earth did I ever think that I could command an entire clan?

"Leave us," Keir commanded.

To my surprise it was Gil who hesitated. I sent him a smile and nodded.

I stood with a sigh when both Emery's and Gil's footsteps receded down the hall. Keir's hand cupped my face and forced me to look at her.

"Why don't you want this?" she asked. Instead of the harshness of before, her tone was gentle and her expression had softened.

It made me panic. She always saw right through me.

I pushed her hand away and glared at her. "Just because we slept together doesn't change this," I said. "I never wanted to rule. I *never* wanted this responsibility."

"Then what do you want?" she shot back and rounded the desk. I stood still, my eyes falling to the papers in front of me.

What did I want?

"I want to find out who's responsible for my parents' death," I answered, but it felt thick on my tongue. It wasn't a lie, per se. I *did* want to find out and pay them back tenfold. But I wanted more. . . I wanted to be free.

Truly this time. I didn't want to run anymore. I was tired of constantly being on edge and always looking over my shoulder. But once I took this title, even though it would ensure that I never again had to run. . . I still would never be truly free.

Keir clicked her tongue. She moved around me so that she was standing right behind me, her breath on my neck and her hand trailing up my arm. The action sent a shiver up my spine.

When she leaned into me, I didn't push her away. I wanted

to lean into her touch. To rest my head on her shoulder and curl into her. But I didn't. I stood my ground.

"What do you want in life, little hunter?" she asked.

"Don't call me that."

"Let's try again," she said with a chuckle and placed a kiss to the side of my neck. Every one of her bites pulsed and caused shivers to course through me.

Such a little *insignificant* action, and I was already acting like this?

"What do you want in life, my queen?" Her voice lowered an octave and was accompanied by her free hand trailing across my stomach. My nipples hardened, and I was forced to suck in a sharp breath of air when her other hand brushed over one.

"Don't try to distract me," I growled.

She placed another kiss on my neck before moving her lips to my ear. "I didn't do anything yet and you're already distracted?" she teased and inhaled deeply. "And *wet*."

I couldn't help but follow her actions and inhale deeply as well.

But it wasn't just my own arousal I smelled. It was hers as well. My mouth watered and my fangs ached.

We had been separated for so many years and *this* was how we acted once we were in the same room as each other? We were no better than teenagers at this point. But there was nothing I could do to clamp down on the feeling. Not when she was so close.

"You could have anything you want," she whispered. Her hand slipped under my shirt and cupped my breast over my bra. Her thumb rubbed circles over my nipple, pulling a gasp from me. "Money. Power. *Revenge*."

She used one hand to rip my bra off me entirely and the other to lift my shirt up, baring my breasts to the empty room.

She nibbled on my ear as she took both in hand and began pinching my nipples and rolling them between her thumbs and forefingers.

I leaned back into her, my head resting on her shoulder. My breathing came heavier now, and wetness pooled between my legs.

"This won't make a difference," I moaned. She pinched my nipple, *hard*, pulling a strangled yelp out of me.

"Think of it," she said and turned me around.

I whined at the loss of her hands but was delighted when they came back to pluck at my nipples while she pushed a leg between mine, creating a delicious friction on my aching pussy.

"Me and you. Like this, for all eternity. There is nothing between us now."

I swiveled my hips, chasing the bursts of pleasure that shot through me. Her lips ghosted mine, but when I opened my mouth for her, she pulled away and pushed her knee into me. I cried out, far too loud. The others probably heard what we were doing.

I tried to muffle my moans with my hand, but she slapped it away. I glared at her only to catch her ducking her head to pull my nipple into her mouth.

"Fuck," I moaned.

She pulled away releasing my nipple with a wet plopping sound. "We don't need to be quiet anymore," she said. "We could be as loud as we want. Fuck as often as we'd like. Wherever we'd like. Just say the words."

"This is not up for debate," I growled.

"Stubborn," she muttered and slipped a hand into my pants. Her face was centimeters from mine, and she watched with hooded eyes as I arched into her as three fingers slid down my folds and pushed into me slowly. She ground her palm against my clit, staying silent as I fell apart in front of her.

I placed my elbows behind me and lowered myself as she began to slowly fuck me against the desk. I let out a moan as a hand came to tease my nipple again.

It was not the anger-fueled fucking we had before. This was slow, deliberate. Each movement was feeding fuel to the raging fire inside of me, but it was all so very intimate that it made every shift, every breath, feel that much more intoxicating.

"Stop lying to yourself, Silvia," she said. "It's okay to want power. It's okay to want to stay here with me. We don't have to hide anymore."

Just as I felt the slow buildup of my orgasm come to its head, she removed her fingers.

"Don't you dare," I growled.

A smirk spread across her face, and she slid the three fingers coated with my wetness into her mouth, moaning at the taste.

I shot up and grabbed her wrist, fully intending to put it back between my legs, but she simply stepped back and released herself from my hold.

"Ceremony is in a week," she said. "Don't try to leave. I won't be as forgiving next time."

I was left there in shock as she turned and left the room.

With a growl, I grabbed the nearest thing, the nameplate on her desk, and threw it at the door.

Her laugh echoed down the hallway.

CHAPTER 8
KEIR

Silvia may not have wanted to meet with her people, but could she at least try to look happy?

Gil and I had taken her out to the garden, giving her a bit of space. It'd been two days since she'd agreed to sign the contract, but she hadn't made the move to actually do so.

Instead, she sulked in her—*my*—room, refusing to leave. I'd tried to coax her out with blood, but she hadn't even budged. She just stayed on the couch, flipping through book after book, and then when she got bored, she would stare off into space.

Hence the plan to get her out of the fucking room.

She stared longingly at the café kiosk that stood toward the right side of the garden. Many humans and half humans were sitting there to enjoy their coffee, but as soon as we made an appearance, they all started to stare.

Some even came up to talk to her.

"Is there a reason why you keep your weapons, my lady?" a young vampire asked. She was but ten years old if I remembered correctly, and she stared at Silvia as if her new queen was the most awe-inspiring thing on the planet.

In some circumstances, I may be inclined to agree with her, but not when she was giving the girl the cold shoulder.

The older lady next to her, who I assumed was her mom, smiled gently at her and tried to pull her away. Silvia's eyes snapped toward the young girl. Her gaze was too harsh and caused her to flinch.

"Habit," Silvia answered, her hand going to her dagger and pulling it out. I had half a mind to confiscate the offending object from her, but I let her have her fun. Now, if she tried to pull it on someone then we would have to have a talk.

The images of her threatening me with a similar dagger during our first meeting flashed through my mind and warmed my chest.

Maybe I could goad her into pulling it on me again.

She held out the dagger to the young vampire. Her mom's eyes shot over to mine.

Should I step in?

If I did it would look like I was going against the clan head's wishes. I looked over to see the others who were watching us. Many were already whispering behind their hands, though their words reached my ears with ease.

Is she going to attack the child?

She was a hunter before, you know? Old habits die hard.

Gil was next to me in an instant, his hand on my shoulder. He was stopping me. I hadn't realized that I had taken a step forward.

The vampire girl looked at Silvia and then her dagger. Her eyes were wide with wonder. She showed no fear at all and even reached her hand out to touch it.

"This dagger was not originally mine, but it was used to protect."

And kill, I wanted to add but bit my tongue.

"It's dangerous, and if you ever see someone who is not me wearing something similar, you should be wary."

The girl looked up at her. "But why do you keep it?" she asked. "The clan will protect you."

I stood frozen, watching as Silvia digested her words.

"Because I don't want anyone to protect me," she said softly. "I protect me. I always have."

Her eyes shifted. Her head was tilted so our gazes didn't meet, but I knew she was thinking about it. I could feel the weight behind her words.

A heavy feeling of sadness washed over me. *How many times over the last few years has she been forced to protect herself with that dagger?*

"Your clan head is strong," Gil said by my side. "She will protect all of us."

Silvia's gaze snapped over to him, a scowl on her face.

I could almost hear the words, *Like hell I will* shoot through the space between us, but she stayed silent.

The girl's eyes lit up. Before she could launch into more questions, her mother pulled her away with a forced laugh.

"Thank you, my lady," she said quickly. "Sorry to inter—"

"Silvia," she interrupted.

I almost groaned.

"What?" the mother asked.

Silvia turned to her, the scowl gone but her face giving no more emotion away than it previously had. "I don't like *my lady*," she said. "Call me Silvia."

The older vampire nodded but didn't say it. She bowed slightly to Silvia and then to us before running away.

"You can't just give her permission to use your name like that," I said and stepped forward to grab her arm, but she evaded me. Her knife glinted in the sunlight, and I thought for a moment maybe she would make my wish come true and hold it to my neck once more, but she placed it back in her strap with a smirk.

"Well if you don't like it, now I am definitely going to do it more," she said, then turned to look back at the coffee kiosk.

"Do you want one?" Gil asked from my side.

Her lips formed a frown but she nodded anyway.

"Ever since I have become a. . . *vampire*, I have missed out on the one thing I love the most," she said with a sigh. Her expression was forlorn.

Besides when we were fucking, this was about the most expressive I had ever seen her.

A sudden, violent need to get her all the coffees they sell at the godforsaken café ran through me. My chest felt tight and my shoulders tensed.

"Get a few cups," I told Gil without looking toward him. "She may not be able to enjoy the taste, but she can smell it."

Gil left our side without a word, and Silvia turned to look at me.

"I won't forgive you over coffee," she muttered.

I let an easy smile show itself on my face. "Then tell me what I can do," I said and reached out to grab her hand. She tensed before letting me thread my fingers through hers.

I knew both of us could hear how that made my heart pound in my chest and the thick vampire blood rise to my face.

It is pitiful, how obsessed I am with her.

And I always had been. Even from the start when I'd been trying to get rid of her, it was all empty threats. She had been the one person who I knew would make this existence worth living.

I didn't care if it took a few months, years, hell the rest of our lives. I didn't care. I would spend every moment I could basking in her attention.

She looked me up and down, a slow smirk spreading across her face.

"Nothing. You roped me into this hell. You really think I can forgive you for anything?" Her voice was cold as she spoke. The smirk wasn't one of amusement, it was one of bitterness.

It deflated everything that had been building up inside of me. A low growl rose in my chest.

I couldn't hide it anymore. Her words *hurt*. But I guess that was the point, and just another side effect of the life we now had to live together.

Gil was back with coffee before I knew it. He had one for himself and one for her. She sent him a small smile before accepting it and taking off the top to smell it.

Her entire body relaxed as she inhaled deeply.

"I would like to bring back our morning coffees," Gil said in a hesitant tone. "I would like to start again. Maybe be friends again."

Just like that I saw the part of Gil that he kept hidden from the world again. The child who wanted nothing more than companionship.

"As long as you are buying," she said. Her tone was cold, but the light in her eyes told me that she was looking forward to it as much as he was.

It made bitterness explode on my tongue and heat to flush through my veins.

"She's gonna bolt," Emery whispered as we both stood, arms crossed, against the wall.

Along with getting Silvia out of the room, it was also time for her fitting.

Not all ceremonies required something as extravagant as

this, but our clan had a tradition, one that I was going to uphold. Every new clan head got fitted for something they would only wear twice.

Once when they take the title of clan head.

The next when they transfer the power to their heir.

Silvia, the seamstress, and Gil were in the same room, all critically looking at Silvia's newest garment. I expected her to flush under the pressure, but she stood there with a cool expression and spoke in a low, controlled tone as she gave feedback to both Gil and the seamstress.

This was not the same girl who I thought would be in this position. The one who was *scared* of this title.

She fell into this role easily. *Too* easily.

I'd hoped that she'd choose a dress, but I was almost glad that she didn't. It wasn't like her to choose one, and the last thing I wanted was for her to pretend she was someone she was not. She'd picked a one-piece jumper that hugged her hips and ass while the front dropped in a low V. The fabric was black and shimmery and fell elegantly around her breasts and down her arms.

The seamstress was trying to pair it with the ceremonial robes. The same ones I would drape across her shoulders when the time came. They were bloodred. A symbol of all of the blood spilled by the kings before her. Something we were meant to wear proudly.

It was all a farce. Everyone knew Silvia was the clan head regardless of whether or not we did the ceremony, but this needed to be done to show that not only I accepted her, but the other clan heads as well.

We didn't need any more division.

"I don't think she will," I lied. I was terrified she would.

The seamstress was out of our compound and closer to

Seattle than I would have liked. It still may have been my clan's territory, but it gave her the perfect chance to run.

Gil said something to the seamstress, and she nodded and bent down to pin the fabric at Silvia's ankles. My eyes drifted to the mirror, and a bolt of electricity ran through me when I caught Silvia's silver-blue gaze. Her eyes had just a hint of red in them, but for a moment there, she looked just like her human self.

"Are you sure this is what you want?" Emery asked and effectively ruining all the warm and fuzzy feelings that had been rising in me.

"What are you on about now?" I asked with a huff.

She hadn't hidden her dislike for Silvia and had more than once made a comment to me about just how much she thought her new clan head was not up to the task.

"An outsider as clan head," she said. "Someone taking your birthright."

I held Silvia's gaze for a moment longer before turning to Emery. For the first time in a long time, she was looking at me without an ounce of humor in her expression.

I would have liked to think of us as friends. Of course she had to respect my title, and there were times our work relationship got in the way of things, but I wanted to be friends.

Maybe I am more similar to Gil than I originally thought.

But if she didn't accept Silvia as the new clan head, then trouble was on the horizon.

"You're an outsider as well," I noted.

She turned toward me and dropped her voice in a whisper.

"But I am not the new *clan head*," she said. "You have been waiting, what? Three hundred? Five hundred years for this? And she just comes in, stabs your father in his face until he dies, and you just accept it?"

Two hundred but I didn't correct her.

I ground my teeth together. There was a time when I wanted the title. When I wanted to prove my father wrong about everything. I had dreams of punishing him. Dreams of showing him that I could be a better king than he could ever be.

But a bigger part of me didn't want it. I didn't want the responsibility, and I knew I wasn't fit for this position. I wanted it for shallow reasons that would've only satisfied me for maybe a few months before I realized that I'd never wanted this at all.

I would've been alone save for Gil by my side. It wasn't the life I wanted to live.

"I was never fit for the position," I told her. "And even if I was, I wanted more for myself than this. I wanted freedom, I wanted the ability to come and go as I pleased. To *love* as I pleased. The throne is a lonely place to be, but I am hoping with me, you, and Gil that Silvia will never have to feel the same loneliness that causes people like my father to corrode from the inside out."

She digested my words and turned back to look at Silvia with a hard expression.

They were just about done now. They pinned a mock robe to her shoulders and had her twirl around in it. The real robe was hidden deep in my father's old room and locked in a safe. It would come out only the day of, but even so, I could just imagine how good it would look on her.

Unlike me, she was made for this. No matter what anyone else thought, even her. I could feel it. There was something awakening inside of her. Something that I had never seen before.

Her chin was held high and her eyes trailed down her own form, critically assessing every single wrinkle and stitch.

This was the vision she would show our clan, and I had no doubt that they would fall for her.

"She has not an ounce of diplomacy in her," Emery grumbled. "She cut Vance's dick off. You remember that right?"

A smile pulled at my lips, and I pushed off the wall.

"Maybe that's exactly what we need."

CHAPTER 9

SILVIA

M*orning coffee.*

Though this time Gil and I had taken it alone. Something I was grateful for. Being around Keir the last few days had been far too much for me to handle.

"You should have come with me back then," I said as I held the coffee in my hands and inhaled its scent.

The morning air was chilly, but my turtleneck protected against it for the most part. Gil had insisted we stay out of the garden for our first coffee together and offered up the balcony connected to his room.

Outside there was a single table and two chairs overlooking the west side of the compound and the trees surrounding it. The French doors to his room were wide open, and his scent lingered all about.

It was a warm, homey scent that made my chest twist.

A smile spread across Gil's face. "I would've just been deadweight," he said softly.

"But you would be free," I said. "Maybe we both would've been."

"Or dead," he countered. "But besides that, Keir needs me more than you ever did."

Bitterness filled me. *Keir* was a spoiled heir who'd gotten exactly what she'd signed up for. Shackling Gil to her seemed almost cruel and entirely too selfish.

"Keir never needed anyone," I said before I could stop myself.

I bit my tongue after the words spilled from my mouth.

There was a heavy silence between us, and I felt the ridiculous need to apologize.

"She needed you," Gil commented after a while. "But I would suffice in the meantime."

I looked out at the people walking around the compound. Mothers and fathers were hand in hand with their children. Couples were walking arm in arm down the pathways. If I didn't know any better, I would say this was not a clan plagued by the lack of blood, but one filled with happy, loyal people.

I jumped when Gil's hand brushed my arm. I snapped my head over to him and caught sight of a sad smile.

"I'm sorry," he said. "Maybe you did need me in the last two years. Or a friend at least."

Why did his words make my throat tighten? Why did it make me want to hug him?

I vividly remembered how much it hurt when he pulled me out from the torture chamber in the basement, but I also remembered the warmth and relief it brought me.

I cleared my throat and brought the unlidded coffee closer. It had lost it warmth, but this small action was all I could do to stop whatever horrible emotions were creeping along my skin.

"You're not someone who needs to be at the service of people," I said and jerkily put the coffee down. He did the same before snatching my now-free hand.

"It's called being a friend, Silvia," he said with a small smile. "Which I'd like to think we could be again. Title or not."

I couldn't continue on with this conversation. I nodded and pulled away from him, missing his warmth almost immediately.

"Please tell me this won't happen *every* time we have coffee," I said jokingly. Even though it sounded forced to my ears, Gil seemed to let out a genuine laugh.

"It's good to talk about it, Silvia," he said. "Maybe next time we can talk about what it'll take for you to forgive us."

I let out a sigh and sank back into my seat. If this was even a shadow of what I would get the rest of the time I was here, Nat's suggestion to leave was looking better and better.

I was a hunter for God's sake, and for the last two years, between running from the Order and Keir, I was out killing vampires and feeders for whatever insane job Tobias had us doing. I was cut out for that. The action of it all.

I was *not* cut out for sitting in a regal-looking vampire compound and talking about *feelings*.

But a part of me was curious about it. What were they willing to do in order to gain my forgiveness? What cost was too high?

Anything. Keir had said she would do anything.

"What if I can't?" I whispered to Gil.

Gil's smile dropped and he let out a sigh.

"Then I guess it is in your right," he said. "But I have a feeling Keir will be trying her very hardest to get you to reconsider for however long we end up living. She's already lived two hundred years under her father's reign. For you? I don't see an end in sight."

I didn't like the way my heart skipped a beat at his words. Would Keir wait for me? Would she be willing to take everything I gave her and stay at my side. . . forever?

The idea was almost too ludicrous to imagine.

But that didn't stop me from trying.

How comforting it must feel, to have a person waiting for you. Living life by your side. Even if it wasn't the life I would have chosen, it seemed less daunting imagining her with me.

Imagining them all.

"You think too highly of her," I muttered, but there was no heat behind it. I had no energy for it as my mind was still filled with images of us together.

Suddenly the galas we went to back in the day had shifted. Instead of looking at each other with hate, there was laughter, happiness. In these images I wasn't upset about my vampire life but just happy to live here, with her.

I wasn't surviving in those images, I was thriving. Truly living.

And the thought scared me.

"Is it lonely?" he asked. "Pushing people away all the time?"

Yes. The word was on the tip of my tongue, but this time I didn't let it slip.

The last two years, as the Order turned their back on me and Keir hunted me, were the loneliest I'd ever felt, only rivaled by my first years at the Order when I didn't have a team and pushed my classmates away.

"No one is going to like you if you keep trying to dig into their feelings," I teased.

He gave me a hard look before sinking back into his chair. "Someday you'll open up to me, Silvia," he warned. "Until then, enjoy the walls you hide behind."

I let out a scoff. "Such a good friend," I muttered.

He let out a laugh. "You'll realize one day that I do this *because* I am a friend, Silvia."

The issue was even through my anger I already knew what he was trying to do. I just didn't want any of it. Not now, and maybe not ever.

No matter how pretty the pictures my mind painted.

CHAPTER 10

SILVIA

I was back to hating everything about my situation.

Mainly the way my body was reacting to Keir. I wanted to hate her. I wanted to feel disgusted by her touch and cringe away from her. But I didn't.

Every time she touched me, I had no problem leaning into it. My mind and body were at odds with each other, and Keir just seemed to love calling me out on it. Every time there would be that fucking smirk on her face when she heard my heart skip a beat. It was even worse when she smelled my arousal.

This morning was just as bad as any other. I tried to persuade Gil to take me up on the coffee, but apparently we had actual work to do. Though I would've much rather sat with him instead. We'd had a few coffee chats since our first one, and each time he tried to delve into things I would rather not, but I'd take that over *this* any day.

Today meant prepping for the Order contract.

I sipped on my blood as I took in the quietness around us.

The morning sun streamed through the windows and

warmed my skin. I wanted to sink back into the comfy chairs and close my eyes, soaking everything up. It was the closest I could get to sleep in this form, something I missed dearly.

The ability to turn off the human brain was one that I didn't fully appreciate until I could no longer do so myself. At least when I could still sleep, I could forget the world outside.

I wanted to pretend that Keir, Gillard, and Emery were not here and trying to lecture me about what to expect at the Order. It would have been so nice if we could just *live* here in the moment and enjoy the one time that the clan members and Keir's various relatives were not pounding on the door and ordering me to meet them officially.

But as they talked more and more about what was to come, a sense of dread weighed heavily over me.

For the last few years, I had been chased by three different sets of people: Carpe Noctem, the enforcers, and the Order. Each of them had their own motives, and now I was at the will of them all. Keir had me right where she wanted me. The enforcers had already given me a suicide mission. And in mere days the Order would have me in their clutches.

I knew what the Order was capable of, but I didn't know how far they would go with me.

Would they see me as a threat now that I was a clan head? I held years of Order information, and now that there was nothing tying me to them, I could do whatever I wanted with it.

And no matter what Gil said, I still didn't quite understand why it was so important that the clan heads signed with them. The Order doesn't get much out of it. Maybe a bit less fighting here and there... but what else?

All of the unknown questions swirling around my head made me not want to go.

But I am so damn tired of running.

That I was tired in hiding in the Underground where the halls stank of rotting blood. Tired of always looking over my shoulder. Tired of always being so fueled by revenge that the world outside of it meant little to nothing at all.

Was it so wrong for me to want better for myself?

Was it wrong of me to take advantage of what was given to me?

Keir's ankle brushed against mine and tore me out of my thoughts. My heart skipped a beat and the thick blood that filled my veins rushed to my face.

She smirked when she noticed.

Damn.

Her words when we were fucking hit me like a truck.

You can't deny us, Silvia. You may try to hide, but you can't. Not from me.

I hated it.

It'd been like that since the beginning, but it made it harder and harder to separate myself from her.

But do you even want to anymore? a small voice in the back of my head whispered.

"You'll be there with me, right?" I turned my head to meet Gillard's gaze, trying to brush away those annoying thoughts.

He nodded. "I am usually brought to all signings," he said. "But they will bring you to a separate room where you will need to read through everything."

I pouted. "I would feel better with you there," I admitted.

His smile lit up his eyes.

"You will do great, Miss Silvia," he said, bringing back the nickname that annoyed me as much as I loved it.

"Make sure you *actually* read it," Emery jabbed.

I turned to glare at her. I didn't know why her words made me as mad as they did, but just like that, all the warm feelings inside me burned to a crisp. I was not some sort of incompetent random vampire trying to push my way into something I knew nothing about.

"You think this is my first time signing a contract?" I spat. "You forget I was in the Order. I have probably seen more of those than you ever have in your path—"

"Whoa," Emery said with a laugh and raised her hands in the air. "No harm meant."

I glared at her. "You guys want me to be clan head? Then you better start acting like it," I growled. "I have put up with this long enough. You think I haven't heard your whispers over the last few days? Think I will just overlook your words?"

It had been hell here. I wanted this done as fast as possible, but for some reason they wanted me to go to the Order and sign the contract before anything else. It made me nervous, to be around all the hunters again.

And to see the captain.

I hadn't seen him since the last time I was in his office two years ago, and the last present he gave me was a shot to the head by my former classmate. Who knew what he would do to me as soon as I stepped on site.

As Isaac said, *The captain is not happy with you.*

Who was to say that this title would do anything to sway him?

Keir's ankle brushed across mine again.

And there was her as well.

She was at my side at all times and a constant reminder of my past. It didn't help that she'd wound me up last time we were alone together, so now on top of all the nervousness, I had to deal with how I was reacting to her as well.

It was embarrassing. So when I heard Emery's little comments, there was little I could do to stop them from hitting me right where it hurt.

"Emery knows better," Gil said, more of a warning to

Emery than an explanation to me. "She will be better from now on."

Emery's smile told me she wouldn't.

I rolled my shoulders and let out a sigh. "What does the blood contract state now?" I asked.

Gil shuffled some papers behind us and laid them out on the table in front of me, but I kept my gaze planted on both Emery and Keir as he spoke.

"We have carriers that get the blood for us each month from the back," he said. "We report how many people are in our clan to the Order on a yearly basis, and they use that to give us authorization for a month's supply at a time. Lately though, we have noticed that whatever they give us has been sustaining us for less and less time. Especially since we have gotten rid of the feeders. I suspect—"

"You got rid of the feeders?" I asked, looking toward Gil and then back to Keir for confirmation.

She simply nodded but said no more. My chest warmed at the thought. I'd seen far too many feeders have their lives destroyed by what the clans had done to them. To know that we were not contributing to their downfall. . .

"We allow the clanspeople to contract out, but we no longer have them as a clan," he said. "Many of us prefer blood bags anyway as opposed to feeders."

"Speak for yourself," Emery said with a smirk. "Though I do enjoy going out with Keir on the occasion to find some willing ones. What was that bar you took me to?"

The warm feelings disappeared in an instant.

"I see you haven't changed since then," I murmured.

Keir's glare toward Emery was cold enough to make hell freeze over. "That was a long time ago," Keir grumbled. "I don't do that anymore."

"Not like you'd have any time to," Emery said. "Well,

maybe now that the clan head is back you can finally have some fun."

"Where are the new numbers for the clan?" I asked Gil, not wanting to continue this conversation. A bitterness had washed over me, and I didn't want to try and decipher what it meant, nor did I want to fight anymore.

Gil looked through the pile and showed me the current numbers as compared to the previous years, but there was something wrong.

"It's less than before," I noted. "And with fewer vampires they will probably lower our monthly limit."

Gil nodded, his lips pulling into a frown.

"The issue is we are already pushing it," Keir said. "The other clans have the same problems as well. Each month they are getting less and less. This isn't just about clan size. The Order has been targeting us."

I bit the inside of my cheek to keep a scathing remark to myself.

Another time I might even side with the Order, but now I had to think of this from the vampire's perspective. I might not have ever wanted this, and might even plan to leave as soon as the captain was delivered to me... but I would do my duty.

Nat's words still swirled in my head. They were enticing to say the least, especially after all that I'd experienced in the clan so far.

Could I just up and leave after this?

"I know what I need to do," I said and stood abruptly. "Let's go."

The other scrambled to follow me as I charged toward the exit.

"Wait, you don't want to look over anything else?" Gil asked from behind me.

"No need," I called behind me. "I see the Order's game."

And the faster I got this over with, the faster I could end this.

I didn't give myself time to think about what waited me or the fear that was looming over me like a cloud. I focused on one thing and one thing only.

This would be the first step toward my plan, and I couldn't wait to see the captain's face when he realized he was at my mercy.

Hunter Rules

rule 10 sec 5

When coming across a dead
Hunter, no matter the
circumstances of their death,
The Order <u>must</u> be called
immediately to dispose of the
body.
If The Order cannot get to
your location you must <u>burn
the body and all evidence</u>.
If you are also injured and
unlikely to survive call The
Order to notify them of your
death and set yourself and the
body on fire.

CHAPTER II
SILVIA

"You're scared," Emery commented from the front seat.

"Like hell I am," I muttered and pushed out of the car. Gil followed me out, and to my surprise, Keir did as well.

I'm not sure if it was a good idea that we all went together, but it did provide me a small bit of comfort.

I paused when I was met with the stares of all the hunters who lined the Order's perimeter. It was almost eerie in the way they followed our movements. The matching outfits and weapons didn't do anything to combat that.

Was that what we were always like to vampires?

I didn't recognize any of them. And maybe that was a good thing, but at the same time it caused my chest to hollow. The entire world was moving on without me. The hunters I once worked with were nowhere to be seen. I let myself wonder about what happened to the academy students who once used to train with me in the mornings.

Did they ever make it?

The all-black building towered over us, and when I looked

up, I could feel the stares from the windows even though I couldn't see the faces.

No, I can't be scared. I won't. Not anymore.

I'd lived the last few years of my life in terror, and I wouldn't let the Order take anything more from me than it already had.

Without another word, I walked toward the entrance.

The hunters looked toward each other and began to whisper, but I ignored them.

If seeing the outside of the Order for the first time was like a punch to the gut, seeing the inside was like a knife to the heart.

It looked the exact same as I'd left it, but instead of the hunters who lingered in the lobby welcoming me, they glared at me. Their hatred was palpable, and I didn't know if that was because we were vampires or if it was because I'd become a traitor in their eyes.

A throat clearing called my attention toward the elevators. I couldn't help but let out a small sigh of relief when Knox's gaze met mine.

I straightened my shoulders and walked toward him with Keir and Gil following behind me closely. I wouldn't admit it in that moment, but them being by my side was the comfort I needed to push through this.

"The captain is waiting for you," he said as the elevators opened.

We were silent as the elevator ascended. I held my breath when it finally reached our floor and we were motioned out.

There were only two hunters in the hallway, but both of them stopped when they saw me. I didn't recognize them, but my name slipped from their mouths in a whisper.

If I was being honest, it fed my ego.

The walk to the captain's office was far shorter than I

remembered, and before I knew it, I was being pushed into his room. He was looking out the window when we entered, but as soon as the door clicked shut behind us, he turned to greet us.

"Silvia," he said with an almost curt tone as he rose. It caused anger to swirl inside me and my hackles to rise.

"Captain Moore," I greeted back, but instead of matching his tone, I ended my greeting with a smile. "Have you missed me?"

He let out a huff of a laugh. His face remained the same, and the unexpected comfort it brought only caused the open wound in my chest to ache even more. His hair had more streaks of gray in it than before, but it was hardly noticeable.

All in all, he'd been taking care of himself in my absence. Something that should have made me angry because I'd been fighting for my life while he lived his in luxury.

"You are a hard woman to find," he said and motioned for us to sit. I took the seat I normally did and was surprised to see that the picture of my family's graduating class was still on his desk.

The entire situation felt so surreal it was almost as if I were dreaming.

How could the world I once knew stay so stagnant while I had been violently molded into something completely different?

The hunter who'd sat in the same seat that I was and glared at the vampires while confiding to the captain was no longer here. But in that moment, I was glad she was nowhere to be seen. Because the new me had the strength to grab the picture frame from his desk and start to dismantle it.

"Yes, well," I said with a sigh as I popped the picture out, "I am here now, and to talk to you about my clan's lack of blood."

I all but threw the picture frame onto his desk and stared at the picture. I was surprised to see not only were my parents woven into the crowd of hunters, but so were Isaac's, Knox's, and Jase's.

I let my fingers brush down my mother's hair. The same locks that I had. The image of my father's hand on her hip caused a sadness to run through me. They had always loved each other so much.

"If you want to sign the new contract I can have Knox—"

"Not yet," I said and gave him a forced smile while folding up the picture and tucking it into my pocket. He followed the movement with clear distain on his face.

Knowing that my actions bothered him caused a thrill to run through me.

"Our contract has not been renewed, but that doesn't mean it expires," I said. "I looked it over just this morning, and there was no mention that if we should not renew the Order would limit our supply. So tell me, why is it that we are receiving only but a third of what we had negotiated previously?"

The captain let a smile tug at his lips, but it wasn't the one I'd seen in my fuzzy memories. This one was full of malice.

"The contract may stay the same, but we have every right to end it based on your clan's *unsatisfactory* performance," he said. "You have been running around murdering my hunters. Limiting your blood supply has been a slap on the wrist."

I clicked my tongue. "There is nothing in the contact that outlines such a clause," I said. "My actions were in self-defense. Your hunters have tried to start an unjust war with my clan. The Order is lucky I haven't brought my allied clan heads here to have a *talk* about how unfairly you've been treating us." I leaned forward with a smile. "And I've heard you are shortchanging them as well. They couldn't all have been running around and murdering your hunters? Or am I mistaken?"

His face turned the brightest red I'd ever seen. His body was shaking with the effort it took to restrain himself.

I had to hold in my giggle.

Maybe messing with the captain was worth the effort it takes to run a clan.

"My hunters tried no such thing," he argued.

I leaned back with my brow raised and crossed my arms over my chest. "No?" I asked with mock surprise. "The last one told me *you* personally asked him to put an arrow in my head. Damon wouldn't have lied to me on his deathbed, would he? He was even nice enough to offer to see me through until the end."

He opened his mouth to speak, but I raised my hand.

"Let's not, Captain Moore. Let's just get this contract signing done with, shall we? And don't try to trick me with this *less blood* shit you've been doing while I've been gone. You should know me better than that."

His heart was hammering in his chest, and his blood was rising to his face. I could hear every movement and could see the struggle as he waved for Knox.

"He will take you up to the twentieth floor to sign the contact," he said. "Your lackeys stay here."

I gave him the sweetest smile I could muster before getting up and waving him a goodbye.

Knox motioned for me to follow him, but instead of leaving the room and taking a left back toward the elevator we came in, he took me to the right and farther into the building.

There was no one in the halls, but I knew the cameras were watching us like hawks. I wanted to talk to him about finally getting up to the twentieth floor, but all the questions I had would have to wait.

He brought me to another all-black elevator nestled inside a forgotten corridor. It was fancier than the last, complete with sparkling tiled floors and walls that peered out across the city. I wanted to focus on the pretty views, but the terror had already set in.

"In the signing room," Knox said, calling me from my panic, "there will be a few men for you to meet."

I swallowed thickly. "The higher-ups?" I asked.

He nodded. "They call themselves the council. While Captain Moore oversees all the contracts with the hunters, the council is in charge of the ones for the clans. He acts as a third party, and this is usually the only time a clan head sees the council."

I nodded.

The high-pitched ding of the doorbell caused me to jump.

I was about to walk out, but Knox's whisper stopped me.

"Be careful, Silvia," he said. "You cannot anger them like you did the captain. For your clan's sake."

I gritted my teeth and stepped outside the elevator. In front of me was a completely black hallway. Unlike the first floors of the Order, the upper stories were reversed. Black marble floors, black walls and ceilings, and a single white door at the end of the hall.

Knox didn't follow me.

I steeled myself and walked down the hallway, my boots making squeaking noises against the pristine floor.

Without hesitation I pushed the white doors open and froze when I realized the room had not a few people like I'd imagined but *ten.*

The room had windows on each wall with a long table in the middle. On the far end of the room there was a large seating area with three men in chairs that were far too large for them. There were enforcers with silver brooches on each side of them, all of them glaring at me, and four witches standing off to the sides.

I wish it was the scent alone that gave the witches away, but imagine my surprise when I saw not one but *two* familiar faces among them. Cain and Jade now wore enforcer uniforms and serious expressions.

Cain had always had a cold look to him, but never Jade. I couldn't help but compare her to the once-bubbly girl I'd known. Her dead eyes were surrounded with deep, dark circles, and her face had lost all its plumpness.

Whatever she had seen in the last few years had to have scarred her. It hurt to think that while I was on the run, I couldn't protect them like I was supposed to.

I noticed there was not a single gold-level enforcer in this room.

"Silvia," the man from the middle called. He didn't look a day over thirty-five. His skin was clear, his light hair combed back, and his gray eyes were alight with excitement. "Or should I say, 'new clan head of Carpe Noctem'?"

The other two at his side made no movement to greet me, and I realized only then that they seemed to be twins. Both men were of similar age to the one in the middle but both had cropped hair and brown eyes. They wore suits in contrast to the main man's slacks and loose button-up.

"Silvia is fine," I said and stepped forward toward the table. "This is all very cult like."

The man did not laugh at my quip. The contract was already waiting for me on the table.

I didn't take a seat as I read through it. Almost every single line was the same as the previous contracts.

"Who are you anyway?" I asked as I read through the contract. "The council I mean. I never heard anything about you when I was a hunter."

I was planning to look through it in silence but the heaviness of the eyes on me made me antsy.

"We founded the Order," he explained. "Well, at least our families did. And now we preside over the dealings here, including signing with clan heads. Unlike hunter intake, this process needs to have a slightly more *thorough* intake process."

When I looked up at him, he flashed me a smile.

"This doesn't seem very thorough," I noted.

The men behind him shifted in their seats. So did the hunters. No one took too kindly to me insulting their leader, it would seem.

"We know everything we need to about your clan, Silvia," he said. "And you."

I let out a huff and looked back down to the contract. I was about one more page in before he spoke again.

"Do you need me to explain it to you, dear?" The man's annoying voice grated on my nerves.

"No," I said in a curt tone. "But before I sign, I would like to say to you, as I did to Captain Moore, my clan is suffering from blood shortages with no change to the contract. When asked about it, Captain Moore stated it was because of my actions, but mine is not the only clan that faces this." I looked up at the group from under my lashes. "This leads me to believe that the Order has been stealing from my clan."

No one said anything, so I looked back down at the contract. When I caught clause number 374 and something about blood donation, I felt a presence in front of me.

When I looked up, I was met face-to-face with one of the twins. I jumped back, my hand falling to my dagger.

How could I not have heard him come up?

And then his eyes flashed red. A *vampire*. There was a vampire in the council.

Just like there was a vampire in the enforcers. Were my eyes playing tricks on me?

The sound of weapons being drawn around the room caused me to freeze.

"That is a *serious* accusation for a new clan head to make," he said in a low voice. I stood my ground.

"Then do you have an answer?" I asked. "Because the other clans and I are losing faith."

There was a short clap from the man back in his seat, and the twin withdrew himself.

"Enough," the man said. "Continue, Silvia."

My eyes glanced toward him. "Your name?" I asked.

A smile tugged at his lips. "Josiah," he said. "The one closest to you is Marcus and his twin is Mason."

It was my turn to smile. "It's cute that you have matching names," I said to Marcus.

To his merit, he didn't growl. His eyes changed back to the brown they had been before, but he did not go back to his seat.

"There is a clause there that states you will divide up the amount of blood based on my clan's current number," I said. "I would like to change that since you have been shorting us. To make up for the loss."

Marcus's growl sounded throughout the room, and a few of the hunters shifted in their spot. Many were looking toward Josiah for an answer.

"It's only fair," I added after a moment.

Josiah stared down at me, and just when I thought he was going to make me regret it, he let out a light laugh.

"You have always been known for going against authority," he murmured. "And think of this as a thank you for your service. After all, if you had not killed Raphael there was no doubt he would have caused this organization a mountain of problems."

I averted my gaze as a witch came over and ran their hand

across the paper. I was too afraid of meeting their eye for fear that it was one of my previous teammates.

There was no way to tell why the council, and essentially the entire Order, hated the royal vampire family, but I had a feeling it had something to do with the pile of redacted documents the enforcers found in the captain's office.

I stepped forward again and looked at the contract, but when I caught sight of clause 373, I realized it was the last one. It was about quarrels between clans being their own and having no reflection on the Order, but nothing about blood donation.

"There is no clause 374," I said and looked back up to Josiah. "Did the witch remove it?"

"There are only 373 clauses," he said. "Are you done?"

He waved the witches over.

I tried not to make a face as Cain and Jade stood on either side of me. It was hard to look at what my former teammates had become. They were but husks of the people they once were, and it was all the more obvious when they got closer.

Was this the project they were working on when I'd left?

"When you sign, the four of us will use our magic to make this a binding contract," Cain said. "You will feel burning and discomfort, but it will end as soon as you're done."

"I didn't know that these were bound by magic," I said to Josiah with a glare. "What happens if I break it?"

Josiah's smiled widened.

"It's a new addition to our signing process," he said. "If you break it, it will signal one of the witches surrounding you, and we will then take you in for questioning. It doesn't hurt much, I promise."

I didn't like this. I understood now all too well why the previous clan head didn't trust witches.

But what choice did I have?

"Fine," I grumbled and looked for a pen but there was none.

Jade handed me a glowing cylindrical object that lacked any detail. The air around it buzzed to life, and the heat coming off it wafted across my skin.

Is this magic?

It was blue and wavered in and out of existence as she held it.

"Magic," she explained. "Use this to sign."

I nodded and took the pen from her. I was almost brought to my knees by the burning pain it shot through me. I let out a yelp and tried to drop it, but it remained stuck to my hand.

It was a pain unlike any I had felt before. My entire body was vibrating, and the blood in my veins felt like it was starting to boil. My nails dug into my thigh but even as they broke my skin and blood started to spill, it gave me no reprieve.

"Get it off!"

"Sign and it will disappear," Cain said from my side. "The longer you keep it the more it will hurt."

Why? Why did they give me this?

I cursed under my breath and leaned over to sign the document, but my eyes were blurry as I tried to make out the place for me to sign.

Shit, am I going to pass out?

Cain's hand touched my back and only caused more pain to stem from where he touched me. I know he was trying to comfort me but I was ready to crush that offending hand of his.

I gritted my teeth and forced my hand to the paper. As I signed, it felt like every part of my skin was being flayed off. My knees were ready to give out, and my chest was constricting. My jaw was clenched so tight I could hear my teeth cracking.

I don't know how long it took me. A minute, maybe five,

but it felt like an eternity until the magical pen disappeared. The pain left with it, but I felt weak enough to pass out. Vampire *didn't* sleep.

"Great," Josiah said. He was in front of me now and grabbed the contract before I could even stand. I didn't even get a chance to make out my signature.

I let out a growl.

"That was *not* a bit of discomfort," I said to Cain. His mask was back on, and he had removed his hand long ago.

"It is the process now," he whispered.

"Here is your copy," Josiah said, handing me the stack of papers as I struggled to stand. "Now if you have any questions, Captain Moore will be happy to assist you. Your clan will get the scheduled blood accordingly."

I took the papers with a scowl. He stood there staring down at me for long enough for me to realize that this was a dismissal.

With a sore body and a heavy heart, I turned and left, leaving my former teammates in the den of lions.

CHAPTER 12

KEIR

Fury did not begin to describe the violent onslaught of emotions that took over my entire being when I saw Silvia's pale face and shaky frame enter the captain's office.

When I heard a pair of feet shuffling down the hall and heavy breathing, I assumed it was some wiped out hunter, not the clan head.

She pushed open the door with far too much force, and it flew back against the wall, hitting it so hard the doorknob was embedded into the wall, leaving what was going on in the office open to anyone who walked by. She had a stack of papers in her hand, which she held out to us. There was blood on them. *Her* blood.

Gil's breath caught, and he was up in an instant and helping steady her in another. She leaned into his frame with a small moan, the act causing even more fire to burst through my veins. Gil took the papers from her while trying to keep a hold on her.

I was seeing red. My hand dug into the armrests at my side.

I wasn't able to stop myself from breaking them off.

Her tripping over her own feet was my last straw.

I stood and threw the chair across the room before lunging over the table, grabbing the captain's collar, and pulling him to me. I didn't care that his heart startled enough to indicate a heart attack. Nor did I care that his breathing was cut off by the angle at which I held him up.

"You have two seconds to explain, or I will bury my hand in your chest and stop your heart myself," I growled.

He struggled for words, his eyes bulging and mouth flapping open and closed like a fish out of water.

"Hands off," the witch's voice said from far too close for comfort.

I hadn't even heard him come in. But, to be fair, I hadn't heard anything over the sound of my own angry thoughts yelling at me to end this pathetic human's existence.

A weak hand gripped my wrist. I turned and glared toward the offender but stopped as soon as Silvia's pale complexion filled my sight.

I dropped the gasping man immediately and tucked her under my arm, growling at the witch behind me who'd taken a single step closer.

The world quieted when she placed a hand on my chest.

"Who knew the once-feared heir could be tamed?" the captain remarked through coughs. He sat back down in his chair with difficulty and forced a smile. "By an ex-hunter she liked to play with, no less."

"You're a disgrace," I spat. "We come here to work with the Order, and my clan head comes back like *this*?"

Silvia cleared her throat and slowly unwound herself from me. I stiffened only to relax again when she stayed close enough that her arm brushed across mine.

"You didn't say that there would be binding magic that would *burn* me from the inside out," Silvia hissed.

Burning magic?

I shot a glare toward Gil for confirmation, but he looked just as confused as I was. I took a deep inhale, and sure enough, it was there, just under the surface of her skin.

"It's a new initiative," Captain Moore said and motioned for the witch to come closer. "Pioneered by your old teammate actually. Ingenious. Never again will we have trouble with clan heads breaking contracts." He sent a knowing look to me. "Like your father. He was a pain."

"Enough," Silvia said, then grabbed ahold of my arm. "Let's go."

I reluctantly let her pull me toward the exit. I glared at Knox as we passed. I knew he wasn't truly our enemy, but I was pissed at anything and everything in that moment.

"No questions?" Captain Moore called from behind us. "I'm sure there are many things swirling around that head of yours."

Silvia stopped when we reached the door and turned back to give the captain a smile that caused even my own blood to freeze.

"I'll see you soon, Captain," she said.

The captain didn't know how to respond. I let a smile pull at my lips and turned to pull the door out of the wall and close it behind us, but it quickly fell off its hinges as I let go.

The small laugh Silvia let out as we made our exit was enough to set my heart alight.

"I'm fine," Silvia grumbled. "You can leave now."

Even if I *could* leave my own room, I wouldn't.

I sat down on the edge of the desk with a smile, though it was somewhat forced. I tried to keep the playful mood, but Silvia was obviously not fine.

It had been six hours since we'd left the Order, and she'd only drunk a single cup of blood. She had gotten somewhat better, but I noticed the small tremor when she was shuffling through the contract for the fifth time that day.

"Drink another cup of blood, and I'll be out of your hair," I said and grabbed the full one she'd discarded on the side of her desk.

She frowned when I pushed it in front of her.

"Isn't there like a shortage or something?" she said and pushed it away. "I don't need more."

I rolled my eyes and gently grabbed her chin. I was careful not to put too much pressure as I held it or as I brought the cup to her mouth.

"You're clan head," I reminded her and tilted the cup. She opened her mouth for the blood, but some quickly fell down her chin and stained the papers in her hands. "You will get blood even if I lie starving at your feet."

She was quick to take the cup from me. What I didn't expect was for her to get up and grab my chin just like I had. From my position sitting on her desk, she was still shorter than me, but it brought her face closer. I could smell the blood on her breath as she exhaled.

Even after everything that happened today, her being this close to me was intoxicating.

"And as your clan head," she mumbled and started to pour the blood into my mouth, "I demand respect. So when I tell you I don't want to drink, I expect you to listen."

Sweetness burst across my tongue, but I barely noticed it. Her eyes were trained on me, and the twist of her lips caused heat to unfurl in my belly. I couldn't keep up with the speed she was pouring, and blood flowed from my mouth, down my neck, and soaked into my clothing.

I didn't fight her, instead I was a good loyal subject and took every drop she gave me. It didn't matter that I couldn't breathe. It didn't matter that we were making a mess.

I was loyal and I would show that.

She could demean me. Spit on me. Beat me into my own grave. And I would still kneel for her. I wasn't angry like I once had been, instead I accepted this.

Accepted the new her.

When the final drop was spilled, I swallowed what was in my mouth and waited for her command. Our hearts were beating fast, but they were in sync. Both of us were breathing heavily, and the world around us began to drift away.

She was mesmerizing when she commanded. Even more so when she was covered in blood.

"Not clan head," I said and inched closer to her. "*Queen*."

Her eyes widened, and then she stepped back, breaking the spell between us. Disappointment welled up inside me, and I felt humiliated, sitting there on her desk while she walked back to *my* chair and sat down. She maneuvered the chair to the side before crossing her legs and patting her lap.

When I didn't move, she let out a small chuckle.

"I still feel that there is a lack of respect here," she said and motioned between us. Her tone was light, almost joking. "You walk around this place like you run it. You give *me* orders. You push me around all you want, leave me wanting, and you think somehow this is you respecting me?"

Leave me wanting. I cursed internally. Who knew the *motivation* I'd wanted to give Silvia would come back and haunt me in such a way.

"How can I prove it to you?" I asked. "I am not vying for clan head. I meant it when I knelt to you. You are rightful—"

"*Crawl.*"

I licked the excess blood off my lips. She quirked her brow when I didn't move right away. She was testing me in a way she thought I couldn't handle.

It was laughable.

"So you can't even—"

I jumped off the desk and slowly fell to my knees. When she realized she was staring with her mouth open, she snapped it shut.

"And what do I get after this?" I asked and placed my hands on the carpet in front of me.

My clothes were sticky and clung to my skin. The carpet itched against my palms. It was humiliating and nothing that I thought I would do in my life. . . but there was also a satisfaction curling inside of me when I saw her swallow. The sound could be heard through the silent room.

"What makes you think you get *anything*?" she asked. There was a slight quiver in her voice.

I started to crawl to her, a smile spreading across my lips as she straightened in her seat.

She didn't truly think I would do it. She remembered the old Keir. The one who would have scoffed at this. The one who, while playful, wouldn't demean themselves this way, *for her. . .* but I wasn't like that anymore. I would give anything to prove myself to her.

It hurt to see the way she looked at me now. So guarded when before all the emotions she had would play across her face.

That wall was my fault. I broke her trust, and now I wanted to repair it. Having her here in this position would mean nothing if I couldn't have her in my life, for real, and not just the locked-up version of her.

Each shift of my knee against the carpet caused a thrill to

go through me. Such a short distance seemed miles away, but I was enjoying every moment of it. Especially as the shame and embarrassment of it all mixed inside me and heated my skin. Her breathing came faster now, and desire began to cloud her eyes.

"I have shown my loyalty," I said as I got to her feet. I sat back on my heels, squared my chest, and grabbed her right ankle.

She let out a small gasp when I pulled it to my lap.

"That doesn't deserve a prize," she muttered. She was trying to sound cool, and maybe a bit angry, but I could hear the way her heart was reacting to me.

Slowly, I began to pull off her shoe.

"Then I guess I better try harder," I murmured.

She stayed silent as I pulled her shoe and sock off. Only when I began to knead her foot did she let out a groan. I had never done this before, but having her at my mercy and melting into my hands with a single move, I may be inclined to do it for the rest of eternity.

"Could you ever imagine?" I asked, looking up at her. Her eyes were hooded now but fixated on me all the same. "*Me* kneeling in front of you like this?"

"Maybe you like a bit of humiliation," she muttered. "Though an heir, being degraded in such a way? I could never imagine."

Her voice was heavy with sarcasm until I pushed on a spot that caused her to moan.

"Degraded?" I asked and moved to her other foot. I started the task of taking her shoe and sock off with a smile. "Never. Kneeling at your feet, bringing you pleasure, hearing your moans because of something *I* am doing. It's an honor."

My words were playful, but I meant them, and by the look in her eyes. . . maybe she would believe them finally.

"What happened to you?" she whispered.

I forgot about the foot massage entirely and positioned myself between her legs. I leaned up so that I was just under her and wrapped my arms around her waist.

She had yet to push me away.

"Tell me you don't feel this," I said, my eyes trailing to her lips. "Tell me you haven't missed me. Tell me you haven't thought about me *at all* while you were away."

"What I feel is *want*," she said. "*Lust*. What you are doing is—"

"More than that," I finished for her. "It always has been. Maybe not in the beginning, but we got there. I know what happened between us was un—"

"I was tortured," she growled. "By your father. You lied, and whatever fucked up relationship you tried to build with me only brought me pain. *Your* selfishness turned me into what I am today."

"And I can never apologize for it enough," I said and tightened my grip on her. "But I would do it again."

Her face contorted with anger, but I quickly covered her mouth with my hand.

"I would do it again because it would ensure that you were here with me for an eternity," I said and slowly removed my hand. "I could not handle a life without you. My words may seem shallow, but quickly I realized back then that our relationship was much more to me than I portrayed. It meant everything."

She paused for a moment.

"You know Gil asked me what it would take for me to finally forgive you," she said. Her hand fell to the dagger strapped to her thigh. With quick movements she pulled it out and pointed it to my chest, right on top of my heart. "How far would you go, Keir?"

My breath caught in my throat.

"Anything." I breathed and covered her hand with both of mine and pushed the tip of the blade into my skin.

If this is what she required, I would do it. I doubt I would die from it, but it would hurt like hell.

Her eyes widened as I helped her push it through my skin. A burning pain ran through my chest, and I let out a shaky breath.

"This is but a fraction of the pain you went through," I murmured. "The sounds of your screams, the look on your face as you lay there helpless, it has been haunting my being since that night. I will never be able to forgive myself for not standing up for you, and I promise no one will ever hurt you again, not under my watch. Even allowing the Order to get as far as they did today was unacceptable—"

I thought that she was ready to attack me, but instead she lunged forward and covered my lips with hers. The taste of blood on her tongue caused me to moan. She threw the dagger across the room. The sound of the metal burying itself into the wall was drowned out by my gasp. I threaded my hands in her hair and brought her closer to me.

She pushed us both to the ground, pulling a groan from me as she settled atop.

"Don't read too much into this," she said against my lips. She pulled my shirt up disconnecting our mouths for only a moment before she was back and nipping at my bottom lip. The wound was already healing without a scar. The only evidence of it was the blood staining my chest.

I didn't wear a bra, never felt the need to. But as soon as her bloodied hands were on my nipples I thanked my genius brain for making the decision. Her lips trailed down my jaw where she paused to lick up the blood she'd spilled. I shivered against the feeling of her saliva mixing with the blood.

She was being messy, maybe it was a part of the humiliation. Maybe... I liked it.

She then did the same to my neck and followed the bloody trail her hands made before pulling my nipple into her mouth.

I reached down to pull off her shirt. Again she paused to let the clothing fall past us, and then her lips were on me again. Open-mouthed, wet kisses started small fires beneath my skin, and soon, I was out of breath, struggling to keep up with her quick movements and the way my body was reacting to her.

I was slowly losing control, and I had to fight my instincts to flip us around and worship her like I'd promised. I didn't try to hide my moans. I wanted her to hear them. I wanted her to know I loved every moment of this.

It felt like she was making up for lost time, placing a kiss on almost every bare space of my skin. By the time she kissed down to my pants, wetness was already pooling between my legs.

She rubbed me over my pants and looked up at me with a smile.

Fuck. I wanted—*needed*—her to put me out of my misery.

"If I had any more self-control, I might leave you like you did me," she said.

When I pinched her nipple, she leaned into my hand and quickly started to undo my pants.

"I'll make it up to you," I said breathlessly.

It was difficult to get my pants and shoes off while lying on the ground between my desk and the back wall, but when she finally snuck between my legs that moment was far from my memory.

She licked my thigh as she lowered herself to the ground and pulled my legs over her shoulders.

I kept my hands to my side, digging into the carpet,

worried that if I so much as intruded on this that she would disappear.

How many times had I thought of this? How many times did I get myself off to the memory of her between my legs? Too many to count.

I let out a moan when her tongue ran across the length of my folds. When I arched back the sudden absence of her mouth caused me to whine. I looked down to see her watching me.

"Eyes on me, Keir," she commanded.

Fuck. My name was so simple sounding normally. I'd forgotten how it made me feel for it to come from her lips.

When I held eye contact with her, she rewarded me by latching on to my clit. Two fingers pushed inside of me, and without warning, she began thrusting them into me with a speed and power that I hadn't expected.

She wanted to get me off, and with the way she was fucking me, I was going to come fast.

It'd been far too long since we were last together, and even longer before then. I'd been waiting for her and hadn't dared find anyone else.

"Fuck, faster," I moaned.

She didn't need to be told twice. I wanted to ride this out, but I couldn't. It happened faster than I could control myself.

Liquid heat swirled in my body as my orgasm ran through me. I couldn't make a noise as she continued to fuck me through it. It came hard and pushed me off the edge in a way I had only dreamed of in the last few years. My cunt was clenching around her fingers, but that didn't stop her. She was on a mission and by God was I already ready to start screaming her name from the rooftops.

When my body finally relaxed, I grabbed ahold of her and forced her to sit on my lap. I didn't try and take her pants off but quickly pushed my hand into them and began rubbing her clit over her underwear.

"Kiss me," I all but begged as she looked down at me.

She rocked against my hand, letting out small moans as she chased her own pleasure. When she didn't kiss me, I grabbed her by the back of the neck and forced her to me. When her tongue pushed into my mouth, I rewarded her by slipping into her underwear and teasing her entrance.

She was already so wet it was easy to slide my fingers right into her. She tried to pull away, but I kept a firm grip on her mouth as I pulled forth an orgasm from her.

I wasn't in a rush like she was. I wanted to make this last. This was one of the only times that she would let her guard down around me, and I was afraid as soon as she came we would go back to the way we were.

"You feel it," I said as I pulled away. "You know it's not just sex."

I ground the heel of my palm against her clit pulling a long moan from her.

"Don't try to kid yours—"

She was cut off when I pulled a nipple into my mouth and bit on it lightly. I longed to sink my fangs into my previous bites but would refrain until she asked.

"Again," she commanded.

I changed to her other nipple and bit, harder.

Her pussy clamped around me, and in a last-ditch effort, I tried to pull her down for a kiss again, but she'd seen through it. She pushed me back down to the ground and rode out her orgasm on my hand.

She looked down at me as she came around my fingers. There was a satisfied little smirk that enraged me.

She really thought she won.

CHAPTER 13
SILVIA

"I can feel you trying to run still," Emery said after a long silence. I jumped, not realizing she had snuck up on me.

I leaned against the cool window and exhaled a sharp breath.

The hallway was quiet, but the world outside was buzzing with chatter.

We were mere days away from the ceremony, and it was causing my anxiety to soar through the roof. It made me tense, and the lingering pain of the magic from the contract binding only worsened when my body couldn't relax.

Again, I longed to sleep.

"What are you saying?" I asked with a small scoff.

I peered out the windows and caught sight of Gil directing some of the clanspeople who volunteered to help set up. It was still baffling to me that people were actually excited about my ceremony.

Don't they know what I once was?

"Maybe I should ask why you are in a lonely hallway while

peeping on our workers when a real clan head would be out helping them," she said. "Or better yet, preparing for her take-over."

Slowly, I turned my head to look at her.

She stood with her arms crossed and a glare on her face.

"Go complain to Keir," I said.

Her face contorted and she let out a loud, mocking laugh. "Ya let me just go tell the pussy-whipped vampire that her little plaything is about to ruin the clan," she said. "You think I haven't aired my concerns? You think I haven't tried to tell her over and over again how ill-suited you are for this?"

Her words didn't even hurt, because they were the ones that I'd been telling myself all along.

I knew I was not fit for this role. I had not an ounce of experience, and up until now, all I knew how to do was kill and follow orders.

"I've told her myself," I murmured and looked back to Gil.

There still felt like so much distance between us. It didn't matter that we met for coffee almost every morning. We were not like we once were, and it was almost impossible for me to open up to him. Even if I found myself longing to. I miss what once was.

"You obviously haven't done a good enough job," she spat.

I let out a sigh. I didn't want to fight. I was tired and anxious and overwhelmed.

"You're right," I whispered.

"Not only are you parading around here without a care—*what?*"

Emery's voice changed from angry to flustered in the second it took for the words to spill from her mouth.

"You're right," I repeated with a sigh and crossed my arms over my chest. "I shouldn't be in this position. I messed up. Made my bed, now I have to lie in it, so to say. I never wanted this. I never cared about people before in this capacity. But there are things I have to do, and in return, things I need from you. I dislike it as much as you do, but at least I stopped fighting it."

By the end of my monologue my chest felt tight and my breath came harder.

"The Order, there is something wrong with them," I continued. "Something's wrong with the contracts. I did what I could. I sat through the pain. I negotiated like you and everyone else asked of me. . . but I don't have faith in them. I want to believe in them so bad, but I can't. I can't be the clan head that people want me to be. I can't be a leader that saves the people. I tried, and I am afraid it is all going to end in ruin because of—"

I squeezed my eyes shut and inhaled a sharp breath of air.

Shut up, I growled internally. *Shut up, shut up, shut up!*

There was a brush of air against my arm. I looked up to see that Emery had left my side. Her footsteps echoed behind me, and a sort of mortification and embarrassment filled me. My skin warmed, and a sourness exploded on the back of my tongue.

I did not just let that all out, and to Emery?

She must have been so mortified by my comments that she just up and left.

I sat there in my own pitiful state and tried to think of anything else, but my words just continued to play in my head.

"You just going to stand there?" Emery called from the end of the hallway.

I turned slowly to see her standing there and waiting for me. Her face was cold and held no hint of uncomfortableness at my confession.

"I'm sorry?"

She jerked her head back, motioning for me to follow her as she turned.

I walked at a hurried pace to catch up to her. "Please don't tell me you're going to make me help out," I mumbled.

She shook her head but did not look back at me as she led me through the halls of the manor. "But I will show you something that may. . . help you," she said.

"You want to help me?" I asked and almost tripped over my own two feet. "What can *you* help me with?"

"Watch it," she warned. "Or I may just leave you to your own pity party."

I swallowed my retort and silently followed behind her.

I had no words for the sight in front of me.

I had seen many things in the past two years. Death, lots of it. I'd seen the worst of both humans and vampires. I was no stranger to blood and gore. . . but there was always one thing that would get to me.

Suffering.

I hated watching innocent people suffer. It was why I always gave the feeders an out. But this. . .

"The ceremony isn't for you," Emery whispered as we looked down at the hospital bed. "It's for *them.*"

I'd been to the infirmary once before, but in a very different circumstance.

Last time a single hunter was injured the rest of the beds collecting dust, now I was seeing beds filled with vampires. Vampires couldn't sleep, but the vampires here lay so still in the beds that I almost believed they could.

I would say they were dead, but every so often their hearts would pick up and a small moan would pass their lips.

"What happened?" I whispered as I looked around the room.

There were almost fifteen of these vampires. There were a few nurses running back and forth between the beds and feeding them blood every so often, but they ignored us. The patients were nothing but half of themselves. Their skin had started to gray, and their cheeks were sunken in. I gasped when I saw that their irises were bloodred and the whites were almost pitch-black.

I had been here for weeks now and I hadn't once stumbled across this?

"I brought them," Emery said. "From New York. This is the latest batch. Had to steal a helicopter to get them from my contact in Alberta. They came a long way, and this is only half of what I would have liked to bring back."

"Victor's clan," I murmured and stepped closer to the bed. I paused when the girl in the bed let out a shaky moan. The nurse was over right away with a cup of blood and started the painstaking process of pouring it down her throat.

"He has been running experiments," she said. "Some Keir probably filled you in on, but this one. . . He likes to see how long they can live with small amounts of blood. He would starve them, then feed them just before they went crazy, then starve them again. There is no telling how long this cycle goes on for, but after a few months *this* is what they look like."

I didn't know what to say. There was nothing I could say.

"Why do you do this?" I asked.

"Gil and I come from the same clan, you know," she reminded me. "If anyone was given a chance to leave they would, but not many would return."

"But you," I pointed you. "You are the exception."

I expected her to take it as praise, but her face stayed cold.

"Keir lets me save them," she said. "It wastes our blood, but still she lets me."

Warmth spread throughout my chest. I hated the feeling.

"Do you still feel like you did a good job if they are suffering?" I asked.

She glanced toward me before looking back to the vampire.

"Interesting reaction," she murmured. "Here I thought you would be madder about the blood."

"I couldn't care less about that," I admitted. "But them, how do we know we can save them?"

"I don't," she said honestly. "But I want to try."

I swallowed the lump in my throat. "You said the ceremony isn't for me. What did you mean?"

"Just that," she said. "The signing for blood is for Cecelia right here. The ceremony is for all the other people in the clan. It's to show them that you are showing up, and *are staying*. No more running, you walk that aisle and you show them that you will be the person to fight for them."

But I can't, I wanted to say. *I cannot save them. I can't be the ruler you want me to be. I don't want it.*

"I am scared I can't do it," I whispered.

"That's why you do it for *them*," she said. "It sickens me how oblivious you are. Do you not see how excited those people are for you? Do you not see everyone trying to pitch in and make this a ceremony you will never forget? Even after you forgot about the people here, they never *once* forgot about you."

Her words knocked the breath out of me.

This entire time it'd felt like the world had moved past me as I was stuck trying to figure out my new vampire life while also running for my safety, but here all of these people. . . they never forgot about me.

I was still anxious, but there was a weight lifted from my shoulders.

"I still don't like you," I murmured.

"Ditto."

"I could fire you, you know."

Her response to me was a smirk. "Ya, but you won't."

I hated to admit it, but the gesture truly did help.

CHAPTER 14

SILVIA

E xcited whispers filled the halls and the garden outside
Keir's office window.

There was an air of excitement about the place
instead of the usual tense silence. It'd started early, even before
the sun rose.

Vampires and humans alike were running through the
halls, gathering all the supplies needed for the transfer of
power.

Keir assured me that this ceremony was for looks only, but
as I looked out at the venue that they were setting up just
beyond the fountain and in the courtyard at the front of the
house, I couldn't help but feel like it was so much more.

It had taken a lot of courage for me to venture outside of
Keir's office and to look out the front windows that covered the
hallways. I'd done many scary things in my life. Faced off
against bloodthirsty vampires. Sat through the Order's punish-
ments. Hell, I killed the last clan head. . . but *this* was what
scared me?

The fabric of the specially tailored garment was smooth

but began to feel itchy as I watched the hundreds of vampires scattered around the courtyard get the venue ready.

There was a main stage made from wood and iron. Black and red roses were perched on either side of it and at the very top, a throne. It too looked to be made from wood with black iron swirling in delicate patterns atop the back and on the armrests.

It was beautiful. . . and I hated it all the same.

There were no chairs, but there was an aisle and places roped off for the rest of the clan to watch.

It looked like a dark wedding, and the slow rise of the sun gave way to a cloudy day that only added to that spooky atmosphere.

"Are you ready?" Keir asked from my side.

She'd been silent as she allowed me to take everything in. Out of the norm from her typical demeanor, but I appreciated it, nonetheless. It didn't seem real until now. I truly thought that this was all a ploy, and that my job here would be at most to sit in comfy chairs, sign papers, and maybe even engage in a fight or two with other clan heads.

Look just go there, do your thing, and then when all is said and done and you've tortured the captain to hell and back—just leave.

Just leave, Nat had said.

I could leave right after I was done with this. The captain would be delivered to my feet in a mere day's time, and I could take that chance to leave.

I helped sign the contract and would partake in the ceremony. My main responsibilities would be done.

But that still left the issue of getting to Chase's aunt. I couldn't walk into rebel territory alone.

. . . I *could* it was just that I might suffer greatly for it.

I'd seen what those fancy noise devices they had could do to vampires. If I so much as stepped into their territory and they realized that not only was I a vampire, but a clan head as well— I shuddered thinking about what could happen.

And on top of that, I couldn't get the image of those vampires in the infirmary out of my head. I'd been down there more than once in the last few days and was surprised when I saw that they were getting better. It was small changes, but enough to make me realize that maybe it was possible to save them.

"What are you thinking?" Keir whispered, her voice much closer than it had been.

Her warm hand brushed the hair from the nape of my neck. Bumps rose across my flesh, and I had the sudden urge to lean into her.

You know it's not just sex.

Keir and I were a lot of things. Two people unwilling to give the other an upper hand. Two people who'd had their lives destroyed by the vampires in them. Orphans. Two people who were backed into a corner with nowhere else to run.

Cowards.

. . . but we were not lovers, and we couldn't be.

This went beyond whatever hate I still had for vampires, including myself.

She was right that I craved her touch, craved *her*. But I wouldn't allow myself to fall into her as deeply as I had before. She may not be the one in charge anymore, but there was no denying the power she held over me and the rest of the clan.

"I wanted to run. Still want to," I admitted, surprising myself. "I don't want any of this. The contract process at the Order solidified it."

She stilled. Her hand on the back of my neck paused before trailing down my back. My suit was open in the back, so I felt every brush of her skin against mine.

"For a long time I wanted to run too," she admitted.

"You *did*," I said with a huff. Though there was no anger behind it, if anything there was a sort of amusement tickling my senses. "Don't tell me you forgot how I had to chase after you?"

"Oh I remember," she said with a chuckle. The sound caused my insides to heat, and the people outside were momentarily forgotten. Her lips brushed across the shell of my ear. "I also remember you holding a knife to my throat on more than one occasion, *that* is something I've missed, *little hunter*."

I swallowed thickly and allowed myself to lean into her. The warmth of her skin against mine spread throughout my side.

"Who knew you were into knives?" I teased. "Though given our track record together, looking back I would say it's not all that surprising."

Her arm wrapped around my waist, her hand splaying across my lower belly.

"The only reason I was able to rule while you were running was because I imagined the queen you were supposed to be," she said. "I wanted you to come home to a place that was taken care of, to people who missed you. Every day I thought of what you would look like atop that throne and how it would feel to kneel in front of you once more, my people doing the same behind me. *You* gave me strength."

I didn't like the way her words settled heavily in my chest. Nor did I like the way they warmed. Or the feeling of my eyes stinging.

I didn't know if vampires could cry, I never had. . . but it felt an awful lot like I was going to.

Why did she have to say that, and so easily? There was no stutter in her words. No pause.

She said it smoothly and like she meant it.

"The throne is kinda much," I murmured.

She placed a lingering kiss on my temple. "Tradition," she explained. "And when it's time to hand your power off to our heir, they will sit atop the same."

Our heir.

"I have a present for you," Keir whispered after I didn't respond.

I turned around to look at her with a raised brow. "A present? Since when have you ever—"

I was cut off by my own gasp when she held out the most beautiful dagger I'd ever seen in my life. While it was similar in size to what Tobias had given me, this one was entirely gold, or at least gold-plated. The best thing was that it was in a shape similar to that of a wooden stake. The same ones that were once thought to be the only thing to kill vampires in old lore.

It was years before humans would find out that it wasn't the wooden stake that killed the vampire but the stab to their slow beating heart, but it was one of the stories that fascinated me as a young hunter. Stakes were so crude, yet deadly.

I loved it.

"It's a big day," she said. "I wanted to get you something special for it."

I reached out to touch the cool metal and let out a sharp exhale. "It's beautiful," I whispered.

It truly was, but the worst part of it all was just how crazy it made my body react to her. My chest got tight but then filled with warmth. A sort of giddiness filled me at the same time that a sadness washed over me.

"I have the ceremony," I choked out. I hadn't even taken if fully from her, but the thought of her taking it caused me to miss it already.

"I'll keep it safe for you," she promised and made a show of placing it in the harness she had snuck into her suit jacket. "But promise me you'll wear it every day after this?"

When she wrapped her arms around me, I didn't push her away this time.

I nodded, though found no words to say to her.

Why couldn't she just let this all go? Why did she have to kneel? Say all those words that caused my chest to warm and threatened to make me cry?

She even gave herself to me so fully that she didn't care if I stabbed her in the heart.

It was all too tiring and made me feel too many things I didn't want to.

Our moment was interrupted by a familiar grating voice echoing down the hallway.

"Surprised our clan head didn't make a break for it," Emery called as she walked toward us.

Keir unwound herself from me and we both sent Emery a glare.

"There is still time," I growled.

Emery sent me a knowing smirk that only caused all the rare warm emotions in my chest to burn up in rage, but there was something different about the emotions after the incident in the infirmary. Yes, she annoyed me greatly. . . but I couldn't blame her.

She had come here with the hope to save the people who were forgotten by all that left her clan. She needed a strong clan head who would fight for them. To her, I was not that. . . but she made me want to try.

"You're already clan head," she said. "You signed the Order contract and everything. You can't back out of this now."

Keir cleared her throat.

"And we agreed to help you," Keir reminded me. "We plan to keep up our end of the bargain. Don't think you are getting nothing out of this."

I couldn't say anything else as Keir's stare dug into me. I

hadn't been prepared for all the emotions this morning, and her words earlier were still replaying in my mind.

"Take me through it, again," I commanded. "With the clan head information this time. I need to be prepared."

Keir's smile was enough to stop my heart, but Emery's frown was the fuel I needed to actually go through with this thing.

The vampire clan heads were here. *All* of them. Even the crazed teenager from New York.

They all stood in a line, closest to the stage, with the people from my clan standing behind them. Keir stood to the left of the throne, Gillard to the right. . . and I was all by myself at the end of the aisle as everyone stared at me.

Well. . . Emery was by my side, much to her displeasure. For once I was glad that I had someone by me. I needed something to pull from. But instead of pulling from our resentment toward each other, it was the crowd that pulled my attention. Something in the way they watched me, in the way they whispered excitedly to their neighbors.

That something was what allowed me to square my shoulders and walk down the aisle as if I actually was the ruler of this clan. I found surprising strength in the people I passed. The ones who looked at me with something akin to awe.

True to her words, I caught Nat in the crowd at the far side. I almost missed her due to the shifting bodies as my stare glided over them. She sent me a smile that caused my chest to warm. I didn't expect my own lips to pull at the sides, but they did.

There are people here to support me.

Each and every one of the faces in the crowd was here to

see a new leader take over the title as clan head. It brought me a strange comfort to know that they came here to see *me*. A once-bloodthirsty hunter who was forced to act as the Order's shadow.

Just like Emery said. . .

Not a *single* one forgot about me. All while I was running and trying to live a life other than the one I was about to run into, they still remembered my place here.

When I reached the end of the aisle, I stopped to look at the clan heads. They all stood in a straight line, their eye locked onto me. Xin was the only one to smile and wave at me. Ian gave me a nod, but the others didn't budge.

I sent them a smile.

A slow, sadistic smile spread across Victor's face.

I turned to the stage, and the four steps up to the throne felt like a hundred.

My nerves were on fire, and my heart was pounding as fast as it could in my chest. Everyone's eyes were on me. It became worse when Emery stopped at the bottom of the stairs, and I was forced to go the rest of the way alone.

Keir was there waiting for me and made a show of helping Gillard fit me with the bloodred cape.

The weight of it held the entire clan behind me. It held their hopes, their lives, their future.

It took my breath away. This was something that I'd overlooked.

I thought this was a stupid show of power, but it was so much more.

I was helped into the throne, and Gillard and Keir stood in front of me.

I knew the words by heart now, even if I couldn't hear them over the pounding of my own heart and the hearts of the others.

On behalf of Carpe Noctem, I accept you, Silvia, as clan head.

They knelt on the floor, Emery behind them, and sank their upper bodies into the ground, their hands facing upward.

The clan behind them followed suit. Hundreds of people falling to their knees. The only people who did not were the clan heads.

My tongue was heavy and my throat was dry. It was my turn. There was no going back after this.

Once the words were spoken, I would truly be the ruler of this clan.

"I, Silvia, promise to rule over this clan with integrity and honor until my last dying breath. To fight and protect the people of this clan as if they were my own blood, for all eternity."

Silence filled the air and slowly they rose.

One by one they rose, Keir being the last.

Then there were cheers.

It caught me so off guard that I jumped as the sound assaulted my ears.

They were *cheering. . .* for me. The lost hunter who had killed their previous clan head.

Do they not fear me? Do they know the blood that was spilled on my hands? Vampire blood?

They had to.

But still each and every one of them cheered for their new clan head. An unknown, warm emotion started bubbling in my chest.

They accepted me. *Me* of all people. It was almost laughable. I couldn't stop looking at the crowd in front of me. I was taking in every smile, laugh, and cheer they were giving me, until a movement from the front of the crowd caught my eyes.

Victor.

He was already leaving without caring that the ceremony

was in full swing. Just as he reached the end of the line of clan heads, he turned, that disgusting, slimy smirk still proudly on his face.

I squared my shoulders and gave him a smile. Something a clan head would do in this situation. But it wasn't a meek, embarrassed smile. . . No, I met his with a knowing one of my own.

I knew what he'd done and what he'd proposed. Him along with Raphael were equally responsible for what had happened to me in the basement.

But I was here now, taking the spot of the one vampire he thought he could rely on.

I saw right through it all. He was turned as a young boy and had to fight tooth and nail to get to where he was. It was sad, but he'd allowed the hate and pain to mold him into the type of vampire I used to despise.

His smile faltered before he turned and stalked toward the main house.

"Drink! Eat! We celebrate until the moon hangs high in the sky!"

It was Keir who spoke this time. Her words seemed to only ignite the crowd further, but quickly they were off to celebrate. I wanted to join them, but the patiently waiting clan heads would need my attention first.

After all, they were here for a reason.

CHAPTER 15

SILVIA

The last thing I wanted to do was have a heart-to-heart with Ian, but I was forced into a corner.

We'd cleared out a special sitting room for the clan heads to mingle in after the ceremony where we would drink our fill and then get down to business. Unlike the previous clan head, not only did I hate galas, but we were also running low on blood, so we had to keep this as small as possible.

Though there was nothing small about the room. It was about four times Keirs office with polished marble floors, high ceilings, and windows towards the back. The ceiling was painted with an intricate mural of angels paired with a large chandelier. The large crystals on them left rainbows on the light yellow walls. If I squinted, I could make out the slightly raised floral designs in the wall paper. To top it all off there was a large table in the middle filled with glasses of blood and a single intricate bouquet of flowers.

Many of the clan heads were already talking among themselves, forgetting that I was even here, but there were a few who singled me out right away.

Xin *and* Ian.

The energetic vampire had pulled me into a hug while Ian stood by and sipped his blood. He was probably thinking of all the ways he could tell me off for cutting his son's dick off. I wouldn't blame him. He'd been watching him like a hawk for years, no doubt knowing that I would be back for him.

Ian was a smart vampire, but that didn't mean he would take kindly to someone who hurt his own.

So imagine my surprise when he opened his mouth and started with, "Two years too late but glad you finally got to visit the compound. Here I was thinking you'd stick to your guns about not visiting."

Vampire blood was too slow and thick to cause me to blush right away, but damn did my face feel hot. I never once thought that I would have to stand in front of this man and talk to him about this. I expected anger. He'd been apologetic when he saw me as a human, but I thought for the most part that was a farce, and now that I was a vampire, he would drop the act altogether.

"It was very nice," I said and sipped my own still-full cup of blood. "A bit too big for a main house if you ask me, but you've done well with the place."

Xin looked over her shoulder and to Keir, who was watching us intently as other clan heads surrounded her. Gil was next to her and so was Emery, but they both kept their distance and allowed me space to mingle.

For once, I wished Emery would butt in.

Ian let out a light laugh.

"Yes, well, it will feel a bit smaller now that I have named a new heir. She comes with a family of her own, two kids and a partner," he said and paused to take a sip of his blood. He was letting me digest the information.

"I didn't know you could name someone who wasn't a direct line," I said with a hum.

"I can do whatever suits my clan best," he said with a smile. "And having an heir who can only disgrace the clan would not look good. Come to the compound soon. I'd like you to meet her."

I let an easy smile spread across my face. "We can arrange that."

Ian opened his mouth to say something, but we were interrupted by a loud crashing sound. I peered behind Ian to see that the table in the middle, which had been full of glasses of blood for the clan heads, was now destroyed, and the teen vampire stood atop it with a wild smirk.

He'd thrown all etiquette out the window. I looked at the other vampires around us, and they were looking at him, all with equally appalled expressions. Before this he'd been somewhat contained, but it looked like we were going to be seeing another side of him.

"This is nice and all, but it has been *two years* since Silvia has decided to grace us with her presence," Victor said. His voice boomed across the space. Vampires froze and all eyes were on me in an instant.

I guess it's actually time to act like a clan head.

"If you needed attention, Victor, all you had to do was ask," I said with a bemused smirk, showing him that I wasn't at all affected by his outburst, or the waste of blood.

It was a total lie though. Inside I was fuming.

The Order had yet to send the blood we were promised. Meaning that my entire clan was suffering, especially the ones in the infirmary.

There were a few chuckles here and there, and I almost

motioned for the staff to come help him down, but instead I crossed the floor myself. He worked hard to keep his smirk up, but the closer I got the easier it was to see the hate in his eyes.

When I got to the table, I held out my hand for him.

"Come," I commanded. "You've gotten my attention, now let's talk."

He made a move to jump off the table himself, but not before kicking one of the last remaining glass pitchers of blood. The dark-red liquid splattered across the floor, and glass fell by my feet.

"Oops," he said when his feet landed on the ground. His smile almost looked genuine.

He started to walk away, but I was quick to grab his wrist.

Hisses rang out from all around me, accompanied by growls. There was already a low growl coming from Victor's chest as he turned to look at where we were connected.

"It's quite unfair to have the staff clean up your mess, isn't it?" I asked with a polite smile.

"My mess?" he asked.

"Yes," I said and tightened my grip on his wrist. "You are in *my* compound and went out of your way to ruin the blood we'd prepared for you, in a shortage no less."

"You really expect me, a clan head who has been around since your grandfather was sperm in his father's dusty sack, to drop to my knees like some sort of staff and *clean*?" He tried to pull his hand away, but I kept a strong hold.

Something dark spiked around us. I'd felt this power before when I first saw Keir but was taken aback by how horrible it felt crawling over my skin.

Bloodlust.

"Silvia," Keir said by my side, her hand coming to rest on my shoulder. "Let's keep the peace."

Victor didn't even look at her as he smirked at me. "Yeah, *Silvia*. Let's keep the peace."

I was tempted to show him exactly how angry I was until I heard the whispers of some of the older clan heads behind me.

"New clan heads are always so trigger happy."

"She wants to assert dominance."

"It's because she wants to prove she's worthy, even though we all know she's not."

I gritted my teeth and forced my hand to unwind itself from his wrist.

The victorious little smile he gave me was almost enough to push me over the edge.

But that's exactly what he wants. He wants me to lose control. To show them all that I am unworthy.

I wanted nothing more than to grab a piece of the glass that had fallen and bury it in his eye socket.

I brushed Keir off and motioned for the staff lingering by the exit to come and help clean this up.

"The next room has seats," I said with a forced smile and placed my hand across Victor's back. He tensed under my touch but allowed me to push him to the next room. "Since you are so insistent that we start the meeting, how about I let you lead?"

"Perfect," he said with a smile, though it resembled more of a snarl.

The clan heads followed behind us without even trying to hide their whispers. The next room was smaller than the first and had a handful of comfy chairs sectioned out. This wasn't a normal negotiation, so I wanted to provide a more casual area for discussion.

The staff had already lit the fireplace, and there was another cart adjacent to us with extra blood. I motioned for

Victor to sit in a chair while I moved off to the side. Xin was standing next to me in an instant, followed closely by Ian.

Keir had explained the group dynamics to me, but it was much clearer now that I saw it in action.

Myself, Ian, and Xin were a group, give or take the few other vampires who lingered on the side. During times of conflict or low blood, they would be the first that we turned to.

A few of the older vampires were off to the side, ones that I'd learned sided with the previous clan head.

And Victor was all alone in his chair, the thought seemingly not bothering him at all as he motioned for one of the staff to bring him a glass.

I wasn't in the business of empathizing with people, but I couldn't help but wonder about the teenager he'd been when he was turned. He was a powerful, violent clan head... but did he ever get tired of it? Of having no one by his side? I wondered if his loneliness had ever bothered him. If he had hated himself when he was first turned as much as I had when I was.

"We should talk about your contract first, obviously," Victor said, his tone patronizing.

"No changes," I said while meeting the gaze of each of the clan heads there. "We should expect new stock during the usual time. That is all."

Though the Order still had yet to make up for the drop in blood, but I wouldn't say anything to cause alarm... *yet*.

Victor shifted in his seat, but it was Ian who spoke first.

"Our last drop off has already been depleted, and we were forced to use our reserves," he said.

There were murmurs of agreement around the room.

"We have been able to source from the small clans around us," Xin said. "They've had no trouble getting blood, yet everyone in this room has been subject to the Order's unfairness."

"How long have they been targeting everyone?" I asked.

"Two years," Victor said, calling all attention back to him. "Around the time you bolted."

I couldn't conceal the frown on my face. "Has anyone asked the Underground for help?" I asked.

The silence caused my skin to heat. It was embarrassing the way they looked at me. Shame was heavy in my chest, but I stood tall.

The Underground never had issues with blood, and even though their ways were. . . less than honest, they were able to get blood in other ways than stealing humans off the street.

"The last time I had an encounter with the Underground was when they stole all my feeders from me," one of the older vampires grumbled. I recognized him as the head from the Levesque clan. The same one who'd been abusing his feeders.

His disapproval of working with the Underground made sense, after all I was a part of the team that stole his feeders from him in the first place.

"They don't like clans," another said. "It's because they abhor structure and don't want to be under the control of anyone. A clan head nor the Order would be able to get them to bend."

They weren't wrong, for the most part.

The Underground liked their freedom, but they did have a leader. And one that they listened to.

"Aligning ourselves with the Underground would be suicide," Victor said. "You think the Order is mad that a clan head walked out? Wait till they hear that we have been working with the people who they've been unable to bring in for years."

"I actually think it may work," Keir said. Her intrusion surprised me. "We have a common enemy now."

Victor scoffed. "You only want to work with them because your girlfriend was hiding in their filth for years."

My blood ran cold. How did he know I was there? *No one* should have known.

Our eyes met and a slow smirk spread across his face.

"I am inclined to agree with Silvia and Keir," Ian said, pulling us from our heated staring contest. "We won't last long like this, and the Order will not bend. It would be in our best interest to join forces, putting old grudges aside until we can force the Order's hand."

"I am aligned to working with the Underground as well," Xin said. "Even if the contract works out for Carpe Noctem, that doesn't guarantee that it will work out for us."

Then to the surprise of the group, a vampire who'd once allied himself with Keir's father spoke up. "I am willing to work with them on this," he murmured.

Silence fell onto the group before all of the clan heads started talking at once.

"We will not work with those mongrels!"

"Even if we do work with them, what are we planning to do, stage a coup?"

"This is the only way to get blood for our clans!"

"Think of the people you head."

"We don't have much of a choice—"

I was cut off by more angry shouts. This time they started to fight among themselves. Whoever was for would try and convince the against. The against would then try to insult both the Underground and whoever was for working with them.

Keir's hand clapped my shoulder, giving it a gentle squeeze.

"Let them tire themselves out," she whispered. "Then we can try again."

But the end was nowhere in sight. They were not tiring. Everyone was yelling. . . everyone except for Victor.

He was still sitting in his chair and watching the whole thing unfold in front of him with a mischievous glint in his eyes. Chaos, it was what he wanted. He probably didn't give two shits about getting the Underground involved. If anything, he was worse than them.

He concocted this all and was just soaking it in.

He knew just how to push people's buttons. It started first with the blood and now this. It was all gearing up so that whatever I wanted to accomplish today, he would make damn sure I didn't.

I shook Keir's hand off and walked up to him. He plopped his head on his hand and gave me a lazy smile when my shadow covered him.

His playful demeanor only enraged me further.

"That's a serious claim," I said. "I wonder where you heard that I was being sheltered by the Underground."

He shrugged. "Who knows? Maybe I just said it to get these old farts riled up. After all, it's been so boring when we all politely talk."

"These are serious matters," I reminded him. "We need to figure out blood sources—"

"*You* need to figure out blood sources," he said. "My clan is fine. The only reason I'm here is for a little fun."

I gritted my teeth. "The only reason your clan is fine is because you farm humans," I hissed.

Victor gave me an expression full of mock horror. "Me?" He stood up. "I would *never*." He closed the space between us and leaned forward so he could whisper in my ear. "If you just died in the first place, all the clans here would've been better off. You're a coward and unfit to rule. Their deaths will all be on your hands."

I took a step back and squared my shoulders.

"My hands are already stained," I said and motioned for him to join the heated conversation still raging on behind us. "But I'm not afraid to stain them some more if you so insist."

Victor threw his head back and let out a booming laugh before pushing past me. "In another lifetime I may have liked you, Silvia," he said and made a point to brush across me a bit too hard, causing me to stumble to the side. "Pity it's not this one."

I watched him seamlessly join the conversation again.

"Be careful," Gil said, coming to my side. "He's dangerous."

I narrowed my eyes at the clan head. "I'm not sure how the previous clan head dealt with him," I commented as Victor took the spotlight once again. He thrived under it. Each and every eye on him was just another boost to his confidence. He stood taller now, spoke louder, there was a light in his eyes.

Gil leaned against me. I took comfort in the warmth of his skin. "With eyes on Victor, Raphael could do as he pleased," Gil whispered. "He had a thing about image."

"I remember," I muttered.

Emery appeared on my other side. I expected her to give me a snide remark but instead things took a surprising turn.

"A tip," she said and leaned close to my ear. "If he likes you, he can be easily manipulated. He likes to hold his own, or at least the looks of it. In reality he will latch on to anyone who has power."

He seeks out safety.

Even though he was a powerful vampire who could kill anyone he wanted to at a moment's notice, he too was looking for a way to survive this world.

"Bad news for us then," I said and took a deep breath before jumping back into the fight.

It would be a long day before we were let go.

Hunter Rules

rule 76 sec 1

Conspiring with the rebels
will be ground for termination
of your contract and will be
considered treason.

CHAPTER 16

KEIR

"I don't get why we have to agree with them on anything," Silvia grumbled as I helped her out of her ceremonial clothes.

We'd been stuck in negotiations for over six hours. The sun was already rising high in the sky and the various clanspeople had returned to their homes. For the moment, we were truly alone.

I inhaled her scent, savoring it for this small moment. She did perfectly. It would be a lie if I said I wasn't worried about her. I knew she was strong enough to do this. She would make a perfect queen.

I was just worried she didn't want to. Worried that after everything, she would still walk right out of here and never look back. My heart wouldn't be able to take it. Each and every day I was reminded of just how much I'd fallen for her. There wasn't a moment where I didn't think about her or want to seek her out.

It scared me.

There had been a small shift in her today. Even as she

straightened her shoulders and looked over the clan with a cool confidence I'd never seen before, there was something occupying her thoughts. I chalked it up to nerves, but there was something else going on in that mind of hers, and I was dying to know what it was.

I let my hand linger on the back of her neck as I swept her long curly hair over her shoulder. She shivered against my touch and tried to hide the small hitch of her breath.

I let out a long sigh of my own.

How many times have I dreamed of something like this?

Back when she was a human this was all I wanted. I yearned to lean into her and hold her until the emotions of today had settled. My heart was still pounding in my chest, and the stress of the clan heads fighting still weighed on my shoulders.

"Because uniting with the clan heads is important," I murmured. "In a world where there are organizations built to kill us, and they are very good at their job if I may remind you, we can only rely on each other."

She let the clothes fall to the ground and turned to meet my gaze. Her brows were pulled together and her lips formed a pout. I wanted nothing more than to pull her bottom lip into my mouth and bite on it.

"But the Order is there to protect," she said. "If you follow the rules, they *shouldn't* harm you."

I brushed a lock of hair behind her ear. "They just about killed you, and you still defend them?" I asked.

She bristled at my comment.

"They are not there for protection," I said before she could start arguing. "They never were. They look out for their own selfish wishes. Why else would they keep you tied to them? Why else would they have contracts with clan heads?"

"I'm just—" She let out a sigh. "I just don't understand

what the Order is doing, nor do I understand how these clan negotiations work. Everything just seems so irrelevant to what we actually need to do. We didn't accomplish anything, we just fought until we couldn't fight anymore."

I gave her a small smile. I selfishly took in her almost-naked form. She wore panties but no bra yet didn't try to cover herself or step away from me. We were making progress. I could feel it. But instead of heading back to what we were, we were diving headfirst into new and exciting territory.

"That's all this is," I said and trailed my hand down her bare arm. My mouth watered as her nipples hardened under my touch. "We will talk until we cannot anymore. Sometimes it takes months to come to an agreement on a single point, other times we may never come to an agreement. Sometimes there are even wars within the clans. . . but there will never be a time where they will stand back and watch as the Order destroys a clan we are allied with."

The air was thick between us. Almost too heavy to breathe. My racing heart slowed in my chest, and the heat of her sank into my bones.

"It's been a long day," she said, effectively ending the conversation.

"It has been," I said. "You should relax a bit."

I threaded my fingers between hers.

"How does a vampire relax?" she asked. There was a hesitancy to her voice. One that made me kick myself for not realizing just how alone she had to have been during her first few years as a vampire. "I can't sleep. All I can do is lie down and stare at the ceiling."

"Let me draw you a bath, my queen," I said and leaned down to brush my lips across hers.

Her lips twitched, and I let an easy smile spread across my

face. She liked when I called her *queen*, even if she didn't admit it.

"Go on then," she said. Her voice had dropped an octave and a flush of excitement ran through my body. "I expect to find you naked and waiting for me in there."

Her words hit me hard and it became difficult to think of anything other than devouring her right then and there. But I promised her a bath, so a bath she would get.

"You're coming again?" Silvia asked with a laugh as her thumb rubbed hard circles on my clit. Three fingers were pushed deep inside of me and working me quickly into my next orgasm.

Water sloshed around us in the tub and spilled out over the edges with the voracity of her strokes. I held on to the edges of the tub, my fingers digging into the porcelain, and my upper body was stretched out across the edge. My head was thrown back and my moans tangled with the sound of the water falling to the floor.

How long have we been at this?

I'd gotten two orgasms out of her while in the tub, but now the water had run cold and I'd lost count of my own orgasms.

My insides were delightfully warm, but I couldn't stop the shivers that racked my body. Everything was hypersensitive as she forced my body to her will over and over again. She could tell me to do anything in this state and I would do it without a second thought.

There was something intoxicating about the loss of control, especially when it was taken out of your hands by someone like Silvia. She knew my body better than I did. One moment she would give me a break, leaving burning kissed

ELLE MAE

down my neck, the next she would be forcing me into an orgasm that made my head spin and my thighs ache.

"I asked you a question," she growled and slowed her movements on my clit.

"Fuck *yes*," I moaned and opened my legs wider for her as my core tensed.

She leaned forward and covered my mouth with hers as the first wave of my orgasm overtook me. My fangs ached with the need to bury themselves in her soft skin. It didn't matter that her blood was no longer human and wouldn't taste as good as it once did. All that mattered was the need to feel her writhe against me again as my venom worked its way into her body.

Just as she pulled away, I lunged forward and sank them into her neck. I'd lost all reason. The need to sink my teeth into her had overcome my senses. She growled against me but didn't stop fucking me as my pussy clenched around her.

The burst of her blood across my taste buds had me moaning into her. It was the last thing I registered before I was hit by a wave so powerful my sight filled with white spots.

When my mind finally cleared, and I realized what I'd done, I pulled away.

"Silvia I—"

She cut me off by changing our positions and straddling my lap . She brought my hand down to her pussy and began to work my fingers into her. I didn't stay still for long.

"Fuck me," she commanded.

I didn't need to be told twice. I used two fingers to fuck her while my heel ground into her clit. I tried to lean forward and capture her lips in mine, but her hand had tangled in my hair and pulled it back and to the side faster than I could comprehend what was happening to me.

The first prick of pain washed over me as her fangs buried into the sensitive skin of my neck. An intense heat flowed

166

through me. It was nothing compared to what it was like tasting a human's blood, but it felt damn good. I had never let anyone do this to me before. Something like this was too personal for just any random person to do.

She would be my first and last bite, and I hoped to God it scarred. I wanted the reminder. I wanted her to see it and remember just how good it felt to be together.

I slowed my movements as she drank from me, wanting to ride out this moment for as long as possible.

Vampires drank from humans often, it was in our nature. . . but vampires drinking from vampires? This wasn't the norm and was only reserved for those you wanted to forge a close connection to, or wanted to humiliate.

With her, I knew it was the former.

The venom would work its way into your system and your blood into your partner's. Your scents would become one, and for a few days, it would feel like the two of you were connected in a way that was almost spiritual.

I shuddered again when she pulled herself from me. She arched back and began to meet my slow thrusts with her own. Blood was running down her face and neck until it mixed with the water below us.

Silvia was beautiful, she always had been. . . but there was something about seeing a queen take what she needed with blood running down her body that was just ethereal.

I leaned forward and took a nipple into my mouth before lightly biting it. I could taste my own blood on her skin.

When her cunt convulsed around my fingers, I pulled back with a smirk.

"Coming already?" I asked repeating her words back to her. "Have you deprived yourself of blood for so long that even a vampire's will get you off?"

"Shut it," she growled and glared down at me.

ELLE MAE

"I don't think you want me to," I said and put more pressure on her clit. I upped the pace of my thrusts and used my free hand to still her hips, so I could fuck her properly. "I think a part of you wants to hear what I have to say. Or maybe it's that you're afraid that I may try to convince you that this is more than fucking again?"

She let out a noise and placed both hands on either side of me, steadying herself against the tub. The porcelain started to crack under her fingers.

"You feel that, love?" I asked. "Feel how your cunt is squeezing the life out of me as soon as I tell you there is more to this?"

She shook her head, but the whine she let out combined with the way she shook above me told me all that I needed.

"You don't hate me," I whispered. "If anything I would say that maybe you favor me. To come back after all these years and pick up right where we left off. You missed me, didn't you?"

"Fuck," she groaned. "Stop it. I didn't miss you."

"Well I missed you. I was telling the truth when I told you I was waiting for you. There has never been another who can command me like this, Silvia. Who can make me as crazy as you do. I can't even think straight when you're near me."

"Don't, Keir," she forced out. Her body went taut as the orgasm hit her.

"I will do what I want, Silvia," I growled and curled my fingers inside of her. "If I want to fuck you until dawn, I will. If I want to tell you how much I've missed you, I will. And if I want to tell you that I have fallen in lo—"

I was cut off by her cry. Quickly I looped my arm around her neck and forced her lips to mine. The cracking of the porcelain was barely audible over the sounds that were spilling from her lips.

When she pulled away a part of me was disappointed by the silence that fell over us.

I hadn't planned on telling her how I'd fallen for her. I'd planned to wait until we'd overcome that wall that still separated us. . . but I just couldn't keep it in any longer.

"Silvia," I whispered.

Her brows were pulled together, and there was a pained expression on her face.

"Keir, please don't do this to me," she whispered. "Please."

"Since that night I had a revelation," I admitted. "When I thought you were dead, it was like nothing I'd ever felt before. I was so *scared* and helpless. All I could think was that I was too late. I never want to lose you again, and I need you to know that."

"Keir, I can't I'm not ready—"

She was cut off by a crashing in the other room. We both scrambled to get out of the tub, pulling on our towels. I was out first and paused when I saw that my study was not empty.

In my chair sat a person I hadn't seen in years. His fluffy white hair in stark contrast to the environment around him.

"Hello, Keir," he greeted with a wistful tone. "Bad time?"

"Took you long enough," Silvia growled from behind me. "Where is he?"

I gave her a look. *What the fuck is she talking about? And how the fuck did Tobias get in my compound?*

"He's waiting for you in a location not far from here, but first"—Tobias stood and rolled his neck—"we have to talk about what I get out of this little deal. Keir offered a blind eye, but with the trouble it took to get him. . . I've decided to raise the price."

I looked toward Silvia, but she was glaring at Tobias.

"Who is waiting for you, Silvia?" I asked.

Tobias clicked his tongue. "Keir," he drawled, "you can put two and two together."

"Silvia," I warned.

We had *just* gotten through the ceremony and started to negotiate with the clan heads, and she was about to throw it all out the window?

"What do you want?" she asked him.

I let out a growl and turned her to me.

"Silvia," I warned one more time. "*What. Did. You. Do?*"

Each word was forced through my teeth, and everything that just happened in the bathroom had gone up in smoke.

"We had a deal," Tobias said. "Something for the Underground in exchange—"

"For Captain Moore," Silvia said, cutting him off.

I let go of her, my stomach filling with lead.

I looked up to the ceiling and let out a loud sigh.

Shit.

CHAPTER 17
SILVIA

"We need to talk about—"

"No we don't," I hissed at Keir as we loaded out of the car.

We were in rebel territory, and we didn't have time to argue about what Tobias wanted. Though I wasn't totally surprised that he'd changed his mind. He was untrustworthy. It was his entire brand. It was why the others reacted the way they did when I told them that I wanted to work with the Underground.

"You cannot just make decisions like that. It will jeopardize the entire—"

When Emery reached out to grab my wrist, I jerked it out of her hold and turned around to growl at her.

"We are in *rebel* territory," I hissed. "Right now is not the time to be discussing clan matters, and as far as I am concerned, *I* am the clan head, so if I say I will recognize Tobias as a clan head, making the Underground a clan, I will."

Both Emery and Keir stopped in their tracks. I wished Gil was here to defuse the situation, but there had to be someone back at the clan in case this all went wrong, and I would be damned if I died and left Emery in charge.

Keir ran a hand through her hair.

"Couldn't you at least tell me this beforehand?" she asked.

"I didn't agree to anything yet," I said, though we both knew what I was going to do. I looked over my shoulder at the town behind us when I felt a prickle on the back of my neck.

When we'd driven through it, it looked like a random small town. There were normal people walking the streets, a gas station, a few buildings in the downtown, and houses on the horizon. But as we drove through, the people got fewer and fewer, and the feel of the entire town changed.

Things were more spread out, and even though some of the houses looked like they were falling apart, there was a sterility to the place that was too obvious to ignore.

There was not one movement as we stood outside the house. Not a stir, nor rustle of the wind, but the feeling of eyes on us had been hard to shake. The Order training had me looking for the possible targets, but even with my advanced hearing, there was not a single heartbeat I could make out.

I'd come to learn more about rebels in my time in the Underground, but the majority of their activities remained on a need-to-know basis, and that didn't include the bloodthirsty vampires who hid in the dirty sewers and stole the clan feeders.

They'd stayed out of the news for the most part. Stories about their sound devices leaking to the black market were posted over a year ago, but there was rise in attacks that we'd seen.

Or at least that the Order had reported.

So for all intents and purposes, we were walking into the unknown.

I turned to look at the house behind us. It was two stories

with a large porch, and behind it was what looked like sprawling farmland, but there were no animals present, or crops. Another example of the run-down yet sterile environment. It looked like the land hadn't been touched in years.

There were no cars in the driveway and all the shutters were closed. The next house was miles away, leaving us uncovered with nowhere to hide but back inside the SUV.

This was the place that both Ash and Chase were last known to visit. Two formidable hunters were taken and never seen again. There was no evidence that a battle took place. No hint of a witch's smell or the blood of a human.

They didn't exist here, and it made the whole thing that much more unsettling. My gut twisted as I thought of all the possible ways they could have been ambushed.

I walked toward the house with Keir and Emery hot on my heels.

We couldn't waste any more time. I'd been entertaining Carpe Noctem for weeks, and that meant the trail was steadily becoming stale. My main goal was to get information, but I would be a liar if I said that Knox's pleadings were not a constant in the back of my mind as I approached the house.

I thought of Jane in his brother's place. I would have pleaded for her. Would have begged whoever was capable to save her. This was the least I could do. If not to try to get to the bottom of this, but to also reunite siblings.

Just as I stepped onto the porch steps, the door was jerked open, and I narrowly missed the arrow being shot at my shoulder. Keir and Emery jolted forward, each just a hair's breadth away. They were ready to pull me out of there faster than another attack could come, but I held my hand up to stop them.

Narrowed blue eyes looked at me through the crack of the door. They didn't attempt to fire another arrow as I raised my hands in a gesture of surrender. The smell of old magic and blood hit my senses.

"I am Silvia," I announced and took another step toward the door.

The sound of heartbeats and shuffling within hit me as the door was cracked open even more. My heart began racing.

Maybe they were never ambushed in the first place. Maybe they walked up those steps just like I had.

Did they fight? Did they spook them? Am I next?

"Fall back," Emery growled.

I ignored her.

"I am the Carpe Noctem clan head," I said and inched forward. "I am here to ask some questions about what you know about the children of hunters being murdered by vampires. Or at least what seems to be vampires."

"Did the Order send you?" a voice called from inside. It was distinctly female, and I had a funny feeling that this was the exact woman I was looking for.

"I do not ally myself with them," I said and stood tall.

"Then why do you want to know about the hunters?" she asked.

"I was one," I said and took a startled step back when she pushed through the door with two other rebels behind her.

The woman's face was partially concealed by her silver mask. She held a long sword in her hand, and the other two other held bows and arrows. Each of their gazes was trained on me, and they went so still even their breathing paused.

"Listen, I know you don't trust vampires, but I was like you once," I forced out, feeling a strong anxiousness washing over me. I couldn't fight them. I needed them alive, and I needed to get answers. "And now I have no choice but to come and ask what you know about them. My parents. . . they were killed by vampires, and ever since I've been trying to understand why hunters like them could fall so easily."

"What does that have to do with me?" she asked. Her eyes were on me while the others were narrowed on the two vampires behind me.

"Enforcers are dying," I said. "Just like their parents, and you are the only person we can track down who has a connection to them. You're Chase's aunt, right? He was supposed to come here—"

She waved the other two off and moved back to the door.

"Wait," I said in a panic. "I need to know what happened to my fam—"

"What does a clan head know about Chase?" she growled and paused but did not look back to me.

"I worked with him," I said, though the white lie tasted sour on my tongue. "As an enforcer. I was to join his team before. . . before I was tortured and turned against my will."

She turned back to look at me with a hard expression.

"How does a hunter-turned-vampire become clan head?" she asked.

I swallowed thickly.

"I killed the leader as payback for what he did to me," I answered truthfully.

A small smirk spread across her lips, and slowly, she turned and pushed the door open, motioning for me to come inside.

"I soundproofed the house for a reason," she warned. "Now if you want to talk about this, I suggest you get inside."

I nodded and swallowed my fear before stepping forward.

"Silvia," Keir called.

"Don't worry, dear," the woman said. "I suspect if she's strong enough to kill a clan head, she's not someone who I'd want to mess with. Besides, I'm quite curious to hear about your journey. It sounds. . . interesting."

A small smile pulled at my lips, and I followed her inside.

———

"My sister and her husband met in the Order," Chase's aunt, Krista, said and turned to thank the rebel who set a glass of iced tea in front of her. He smiled at her and joined his partner, who was leaning against the kitchen counter.

They had all taken off their masks by now. The boys had young, roguish faces that had seen far too many battles. They looked related, but I wasn't interested enough to ask.

Krista had a few scars on her face and there was a light tan line where her mask normally ended. Her smile was warm, and she was not at all what I'd expected under the rebel mask.

We'd moved to the kitchen, but it was only Krista and I who sat at the small table. Both our people were watching the other's with open suspicion. It was an uncomfortable truce, but it would have to do.

"Most Order couples do," I said, recalling that my own parents met there as well.

She nodded with a faraway smile.

"They got married fast and had a baby even faster," she said. "I would watch Chase once in a while, but he came over less and less as he grew and was able to watch himself. His parents also grew further and further away before their death. It was unfortunate."

"I know how that must feel. It was out of the blue, when my family was attacked. One day they were calling me and checking in and the next I walked in on a vampire attack," I said and shifted in my seat. "Speaking of vampires, I know it must be hard with us here. So thank you and we will make it—"

"Vampires were never the problem," she said, cutting me off. "You don't know much about us, do you?"

I shook my head. "I was around and in the Order for most of my life," I admitted. "To us you were just the people who protected the humans from vampires and made tech that hurt their ears. The Order may have found it. . . annoying, but I knew many a human who appreciated your efforts."

She gave me a bitter smile and let out a sigh. She tapped on the table absentmindedly. I would have related it to nerves, but it felt more like hesitation than anything else.

"We never had anything against vampires," she said. "The sound devices. . . they were used for protection, for us to run. Not to kill."

I sat straight as a rod. "But I saw—"

"We are here to keep the peace," Krista said. "That has been our goal all along. We fight for both humans and the vampires. We want everyone to coexist, and we are against big powerhouses that try to hurt and steal from the people. At least that's what *we* believe."

Unease crept up on me.

"Are there. . . *others* we should be worried about?" I asked.

She shook her head and took a sip of her tea before answering.

"What you know as the rebels started out with the ideal I mention," she said. "But easily it began to crumble when people were being bribed and offered better positions elsewhere. So no there is no one *else* to worry about. Let me ask you, Silvia, do you know who our true enemy is?"

My skin felt warm, and the unease had become something akin to a full-blown panic. I knew what she was trying to say, but I didn't want to hear it. I didn't understand it.

I knew the rebels. They hated vampires and wanted them all dead. *Everyone* knew that.

Maybe coming here had been a mistake.

My eyes shifted to the rebels behind her, but they were still watching Keir and Emery. My gaze darted to the windows and doors before coming back to settle on Krista, who had never taken her eyes off me.

Seconds ticked by before I got the courage to speak again. "No," I said. "I don't know who the true enemy of the rebels is."

"The Order," she said, her eye never wavering from mine. She gave me a moment for her words to sink in. "They *always* have been. They are not what they show the world. *You*, as an ex-hunter, should've had this feeling if you know my Chase. They spin lies about us to keep the hunters from seeking us out for help."

"Why would the hunters need the rebels' help?" I asked.

She raised a brow at me and took another sip as if to tell me that she would allow me to reconsider my idiotic question.

Instead, I tried, "I saw rebels before targeting vampires, so with you are—"

"How do you think the Order would work to spin their narrative?" she asked. "After they took our people with promises of riches and luxury. All they needed to do was keep their masks and run around causing strategic havoc that made it look like we were against the vampires."

"Why would they—"

"Power," she said. "They want to control the narrative in all ways possible. Want to get rid of vampires who haven't broken the contracts? Send the rebels in. They don't want the people to know how many clans have been trying to leave. They need to look like the superpower. It's all a part of their carefully crafted disguise."

I paused with a frown.

"Did your sister know?" I asked. "With feelings so strong

against the Order I cannot imagine you would stay quiet about her involvement there."

Her lips twitched and she took a long sip of her tea before answering.

"I didn't join until she was late into her career, and that's only because of how badly I saw her treated, and what they did to the vampires and even their own people," she said. "It was sickening. We were so close and then—"

She cut herself off with a sigh.

"Well, she died," she finished. "I'm sorry, what else do you want to know? I went on a tangent there."

"It's okay," I said quickly. "I also want to know about the enforcers going missing. All of their parents were killed by vampires, like mine. We thought that maybe, because you were the closet living relative, you may have known something about our parents, Chase's maybe. And who they spoke to, and why this would be happening to their children."

She let out a hum. "I have my own theory about Chase's parents, but I am not sure it would help you with the answer about the enforcers."

"Anything you have would help."

"Well," she said, then paused. "I think my sister was a proficient enough hunter to not get taken down by a vampire. In her own home specifically. And with all that she told me about the Order. . . I couldn't help but think they were trying to get rid of her."

I leaned forward, holding my breath.

"What do you mean?" I breathed. "What did she tell you?"

"The Order was targeting her," she said. "Giving her tougher and tougher missions with little to no downtime. She was being overworked. So much so, Chase was at my house almost all the time."

"Do you think that overwork led her to not be able to protect herself against the vampires?" I asked.

She shook her head. "I think the Order was trying to kill her. And when they didn't succeed, they sent in vampires. More than they both could handle."

My blood ran cold.

"But the Order doesn't work with vampires like that," I said.

She raised a brow. "I think you and I both know that is a lie."

I cleared my throat. "I also thought it was suspicious that my parents and sister died the way they did," I said. "And apparently all our parents have been pictured together. All of them dead and their kids slowly being picked off as well."

She was silent for a moment. "Any more questions?" she asked. When I paused, she continued. "Maybe I can ask one of mine then?"

I nodded.

"You said you were going to work with Chase. . ." She trailed off. "Have you heard from him? You said he'd come here? I've been trying to reach out for months, but I haven't been able to get in touch with him."

Months. Not years like our early conversation had led me to believe. *Months.*

"What do you mean you've been trying to reach him?" I asked. "You said you'd grown apart. I assumed that meant you hadn't seen him since he was young."

She shook her head. "I babysat him until he was about twelve. In this house actually." Her words were like a punch to the gut. "He may have left, but that didn't mean he didn't stay in touch. Though as of the last few years it's mostly been phone calls. I usually talk to him every few months as a check-in, but I haven't heard from him in a while—"

"Wait, Chase knows you're here?"

"Yes," she said. "He used to come over often, too, but the Order has him roped into some stuff. It's why I let you in in the first place, I was hoping you could tell me about him."

Chase had been here. He had come before, but the enforcers never knew. He had been in touch with his aunt while he let his teammates search for her through file after file they had *stolen* from the captain.

All this time they had been putting themselves in danger while he already knew her. They thought the rebels had taken them, but if they hadn't even seen him then—*shit.*

The Order had to have been behind their disappearance. It was finally their turn.

CHAPTER 18
KEIR

S omething changed in Silvia. I should like it, but I was silently loathing every minute of it. Ever since she stood over us and repeated her vows, there was something that had slowly begun to change.

It started small in the days following the ceremony with the polite smiles toward the clan members, human and vampire alike.

Then it changed to small conversations about the clan members' lives outside these walls. She listened intently as many of them complained they would have to commute to the nearby city in order to work, and to everyone's surprise, she'd ordered Gil to help us get some contractors out to repave the dirt road that led up to the compound to give the people easier access to their work.

And now I had to watch as the young children pulled her though the garden while their parents set up a small picnic in the center. The golden dagger I'd given her was strapped to her side. It was the only small bit of satisfaction I got.

Even if she all but ignored me, she never went anywhere without that dagger, just like I asked.

Seeing Silvia like this was so odd and like nothing I'd ever experienced before. My father's previous reign was nothing like this. Xin was close in how she ruled over her people, but I'd never come close to integrating into my own clan as easily as Silvia had.

I liked to visit the clan when I could, mostly focusing on the guards' families and others who contributed to the clan in various ways, but this would be the first time we visited just normal clanspeople for. . . a tasting?

I followed closely behind Silvia as I looked over the arrangement. Small cakes and tea with a few vials of blood on the side.

Half vampires, I realized after a moment. It took an even longer moment for me to realize that I didn't know their names, but Silvia did.

"Moira, Jess, this is *too* much," Silvia said with a slight frown.

The two children pulled Silvia down with them.

The contrast between the girls, flowers, and cute tea set compared with Silvia's all-black uniform she insisted on wearing was almost laughable.

"Think of it as a little *experiment*," Moira said. She had her hair curled and wore a light-yellow dress. Her smile was contagious.

"Maybe we can try it with coffee next time," Jess said with a giggle. Her short hair fell to her chin, and she wore a similar dress to Moira but hers was green.

Silvia turned to me as she settled on the blanket and patted the empty space next to her. The children had already taken their seats by their moms and watched me with little interest.

My heart lodged in my throat when Silvia sent me a small

smile. I was sure it was for the image, but the lie of it being all for me was too sweet to dismiss.

I made quick work of sitting down next to her on the blanket. I didn't miss the two women's faces or how their hearts each skipped a beat in their chests.

"No entourage today?" Jess asked. It took me a moment to realize the question was being asked to me.

"No," I said quickly. "Gil and Emery both have things to do."

And by *things to do* I meant "prepare for the shit show that would be the next clan head meeting." We would do what Tobias asked. It had the possibility to turn all the clans against us in one fell swoop, and whatever ones didn't turn outright against us on the first try, Tobias was sure to do on his own.

That vampire had a horrid personality.

But none of that seemed to bother Silvia, outwardly at least.

For all intents and purposes, just like with her new position, she just seemed to accept the world as it was now. She even seemed to have internalized the meeting with the rebel clan.

I watched in silence as the women chatted with Silvia and tried to feed her. Silvia complied with only a small grimace here and there to show how much she didn't like to eat the food.

I didn't understand it. Not one bit.

This picture of her, here with my people, was the thing that I had wanted the most for the past two years. I had dreamed of this, of her. . . so why did this feel so wrong? Why did it feel like I was shackling her here?

She showed this playful, happy mask to others, but I didn't want that mask. I wanted the real her. I wanted her to show me how displeased she was with everything, how much she hated the spotlight.

What changed to make her this way?

If anything, she had more to hate now. With the visit to Chase's aunt, and with all the demands coming from all sides, she should loathe her work here.

So why wasn't I hearing about it? Why was she sitting at my desk every night looking through the contracts we signed previously without so much as a sigh? Why was she meeting with new people every day? Sitting and having tea with them? Doing things we never asked her to do?

Yet every day she also didn't so much as glance my way.

A cup of tea was forced into my vision, and I jumped away, not realizing that I had been staring at Silvia so hard.

Silvia looked at me with a raised brow and motioned for me to take the cup.

"Try it," she commanded.

I didn't even think twice about taking the cup and drinking a hearty gulp. I probably should have because the taste of something like burned grass water with a hint of blood exploded across my taste buds.

I stood frozen with the drink in my mouth, my eyes darting from Silvia to the women who were now watching me with amused smiles.

"How does it taste, Keir?" Silvia asked with a rare smirk on her face. "I thought you may have been feeling left out, so I made you a cup."

It took great effort to swallow down the offending liquid, and I couldn't keep the disgust off my face.

"What the fuck was that?" was out of my mouth before I could think twice.

I shot a panicked look over to the women, who's faces were

now drained of amusement. One reached out to pull her child closer.

"Tea," Silvia said and took the cup from my hand. "Excuse her. She has no manners."

Moira let out an awkward giggle, but before I could say sorry, a vampire man who I hadn't the barest memory of came to speak to us.

"Sorry to interrupt, Silvia. But the blueprints for the roads have been finished, and we've marked where the adjustments need to take place. We wanted to get started right away, so the road can set and dry before the weekend ends."

"Ah, sure," Silvia said and moved to get up. "Sorry, ladies. Thanks for the fun, though quite truthfully, I never want to do this ever again."

Her comment earned some soft giggles, and they waved us off as we followed the young vampire.

I was still lost in watching how Silvia interacted with them by the time we made it to the front of the compound. There were others waiting for us who waved to Silvia as we passed.

I didn't even hear what they were talking about. Again I was lost in Silvia. But the more I got lost in her the more worried I became. What was she hiding underneath that mask?

Should I be more worried that she hadn't outwardly said anything? I wanted to trust her, but something didn't sit right with me.

We walked back to the house in silence after hours of being stopped by people. Silvia went along with all of it. Added a new plant to your yard? Had a baby? Needed an opinion on drapes?

It seemed that every little chance they got, people would flock to Silvia while I stayed silent in the back.

The sun was setting by the time we got back to the main

garden, but instead of lingering in the main area, Silvia looped around to the back where a familiar, comforting tree lay. She stared up at it, not saying a word.

"You did good today," I said. Her face stayed neutral.

"They have come to accept me easily," she said. "It's almost like they really hated their previous one."

A growl erupted from my chest even through her tone was teasing.

"I did the best I could," I hissed.

"Touchy," Silvia muttered, turning to look at me. Her silver-blue eyes had been red for the last few hours, but now they seemed to glow under the light.

"I just tried to tell you that you did a good job," I said with a huff.

"I don't need your praise," she said.

Her dismissal caused anger to surge through me. I grabbed her shoulder and forced her to face me. "What is your issue?" I growled. "Ever since the ceremony you have been acting like this."

"Like what?" She scoffed and pushed my hand off. "Doing my job? Isn't this what you wanted all along, Keir? For me to be a good little clan leader? Or is it just that you are tired of me doing my job better than you?"

I hadn't realized that I was stepping toward her until her back hit the tree. She was glaring at me, and her chest was rising and falling rapidly. Her lips were parted and I could smell the remnants of blood on her breath.

My hand fastened around her throat, not hard enough to block her airways but enough pressure for her to know I wasn't kidding.

"You're walking on thin ice, Silvia," I growled. "I wanted a clan head. One who cared about her people, one who wasn't always bringing trouble to this clan. But let's face it,

Silvia, you hate this. The others may not be able to see it, but I *can*."

Cool metal pushed into my skin, the tip of the weapon I'd gifted her digging into my flesh hard enough for a prick of pain to travel up my neck. She pushed the dagger harder against my jugular when I didn't move.

I didn't like how it felt when I realized that she had reached for *my* dagger first.

"I *am* caring about them, Keir," she growled. "I have been with them every day, listening to their every word. You wanted this, and it never matter if I *liked* this, so what is it now? Back off or I'll make you regret it."

I let out a growl.

"You show them a mask, Silvia," I said. "They deserve the *real* you."

The grip on her dagger faltered in her hand, and in a blink my back was slammed against the tree. She'd switched our positions so now it was her glaring up at me while I was stuck, immobilized against the bark.

Fuck.

How long ago had it been that we found ourselves in this same position? A deep desire to lean forward and take her mouth into mine overcame me. I wanted her to push the dagger farther into me, play with me like she once had. Most of all, I wanted her attention. I wanted to consume all her thoughts and feelings until I ran as rampant through her head as she did mine.

It wasn't fair that I was the only person who was consumed by her.

Her eyes warmed and a smile played at her lips.

"You're jealous," she teased.

"I am not," I sputtered and tried to avert my gaze, but she forced me to look at her by pushing the dagger farther into my skin. I let out a hiss of pain. Heat from the wound traveled down and started to coil in my belly. It took everything I had to hold in my moan.

What the fuck is wrong with me?

"Are you upset that I am showing them kindness but not you?" she asked. "Are you upset I still hold on to a two-year grudge instead of returning your feelings?"

Ouch. I hadn't put the feelings to words yet, but it seemed that she could read me even better than I thought.

"And if I am?" I asked.

She leaned forward, her lips just barely brushing across mine. "Are you?" she asked. "Is Keir jealous and needing attention?"

The mock concern in her voice was what snapped my thread. I ignored the pain of the dagger in my neck and leaned forward to kiss her. I grabbed her by the waist and pulled her flush against me while I ravaged her mouth.

She wanted to work me up. She enjoyed seeing me like this, so she would get it.

The dagger was slowly pulled from my neck as she melted into me and gave me the perfect opportunity to flip us so she was back against the tree. I kicked her legs opened and pushed my knee between them.

"If this is the type of attention you were looking for all you needed to do was ask," she said after prying her lips from mine.

I used my two hands on her hips to rock her against my thigh.

"What I need is for you to listen to me," I growled and leaned forward to lick the expanse of her neck. Her turtleneck had fallen slightly in our scuffle, giving me some access to her neck, but with her current attitude, I was seconds away from ripping the entire thing off.

She let out a small gasp when I dug my thigh into her

harder. The scent of her arousal filled the area and caused me to groan.

"I've been listening, *Keir*," she whined.

"Lift your shirt," I ordered. "I need to bite."

She shuddered against me but complied anyway. When her breasts were bared to me, I quickly pushed up her bra and leaned forward to take a hard nipple into my mouth. Her hands flew to my hair, and her back arched into me.

Sinking my teeth into her flesh was probably one of the best things I'd ever experienced. Her skin was harder now as a vampire, but it still tasted just as sweet. Even her blood tasted far better than any vampire's I'd ever had.

I slipped my hand into her pants to cup her pussy as I sucked the blood from her tit. She was already so wet that her damp underwear clung to her. I ran my fingers across the length of her slit, enjoying the way she arched into me.

I dislodged myself from her breast and licked the wound clean before biting down on her nipple. A flood of wetness spilled into my hand. I used the heel of my palm to rub her clit while my fingers teased her entrance.

When I pulled back to look at her, I was met with a breathtaking sight. Her hair had fallen out of her ponytail and spread out around her head. Her eyes were almost closed as she rode out the pleasure from my bites, and her soft lips were open and letting out delicious-sounding moans.

I inserted two fingers into her, curling them sharply.

"What I wanted to tell you is that I have been falling in love with you," I said as I started to pound into her wet cunt. She worked to push down her pants so she could spread her legs farther, and as soon as she did, I picked up the pace on my thrusts, my palm hitting her clit with each one.

I wanted her to feel this afterward. Wanted her to

remember how it felt to be at my mercy. To fucking remember *us*.

She let out a strangled moan and tried to look away, but I grabbed her face and forced her to look at me.

"I love you," I repeated. "I have loved you and that will not change. You can run again, as far as you'd like, I will always bring you back. You can't hide from me, Silvia."

"Keir, I—"

"I don't care what you want to call us, but we are past this fake hate," I growled. "I love you, Silvia." I timed my thrusts with my words. "I've *loved* you for years, and I can't take it anymore."

"Please," she begged. "Please stop talking."

"Never." I brushed a kiss across her lips, searing her own blood on them.

I fit another finger in her.

"I'm going to bring you back to the room and fuck you until nothing but my name comes out of your mouth," I threatened. "If this is the only way you'll listen to me then so be it."

"Keir, I can't," she moaned as she clenched around me.

"Come for me, love," I purred. "Show me how much you love it when I bury my fingers in this needy cunt."

She unraveled in a flurry of movements, and I had to cover her mouth with my hand as she cried out. Her orgasm was so beautiful, but it wouldn't be the only one she had tonight, not by a long shot.

I pulled Silvia's hair and forced her to stand flush against me as I thrust into her.

"Fuck," she moaned. "Since when did you get a strap?"

I never needed—or liked—one if I was being honest, but

one day I had the oddest feeling that I needed to see what Silvia would look like stretched around a silicone cock, and it was mere hours before I had one in my hand. Though this was the first time I put it to use with her.

I leaned forward and began to play with her clit as I fucked her slowly from behind. She was so wet she was dripping on me and the floor, making it easy to slide the dildo into her tight cunt.

She whimpered when I plunged it fully inside of her. Until then I'd been doing shallow thrusts to get her used to the feeling, but it was testing my patience.

"Not long ago," I answered truthfully and peppered kisses down her bare neck. "I would ask if you like it, but by the way you're dripping, I can tell that you do."

I pushed her onto the bed and guided her to raise her hips and drop her chest.

"Yes," I praised as the strap slipped deeper inside her. The position would be tough to hold, but I sure as hell would make it work. "Just like that."

"Harder," she commanded. "I want to feel this tomorrow."

I let out a laugh and pulled out almost fully, then snapped my hips into her. She let out a cry.

Her clit was swollen and pulsed under my fingers as I rubbed circles on the sensitive nub. I'd lost count of how many times we'd gone at it. I was addicted, plain and simple. Her moans fueled me, along with how easily we melded together.

During this time, we were unified. Our bodies moved in sync, seeking out the other's pleasure as if we needed it before our own. Her hands knew exactly where to trail and her lips exactly where to kiss.

There had never been a time where I'd felt something like this with anyone else. Nor had I wanted to.

"I love you, Silvia," I said for the umpteenth time that night.

She let out a whine and spread her legs farther for me. I pounded into her without mercy. She wanted to remember me tomorrow. Remember *us*. It was a thought that caused my chest to warm and a violent satisfaction to rise inside me.

I didn't know when I was reduced to such a simple calling, but as long as she was here, I was content.

It didn't take long for me to pull another orgasm from her, but instead of jumping straight into the next round, I collapsed onto the bed with her and forced her to me. She didn't fight me this time and instead curled into me.

We were silent for a long while before she spoke.

"I've never told anyone I love them before," she whispered. "Not besides family."

I rubbed her back. "Not even Nat?" I asked, remembering the freckled vampire I was once familiar with.

"No," she said. "We never got that close."

I swallowed thickly. "Do you still hate me for what happened?" I asked. "Resent me?"

She shook her head. "Not like before. But it makes everything much more complicated," she whispered. "After the ceremony things have gotten. . . clearer."

"Clearer in what way?" I asked, afraid for her to answer.

"I don't hate it here really," she said. My heart stopped when she intertwined her fingers with mine. "I also don't hate you, or Emery, or Gil."

"But you don't love me," I said for her.

"I don't know *how*," she admitted.

I wanted to look down at her, but keeping my eyes trained on the ceiling was the only thing giving me courage to ask these questions. "But you could?"

There was silence.

"Maybe," she answered. "I just. . . I like you by my side. I like fucking you. I like that stupid smirk of yours. And I like things like *this*."

My heart soared. "That's okay," I said and ran my fingers though her hair. "I can work with that."

She was silent for another short while. "What will you do?" she asked. "What do you want to do?"

"About you?" I asked.

She shook her head. "About your life," she said. "I am the clan head now, and while I need your help, you aren't tied down by this responsibility anymore. You could do everything you've ever wanted to."

I peered down at her for the first time and found her already staring at me.

She was asking about plans for the future.

"Is staying by your side not enough?" I asked.

A rare small flitted across her face. "It's okay if you don't have the answer," she said. "Because I don't either."

I leaned down to place a kiss on her lips. "We can figure it out together?" I asked.

She nodded. "I can't promise that it'll be an easy ride, and I can't promise to love you the way you want—or *need*—but I would like to stay here with you for as long as possible."

"No more running?" I asked for good measure.

"No more running," she agreed. "For either of us."

CHAPTER 19
SILVIA

Nerves danced on my spine as I got ready for the clan meeting.

The compound was eerily quiet as we prepared. I'd asked for all people to stay in their houses today or leave the compound entirely, including some of the wait-staff and guards. It would be for the best, for their safety.

I was going to keep my promise, but that didn't mean I wouldn't make sure my people were safe. It was the least I could do.

"You should go too," I murmured as Keir came to zip up my jumpsuit.

"Don't be stupid." She placed a burning kiss on the back of my neck as she zipped me up. She paused when she zipped me fully. "You're doing good. I meant what I said the other night. I know you never wanted this but—"

I turned around and covered her mouth with my hand.

"I know," I said and shifted on my feet. An uncomfortable-ness was building up inside me. "I'm sorry, Keir."

I rushed out the last part before I chickened out. It'd been building in me since last night and was a part of the reason I couldn't bear to hear her tell me that she loved me.

I had been awful. For years I had been awful to her, and even now, I wasn't enough for her. She deserved someone who could let go of the past, someone who could love her fully, someone who didn't hate themselves for even just existing.

Shock was obvious on Keir's face, and she opened her mouth, but no words came out.

"I never wanted this, but you can't always get everything you want in life," I said. "And at the end of the day, it was *me* who ended your father's life. If you'd stopped me, I would've been even more resentful. I should be thanking you for even allowing me to take over this position. It should be you with the clan head title."

She closed her mouth before clearing her throat. Her hands dug into my shoulders, and she took a few more seconds before responding.

"I was a coward," she said softly. "I was relieved when it was you who killed him. You asked me what I wanted to do with my life, wouldn't it be enough to just stay by your side? To lead our clan and someday hand it off to someone of our choosing and then travel the world until we are sick of it?"

Her words hit me in the chest and knocked the breath from my lungs. They hurt, because I could so clearly see it.

I could see us together, every day, traveling and enjoying the sunset in secret places. I wanted more of *that* life.

"Freedom," I whispered. "I would like freedom one day too... with *you*."

A smile pulled at her lips. "It won't be all sunshine and daisies though," she joked. "At least not if you pull a knife on me again in public. What will the others think?"

I couldn't help but let out a small laugh. "You liked it," I said in a scandalized whisper.

She leaned forward and brushed her lips across smile. "Maybe we can try it again?"

My hand twitched for the dagger that lay forgotten on the bed, but a loud knock sounded through the room and caused me to groan. One sniff and I knew it was Emery by her hair products and expensive colognes.

"The guests are entering the compound," she said from the other side of the door. "It would be best if you go meet them."

I let out a sigh. I *really* didn't want to do this.

"Let's go, my queen," Keir whispered. "We have a deal to complete."

"Will he even show up?" Xin whispered as she came to stand beside me.

The clan heads were getting antsy. They all had cups of blood, but they had been here for over an hour with no sign of Victor. . . and if even just one clan head was missing, we wouldn't be able to introduce Tobias.

Or at least that was what Keir said.

More of a courtesy than a rule, but best to wait.

There were more clan heads in this room than I'd ever seen before. We extended past our usual invite list to smaller clans, ones that owed us. The rules were simple. A clan head would nominate the newcomer and the others would have to vote. Whoever was allied tended to lean one way, but even though we pulled in multiple clans from the area, it was a hit or miss with some of the older vampires.

And without this, I would never get the captain. I would never make him pay for what he did to me. Or find out what the fuck was going on with the enforcers.

Hatred burned in my veins.

Where is that little shit?

Just as the thought crossed my mind, Victor pushed through the doors with a shit-eating grin on his face.

He sauntered in here like he owned the place and had the gall to look offended when there was no chair for him.

"Aw, did you wait for me?" he asked and stepped toward me.

Emery was there in a second between the both of us.

"Unfortunately the situation calls for it," I said and stepped around Emery to gather the attention of the group. "Thank you all for coming. I know this isn't ideal, but I promise to make this quick."

I motioned to Keir, who'd been standing near the exit for the better part of the time we'd been waiting, to go and fetch our guest of honor.

There were a few people who turned to watch her, but Victor grabbed their attention with a snort.

"You sure are calling us a lot lately," he murmured. "Abusing the power a bit, aren't you?"

It took everything in me not to roll my eyes.

When a familiar white head of hair showed itself, I waved Tobias over.

"I have brought you all here today because it has come to my attention that many of you haven't met Tobias," I said and took Tobias's arm as he stepped toward me. Both he and Victor were glaring at each other as he passed.

The bloodlust between them was evident in the air, and if I hadn't been around Tobias so much in the past, I might have stepped away in fear when it washed over me.

Tobias broke his stare down with Victor to send everyone one of his airy smiles.

"I am Tobias," he greeted. "Though you may not know me

personally, I know that you have heard of me. I run the Underground."

There were hushed whispers that broke out in the area. Even Xin gave me a panicked look. The sentiment was obvious, but there was one key player who looked to him with interest.

Victor.

The young vampire looked like he was about to pounce. He must have felt how evenly matched he was with Tobias because instead of that playful, annoying expression he gave me, there was *actual* interest on his face when it came to Tobias.

"Now that that's out of the way," I said and cleared my throat. "He not only has a formidable group in the Underground, but they have been operating as a clan throughout the years. They get blood for their people, shelter them, the only thing missing is his introduction to this group. So I, Silvia, Leader of Carpe Noctem, nominate him as a new clan head."

Instead of chaos, I was met with silence.

Victor let out a laugh.

"You can't be serious?" he said. "The Underground is full of mongrels who steal blood in order to survive. The Order would have our heads. We talked about this before, Silvia, there are a few who will go along with your crazy delusions, but I am not one of them."

I gritted my teeth and dug my nails into Tobias's arm.

"I have blood," Tobias said. "For every clan that needs it. Unlike you, I am not aligned to the Order, so they do not give me my supply. Some of them are obtained in less than legal ways. . . but you will find that the majority comes through our work with clans and the blood banks."

"He speaks," Victor said in mock awe. "I thought you were gonna stand there and look pretty while Silvia fought on your behalf." He let out a huff. "Well maybe that is for the best, after all. . . *she's not very good at it.*"

"I would ask you not to disrespect the clan head who has invited you to her home."

I jumped when Emery spoke. I expected the words from Keir, not her. I looked toward Keir, who was slowly making her way toward us with Gil.

Victor was about to speak but he was cut off by Tobias.

"I know enough about the inner workings of every clan here to know that there is a blood shortage," he said. "I also have a list of names of many of the people in here who have sought me out for my resources. Recognizing me as a clan head is the obvious next step, and one that could help us greatly. I do not see anyone else giving any solutions."

"Because we don't need to change anything," Victor shot back. "We get blood fine."

"Through use of force with humans," Keir said. "The Order hates you as much as they do the Underground. You steal humans, and their children, and bleed them until they die. This is not the way anyone here wants to go."

No one spoke because we all knew what Keir said was true. The clan heads may not have known his scheme, but they knew enough to know how bloodthirsty he was.

"Vote!" Victor yelled with a pout.

He was losing.

I looked toward Keir to see she was already looking toward me with a smile. She saw it too. The panic.

"I vote to recognize Tobias as clan head of the Underground," I said with my hand raised.

"I do too," Xin said with a clear voice.

"I recognize Tobias as clan head," Ian said.

I looked toward the clan heads I invited. Four more slowly raised their hands and echoed what we'd said.

Slowly another two raised their hands. . . and then there was silence. There were nineteen of us.

Shit.

"I vote no," Victor proclaimed, his voice giddy.

Hands shot up faster than when they were agreeing. I didn't even need to tally them up.

We lost. We had *lost.* The captain, he was gone to me. The answers, the revenge. . . it was all *gone.*

"No one wants him here," Victor said with a smirk. "Now, Silvia, can you please stop calling us over whenever you feel like it? It's about a six-hour plane ride, and I am frankly tired of seeing your face."

Keir let out a growl that only caused Victor to smile.

"Don't try to fight me, Keir," he warned. "Don't you remember what happened last time?"

In a flash, Tobias was gone from my hold. It took me a few moments to understand what was happening, but when I did, I froze.

There was a struggle, but even still, Tobias had gotten Victor down to the ground in seconds. Snarls filled the room as Victor attempted to fight back, but Tobias was both too quick and too strong.

Keir was the first to step toward them, but I held her back.

Emery tried as well, and I pulled her wrist back. When Ian attempted to jump in, I let out a growl.

"Do not interfere!" I commanded.

The entire room froze save for the two snarling vampires locked in a death battle.

No one could interfere. If we did, we would be showing a side, and depending on who won, it could end up very badly for us.

This was a once in a lifetime chance.

Neither I nor Keir had realized it at the time, but what she did was not cowardice, it was a gift. She was handing me the keys to the kingdom, the power to take what was *mine*. . . and now we would do the same for Tobias.

This would be the end of an era. One in which Victor ruled over us all. Where he harmed humans without remorse.

There was a gracefulness to the way that Tobias tore Victor's head off, and in the way he tucked it under his arm and stared out at the group.

The faraway look in his eyes had disappeared, and in front of me stood the most dangerous wild animal I'd ever seen. And he was now covered in a clan head's blood.

"He did not bring any men," Keir said after a heartbeat. "So we will have some logistics to figure out but. . ."

When she bowed it was like a domino effect. Each clan head tilted their head, one after another, giving Tobias the welcome I could only have dreamed of.

When his dark gaze met mine, I bowed as well.

Well that's one way to solve the problem.

CHAPTER 20
SILVIA

"I have half a mind to send you back this instant," I growled to the two vampires in front of me. "Maybe with one limb less each."

We'd found a small room that overlooked the garden to prep for our next meeting with the clan heads. The one that we would take Tobias to. We had many things to go over, all of them surrounding the possibility of the other clan heads rioting and cutting off all ties.

It was unlikely that our allies would cut ties, but we had to be prepared. . . And with the blood shortage, we would have to get creative with the ways that we could ethically source blood.

Tobias was always an option, but the more we relied on that bastard the more control he had over us.

And these two had to just come in here and throw a wrench into everything.

I'd had enough of their attitudes, and not getting the blood we needed was something that required a firmer hand. It'd been over a month since our last blood donation and two weeks since I met with Chase's aunt.

There was something going on here that I didn't like. Something that reminded me all too much of the time right before my stint in the compound's dungeon.

Many of the people in the clan had come to accept me in the short time I'd been in charge. Every day I'd have coffee with Gil, walk the grounds, greet the people waiting for me, and get to work on whatever needed attending to that day.

We'd fallen into an easy schedule, and surprisingly, I didn't find it all that painful.

Even with Keir by my side.

But then we hit the first speed bump. Even though the Order had put me through literal torture to get the contract signed, they still hadn't given us the right amount. They gave us *less* than they'd promised and only enough to feed a handful of families.

"Don't shoot the messenger," one of the vampires said. He had short hair and dressed in casual clothing. He wore an across-the-shoulder cooler that held half of the blood supply that we'd been given for the month, his partner held an almost-empty cooler of his own.

"What did you do when they said that was all?" Emery asked by my side. "Did you just say okay and leave?"

The two shifted and looked at each other. It was all the information I needed to know.

"Put the blood where it belongs," I ordered. "Everyone will be reducing their intake so that we can stock for the families that have children."

The one with the short hair gave me a look.

"This cooler is only enough for the main house alone for the next few weeks," he said. "The others will starve if they are force to live off of scraps."

"*Everyone* will be reducing," I repeated, "including the main house. The only people who will get the normal amount are those in the infirmary."

I motioned for Emery to come closer.

"This better be good," she grumbled.

"Visit Tobias, Xin, and Ian to see if they can spare," I said. "We will even take feeders if necessary. And Gil—"

"Yes?" he asked, closer to my side than I expected.

"Try to contact our enforcer friends," I said. "They may have more information on this. Also remind them we completed our part of the deal and we need to talk."

Gil and Emery both stood straight by my sides, the vampires still lingering.

"Skip us entirely," I told them and stood. "Take what we need from the reserves. We will use what we have stored."

When no one spoke up against me I took it as a good sign and waved off the two vampires. When the doors shut behind them, I turned to the group. Keir was watching me with a smug smile.

"Very selfless of you," she noted. Gillard's lips twitched while Emery remained stoic.

"It's the bare minimum," I said.

"And what will we do?" Keir asked. There was a small light in her eyes that told me she knew exactly what we were going to do.

I rolled my shoulders and let my hand fall to my dagger.

"We are going to visit a friend."

My nose wrinkled when the putrid smell of human excrement and sweat hit me.

It's the least he deserves, my mind reminded me as a wave of guilt threatened to crush me.

"Look what the cat dragged in," Gabriel said with a smirk as Keir and I walked toward where he stood against the wall of the abandoned warehouse.

It had taken over two hours to get to the secluded Underground hideout. But this was a special one that had something very interesting inside, so the trip was worth it.

Gabriel looked at Keir with interest.

"We are not here to play," I said in a cold tone. His eyes snapped to mine, and he ran a hand through his buzzed hair while glaring at me.

"Geez," he groaned. "Still as annoying as ever I see. I would've thought a little time on that cozy throne of yours would've loosened you up enough to get the stick out of you—"

My hand shot forward and grabbed his throat with ease. He didn't struggle against my hold, but his eyes widened and his breath stopped.

"Open the damn door," I growled and pushed him away.

He rubbed his throat with a pout and walked toward the locked door of the warehouse.

Thunder rumbled over us and the scent of oncoming rain hit me. I looked toward Keir and motioned for her to follow me.

I didn't know much about her involvement with the Underground before we'd met, but I was pleasantly surprised to see how comfortable she was to be here. A part of me was worried that the comfy life she'd lived for most of her existence would make the adjustment hard for her, but over the years that we'd been separated, she really had changed.

She kept the overall playful mask on, but she was serious about her clan. She was no longer running away from the responsibility that came with the throne, and not once did I smell an ounce of fear on her.

She truly had grown.

A sudden pain in my chest caused me to pause. It was a mix of loss and disappointment.

It's almost like. . . I *regretted* not being able to see her change. To not be a part of the making of the person she was now.

And it was all because I'd been the one running from all of this.

And now I couldn't understand it at all. I knew why I ran. I was scared. Helpless. The people I knew and had once confided in were after me, and I'd turned into the *thing* that I'd feared the most. . .

But what would've happened if I'd just stayed?

The muffled screams of the captain pulled me from my thoughts.

Gabriel had pried the door open and inside was the captain, strapped to a chair with two other vampires guarding him. I'd never seen these ones before, but with the amount of people coming in and out of the Underground, I wasn't too surprised.

Just as I was about to step in, Gabriel spoke up.

"He asks me to remind you to make good on the deal and that this is him trusting you," he said.

I let out a huff and pushed through the threshold.

"This is not trusting me," I murmured.

He was making good on his word while simultaneously reminding me that he was the one with the true power here.

Tobias had been kind to me, but I would be an idiot if I confused any of his actions as caring or trusting. He'd shielded me from the world for years, and because of that, I would have to slowly pay him back.

One debt to another, though at least he wouldn't try to kill me like the Order. I am more valuable to him alive than dead.

"Leave," Keir ordered the vampires.

The captain's head shot up to look at us. He looked a mess. His eyes were bloodshot. There was blood stained on his face. His clothes had been torn, stained, and his hair was a wild mess on his head. There was a dirty rag tied around his head, effectively silencing him.

He looked pitiful and not like the powerful man he'd once been.

"Captain Moore," I said with a smile. "What a coincidence."

I walked forward, gripping the silver dagger in my hand. Keir's dagger was still strapped to my thigh, but I found myself hesitant to dirty it with this man's blood. His eyes widened and there were muffled pleas spilling from his chapped lips.

I couldn't help the crazed smile that threatened to split my face. The familiar weight of the dagger in my palm was as comforting as it was exciting.

This was the man who'd handed me over to Raphael. Had no care for me. He left me to be tortured by those monsters all while he sat in his comfortable office, not caring about anyone or anything.

My excitement turned into anger as he squirmed in front of me.

"Don't be scared," I cooed and dragged the sharp tip of my dagger against his throat. "You know me, Captain. You know me."

When the metal pricked his skin and allowed a bead of blood to fall down his neck, the urge to plunge the dagger the rest of the way in overtook me.

It would be so easy to end it all. It wouldn't take that much effort even. Just a simple movement and the person who had changed my life would be gone.

Keir's hand brushed across my lower back.

The movement caused the bloodlust to clear. I stood straight and used the dagger to cut off his gag. He sputtered, and before I could even speak, words were spilling out of his mouth.

"The Order will not be happy about this," he growled. "You think that just because you have a clan now that you will be able to get away with this? Silvia, I had so much hope for you. Your parents had so much potential—"

I grabbed his face with enough strength to stop his word vomit.

"Ah, there he is" I cooed. When I put enough pressure for his bones to start cracking, he let out a wail that only fueled my anger. "Since you want to bring my parents into this so much, why don't you start with that?"

I let his face go and bent so we were eye level.

"What are you talking about?" he sputtered.

"You really think that I wouldn't find out sooner or later that my clan had nothing to do with their deaths?" I asked and cocked my head to the side. "Or did you think I would believe the lie this entire time and use it to continue to fuel my hatred for the vampires and be your little brainwashed hunter?"

"Their clan insignia—"

"Was painted in blood on the walls," I finished for him.

"But my clan wouldn't have done that," Keir said. "We looked into it and found the people who actually murdered them, but what we don't know is why."

I pushed the dagger under his chin, earning me a hiss.

"Not to mention every single enforcer has had their parents taken from them in similar circumstances," I said. "So you are going to tell me what you know."

He let out a harsh laugh. "That's what you have me here for?" he asked. "You had my entire office blown up and me dragged from the thirteenth floor for that *stupid* question?"

My lips twitched at the visual.

Leave it to Tobias to make it theatrical. I'd have to keep it in mind for next time.

I pulled back the dagger only to stab it directly into his thigh.

His screams rang in my ears, and a low pounding started behind my eyes.

"Tell me what you know or I *twist* it," I grappled. "Better yet, how about I feed you my blood like you allowed Raphael to do to me?"

He let out a groan, trying to stifle his screams.

"Your parents were killed by vampires," he growled. "How should I know what they wanted?"

I twisted the knife. His blood had already started dripping to the ground and caused my mouth to water.

How long had I gone without to make even his disgusting blood call to me?

I grabbed the discarded gag on the ground and forced it into his mouth to muffle the screams. I pulled the knife out, and against my better judgment, I licked the length of it.

I moaned against the feeling of the hot blood bursting across my taste buds.

I pulled out the gag.

"My blood is next so choose wisely," I warned. "Tell me what my parents' death has to do with the enforcers going missing."

"Your parents and a few others—they were working on something—"

I cut him off by pressing my fingers into his wound.

"Details," I growled.

His tears mixed with his sweat, and he was shaking with the effort it took to keep his screams in.

"It was a top-secret mission from the council," he forced out. "All I know is they had contracts with the clan heads often and they would disappear for days at a time and come back with blood. I don't know what happened or why, but they got rid of the project after a few years and"—he let out a groan—"they put out hits for me to facilitate."

Ice ran through my veins, and I curled my finger in his wound. His screams did nothing to calm me.

"You?" I breathed.

"I'm sorry!" he wailed. "I didn't want to betray them like I did. I loved them. You have to understand, your parents—"

My bloodied hand shot to his throat.

"You killed our parents and now you are coming after us?" I growled. "Is that why you have us join the enforcers?"

"There are things you don't know, Silvia," he forced out. "Things about you, your sister, the others. The council, they planned this all."

"What did they plan?" I asked. "What are you doing to the enforcers?!"

"Silvia," he choked out. "Please—"

"Tell me the truth!" I growled.

"Yes!" he finally yelled. "Yes! The council had us take out your parents. They tied you to us with your debt. We knew you would all be great, so we capitalized on it. We gave you titles, gave you freedom, but it was only so we could monit—"

Hot blood splashed on my face and two strong arms wrapped around my waist and pulled me back.

Familiar black Order uniforms fell from the sky and shouts rung out in the space.

My breath caught in my throat when I made out Cain descending from the ceiling.

"Run," I breathed and turned to Keir. "Run!"

But we were too late.

The same burning pain that had run through my body when I signed the contract exploded in me.

I fell to the ground, barely aware of what was going on around me. Keir's calls for me sounded far away and muffled. The pain had already become too much, and white spots exploded across my vision.

Cain's face flashed through my sight before it was gone.

I tried to turn as my body protested and cried for me to stop.

Keir.

She was fighting and struggling with the hunters as they circled her.

I tried to scream for her, but my entire body was seized by pain. The last thing I saw before my vision went black was them forcing Keir to the ground.

I never knew that vampires could black out from pain, but I found myself unable to keep my eyes open. . . even as Keir reached for me.

Move. MOVE.

But it was useless. *I* was useless.

CHAPTER 21

KEIR

T never trusted the Order.

They showed the worst parts of humanity.

The fear they instilled in the humans was despicable, but the way they used that fear to shackle unwilling humans to them for the rest of their lives?

Even worse.

But the Order was nothing if not thorough.

Even now as they forced me kicking and screaming up to the twenty-fifth floor. They made sure there were two hunters holding me at all times, three hunters trailing behind us, and two in front carrying Silvia's unconscious body.

I prayed she wasn't dead. I couldn't handle it. Not again.

The hunters were a mix of witches, humans, and vampires. Since meeting Jase I'd had my suspicions about how the Order was able to get vampires on their side, but it seemed to all be slowly coming together as we were forced into a dark room with a light shining down on the middle.

There was a circular red carpet in the middle while the rest of the room was shrouded in darkness. Toward the back were three large throne-like chairs, all occupied by people I'd never seen before.

One of which was a vampire.

There were hunters stationed all along the sides, and my heart stopped in my chest when I caught sight of a very familiar vampire waiting for me in the center of the red circle.

Chase.

He stood tall in his black Order uniform. In his hands were two small swords, and he glared down at us with a sickening smile. He looked the same as he had all those years ago. Buzzed hair, annoying smile. . . the only thing different was now his eyes glowed red.

When I connected the dots I fought harder.

"Silvia!" I yelled. "Silvia, wake up!"

But it was no use. They dragged me and Silvia to the middle and forced us to the ground. It was then that I realized that the red circle was not carpet at all. . . but *blood* that had been left to coagulate and dry.

Silvia was thrown to the ground next to me. I growled at the hunters who'd thrown her and quickly crawled to her. Her heartbeat was so soft and low that I couldn't hear it until I got close to her chest, but it was *there.*

I looked up toward the enforcer in front of me with a snarl. "Do you realize how many rules you have just broke—"

"Says the vampire who was watching while their clan head tortured our captain," Chase replied. "But that's not why you're here. We are here to see that your part of the contract is fulfilled."

In a flash the vampire who'd been up at the throne was kneeling in front of me. His cold hand gripped my wrist and pulled it to him.

"Don't you fucking touch—"

I was cut off by Chase's sword coming down to my wrist and slicing open my arm. White-hot pain shot through me.

The vampire motioned for the witches behind me, and colorful magic shone around us as my blood fell to the floor.

There was a loud growl beside me as Silvia rushed forward and tackled the man who was holding me to the ground. Before I could blink Silvia had grabbed Chase's sword from his hand and had it poised over the vampire's head.

Just as she was about to bring it down, her entire body froze and she fell backward.

I shot forward just in time to catch her. She seized in my arms. Her eyes were wide, and her mouth opened to scream, but no sounds came out.

"Stop it!" I ordered, looking around wildly for whoever was doing this to her. "Stop! I'll give you whatever you want."

The men still sitting on the thrones watched us with blank expressions until the one in the middle lifted his hand.

Silvia gasped and began coughing. I helped her to a sitting position and rubbed her back. I didn't even realize that the wound on my arm was still open until she turned to me and her face was stained with my blood.

"You bastards," Silvia growled. "You hid something from me. That missing clause. I knew you—"

"Enough, Silvia," the man from the middle throne said while he got up and walked toward us. "You wouldn't have signed it with the clause still in there. This is the only way."

She moved to lunge at him, but I held her body tight against mine. We'd been lucky that they hadn't killed us.

"What is it that you want?" I asked. "We will comply, just promise that you will let us go after."

Chase let out a bitter laugh. "You are in no position to negotiate," he said. "You have broken contract. We have every right to imprison you, or even kill—"

"Don't scare them, child," the man said with a hum and waved Chase away. "They will get punished as I see fit."

The enforcer-turned-vampire bowed and took a step back, keeping his eyes on the floor. The sudden change in his demeanor caused a newfound fear to sprout inside me.

"Blood donation," Silvia said. "You wanted blood donation. But why didn't you just take it from me?"

The man gave her an almost pitying look.

"You are a made vampire," he said. "Your blood is dirtied, and by the reports you do not have any of the true Carpe Noctem blood in you at all. Now, Keir on the other hand. . ."

My eyes shot to Chase and then to the hunters around us. How many had red eyes? How many had been turned by blood just like what was now caked onto the floor?

"You're making vampires," I whispered and shot a glare at the man. "Whose blood have you been using?"

The man tsked. "That's none of your business."

"Is this what you are doing with the enforcers?" Silvia growled. "Turning them into monsters with stolen blood? Experimenting on them? How many of us do you have hidden? I have been in the Order, thinking my fellow hunters are *dying*—"

"Oh they are," the man said with a sickening smile. "It's a pity you were turned outside the Order. Your parents had such big plans for you. We all did."

He waved Chase forward, and as soon as he got close, the man brushed the back of his knuckles on his cheek.

"There are only a few who have lived through the transformation," he said. "You have to be of strong body, mind, and soul. Beneath you is an accumulation of all the blood we collected from clan heads all across the country, and there is only a handful of hunters who've been able to transform with all of them running through their system."

He turned to look at Silvia who flinched into me at his gaze.

"I'd like to think you'd have been one of them," he said. "The early tests with your parents showed great promise. Your body was so young but took to the blood as if it was nothing more than a fever."

Silvia froze in my arms.

"My parents," she whispered. "You had them— They were putting blood— *No*."

The man pushed Chase away.

"Yes," he said. "Until they rebelled that is. All save for one couple, both of them turned to give birth to the strongest born vampire we have ever had. Died too soon, the blood ate at them from the inside out. Such wasted potential."

"Jase," the word slipped from Silvia's mouth so low I almost didn't hear it, and the man gave no indication he had either.

"So what?" I asked. "I come here to donate blood and let you experiment on the hunters? Then what?"

"Then you go home," he said. "You go home. Take care of your clan. I can assure you the blood will be there waiting for you."

"You really think we will just sit here—"

Silvia was cut off by the man raising his hand. She let out a groan and collapsed into herself.

"Stop," I pleaded. "We'll do it."

"Stay out of the Order's business," he commanded. "The only reason I divulge this information is so you can stop looking into this. If you kill the next captain, we will kill you and your entire clan. If I so much as get a hint of you looking into anything else in the Order, I will imprison Keir and make you watch as I drain every single drop from her."

"You bastards," she groaned. "I don't know what you

think—"

I covered her mouth.

"Please," I begged. "Please no more, Silvia."

Chase let out a huff.

"At least she has some sense," he muttered.

The man stepped forward with a sigh and knelt so that he was eye level with us. It was like he was talking to a pair of children.

"Listen, Silvia," he said with a small smile. "*Leave it be.* You got your answers. We killed your parents after we caught wind of their small little rebellion. We had plans for you, but you escaped your fate with the vampire venom, and now you will live the rest of your existence in the safety of your clan. You have nothing to fight for anymore, Silvia. Let it *rest.*"

Even though there was no way for me to truly understand what Silvia was feeling, his words still felt like a punch to the gut. It was so calloused, so matter-of-fact. . . and that was it?

She may not be willing to take it, but I would.

I stood and held out my arm. He followed suit with a satisfied look on his face that made my entire body go up in flames.

"Finish your collection and we will leave," I said.

The man waved the witches forward, and I gritted my teeth as they opened the wound again. I tried not to look at the one I recognized from so long ago. Or make any movement as I felt him slip something into my pocket.

"You know," the man said with a smile before he turned back to his throne. "You'll be the first to leave this place alive after donating. You should feel grateful."

I licked my dry lips.

"Why?" I asked simply.

He stayed silent, just staring at me as blood poured from my wound.

"Maybe we value longevity of our. . . *work* together over

onetime gains," he said. "Would you like to know how many clan heads we have gone through to get what we needed?"

I didn't say anything even as Silvia cursed behind me.

"The Order's business is the Order's business," Silvia spat.

His eyes lit up. "That's right, Silvia," he cooed. "You always were such a quick learner."

When the blood donation was done, it took all that I had to not rush back toward her and flee.

"We will see you in a month from now," he said as I turned to help Silvia up.

I bit my tongue to stop from lashing out at him.

Once a month. Just like our own blood supply.

This was how they planned to keep us in check.

"Hurry home, Silvia," Chase called out from behind us. "If you're too slow you may not have a home to go back to."

I tried not to let his words get to me, but as we were loaded into an Order van and chaperoned home by a handful of hunters. . . I knew it was bad news.

And before long my fears were confirmed.

Fire was everywhere as we pulled up.

And it wasn't just the main houses. The homes of the extended family and others in our clan were being burned to the ground as we drove though. Vampires ran out of their houses with their kids in hand. Silvia and I tried to open the doors to run and save them, but the hunter in the passenger seat pointed his dagger toward us.

"Don't think about breaching your contract ever again," he warned.

"I get it," Silvia growled.

There was another moment of silence that passed between us before they let us out, but as soon as they did, we both hit the ground running and began the work of saving the clan.

Our clan.

219

freedom to cut this contract
without warning if the clan
heads actions deem necessar

373. The Order is not at fault
for any actions of clans
contracted with the Order.

**374. Once a month the clan
head is to hand deliver the
previous Heir. for blood
donation**

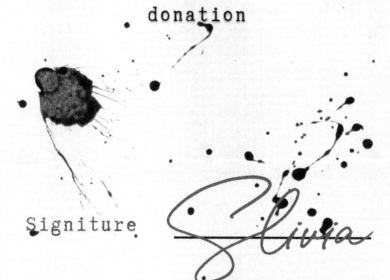

Signiture

CHAPTER 22
SILVIA

Magic. One year.

That was all the note said.

I looked at the crushed-up piece of paper that Keir had handed me with a frown. I didn't even need to her here tell me it was from Cain. I would recognize his handwriting anywhere.

Magic. One year.

It could mean many things, but I was pretty sure what he was hinting at.

Our contract was up in one year, and it would be the only time for us to get out of this. The magic that bound me to the Order would be gone, and Keir would no longer need to donate blood.

There was a knock at the door. I sat straight in my seat and looked over at Keir across from me. Even after everything, she'd maintained her healthy look, and you wouldn't have known what we'd just been through by her appearance.

"Come in," I said.

I was unsurprised to see Vance coming in with a tray of

blood, though the first time I saw him I was so angry after what happened with the Order that I was ready to kill him on sight.

The only thing that stopped me was Ian telling me I could.

Well. . . *that* and the hundreds of clan members who were waiting behind us to see if the Kazimir clan would be kind enough to let us in as refugees.

We'd lost everything. Our entire compound had been burned to the ground. All the blood, history, and goods had been taken along with it. Luckily most all of the clan members were able to flee with their lives. Those who'd been holed up in the infirmary were mostly evacuated.

I could still hear the wails of those whose family members and loved ones had fallen victim to the flames. It felt worse because I knew that I'd caused it. This was them getting back at me for the captain. But instead of discouraging me, it made me all the more angry.

Every life lost only caused the fire in my veins to burn hotter and hotter.

Let it rest, Josiah had said.

Like hell I will.

The only good thing was that we kept most of our valuables in banks behind locked safes, so even though they had taken all of our material things, we could start to rebuild our compound as soon as we were safe.

But that was but a small Band-Aid over a gaping wound.

I almost wished they hadn't kept us in the contract, because then there would be nothing stopping us from retaliating. It was an insult.

The Order was a farce. The anger was almost too much for me to bear. I was angry at the Order. Angry at Chase. Angry at myself.

How did I miss it? All this time?

How was I such a fool?

We'd been lucky everything I'd done hadn't caused Ian to turn his back on us because there was no way we would fit everyone into Xin's compound.

He'd set Keir and me up in a study that would work as our base of operations. Gil and Emery who, thankfully, made it out of the fire had recuperated over the two weeks that we'd been here and were probably out now helping the clan get settled.

Emery had taken a pretty big hit when we realized not all the vampires from her ex-clan had made it. She hid her anger better than I did, but I could sense it rising within her with each passing day.

It was the same with all of us.

"Blood has been delivered," Vance said, pulling me out of my haze. "Enough for both our clans. We were lacking a bit on the last drop off but they made it up in this one."

I nodded but didn't speak as he placed the cups in front of us. The need to kill him had left long ago, but that didn't mean I wanted to be anywhere near the fucker. It was almost exhausting to hold on to the hate I harbored for him. I would never forgive him, but that didn't mean he had to consume my entire being whenever he was near.

Just as he was about to leave, I cleared my throat.

"When are the clan heads arriving?" I asked.

He turned his head to the side, his eyes glancing toward Keir before he spoke.

"Many tomorrow," he said. "The rest the day after. Rest assured, we told them the invite was from us, so everyone should be accounted for."

I nodded and waved him off.

"You should stab him next time," Keir said after a moment. The suddenness pulled a shocked smile out of me. "It would make me feel better at least."

"I don't want to get blood on the carpets," I said with a teasing tone, but it quickly dropped. "Are you sure they're coming?"

Keir's smile dropped.

"I had Emery drop off the message at the spot. The other notes were gone, so we can assume they received them," she said. "But they have been quiet."

I nodded. It was easy to imagine the worst. After all, the Order took no prisoners, and their cover should've been blown long ago.

"What if they—"

"Let's not think about that, okay?" she asked and leaned forward to squeeze my hand. The action did nothing to comfort me. "Let's hope that they're still alive. With the enforcers, the Underground, and the clan heads. . . we have a good chance at making this work."

"But it's a year, Keir," I protested. "We should go while we have the—"

Keir shut me up by leaning forward and covering my mouth with hers. My nerves were already alight with all the stress from the last few weeks, and the feeling of her lips against mine all but pushed me over the edge.

I'd forgotten the last time we were able to have a moment like this. Just the two of us.

What I thought would be a chaste kiss turned passionate as her tongue trailed my bottom lip.

How could I deny her when she asked so sweetly?

I deepened the kiss and let out a groan as her hand found a home on my neck. She gave a gentle squeeze before pulling away.

"I am *not* losing you again," she said. "That magic, it's something else. I don't care if it's one year or ten, I will do whatever I need to keep us *and* our people safe."

My throat threatened to close.

"But that means letting them rip into your skin for eleven more months," I said. "What if one day they realize something is up and go a step further? The Order has never been known to be rational. We have no idea what they'll do when they get what they want."

She let out a sigh. Her eyes fell to the desk.

"We'll figure it out," she said. "First we need help and at the moment that's all we can do. Everything else comes after." Her eyes trailed back up to mine. "Deal?"

I nodded. "Distract me?"

She smiled and leaned forward. "Anything for my queen," she said against my lips, pulling a laugh from me.

"I bet he walks through that door last," Emery whispered from my side.

I elbowed her with a growl.

"Don't jinx it," I hissed.

"I would have to be inclined to agree," Gil said from next to her.

They were on my right while Keir was on my left. We were huddled in the corner of Ian's sitting room as clan heads started to roll in. This was one of the bigger rooms he had, but it seemed to get cramped far too quickly. It wasn't long until there were only a few feet of space between everyone.

It was uncomfortable because of the lack of space but also because there were people here who we normally had nothing to do with. This wasn't a normal clan meeting.

We invited every clan head that we had ever done business with. I recognized a few faces from the galas back in the day, but many still remained a mystery to me. We let Ian do his job and mingle with the newcomers while we stood back to see if our guests would join.

Tobias was one, the enforcers the others.

This wouldn't work without either of them, and each minute that passed I was getting more and more nervous that they may not show.

And there was one other thing that still remained a mystery.

How the fuck did the Order find me in the Underground's territory? This would make two times, only one of which Tobias had warned me about beforehand.

I didn't want to believe that he would do this, not after everything. I understood clan politics enough now to know that you couldn't trust anyone. . . but Tobias should have been different.

"I would like to believe it wasn't him," I murmured. "He may be untrustworthy, but he doesn't just hand over his people like that. And he hates the Order."

Keir sucked in a sharp breath when the three enforcers walked in. The room quieted as soon as the vampires got a look at their pitch-black uniforms and the shiny emblem in the middle of their chests. The news of our compound burning to the ground wasn't well-known yet, but there was one thing we all agreed on.

The Order was out for blood, *our* blood.

Isaac, Jase, and Knox all looked like they'd been through hell and back to get here. Their skin had lost its color, there were dark circles under their eyes—save for Jase—and they were hunched over like they didn't even have the energy to hold themselves up.

But they were *alive.*

The knowledge of it sent a crashing wave of relief through me. I hadn't thought that I cared about them all that much, but

I couldn't help but feel overjoyed that they'd escaped the Order's clutches.

I pushed off the wall and waved them over.

As soon as the vampires clocked my movement, they started whispering to themselves.

The group slowly made their way over to us, vampires moving out of their way as if even just a brush of their skin would burn them. I couldn't help but let my eyes linger on Jase, wondering just how much clan head blood was running through his veins. I wondered how much he knew and, if he didn't, how he would feel about being made from vampires our parents had killed.

I didn't envy his position.

When they finally got to us, Isaac dropped to his knees.

Something I had seen a few times from vampires to clan heads, but never from an enforcer.

I panicked and dropped with him in attempt to grab his arms and hoist him back up, but the other two followed.

"I'm so sorry, Silvia," he whispered. His voice was hoarse, and when his eyes met mine, I could see the pain in them. "By the time we heard, we couldn't get to you in time. Please, *please*, don't think that we planned this. We had no idea Chase would—"

"Silence," I hissed and lifted him while motioning for the others to stand as well. "You *do not* kneel to me, do you understand?"

"Silvia, pleas—"

"Enough. We have things to talk about," I said, cutting off Isaac. I motioned for the others to come closer and dropped my voice to a whisper. "How much do you know about what our parents were involved in?"

"Not much," Jase said, his voice just as cold as it was before, though there was a hoarseness to it that only showed how tired he truly was. "But word got around that Chase was turned into a vampire, and shortly after we saw him, after the new captain was initiated. This was after you were taken."

I nodded.

"I'll explain later," I said, "to *everyone*. This concerns us all. It's not just our parents' issue anymore. The clan heads need to know."

I paused and looked toward Knox. When his gaze met mine, he shook his head.

It was all the answer I needed. Short and simple but enough to make my stomach twist.

"Chase gave us a warning," Isaac said in a low tone. "He let us go as payback for accepting him into our circle. . . and Ash was the payment."

I didn't know what to say.

"They didn't know we were questioning it all, but sooner or later they will," Knox said. "And we need to be prepared, or else they will catch us off guard like all the other enforcers they took."

"I just don't understand how Chase convinced them to keep him," Jase said.

"Or turn him," Isaac added on, his gaze boring into mine.

They don't know the fate that awaits them. They didn't understand that if they stayed in the Order long enough that they too would be subject to the experiments the Order had conducted on Chase.

And who knows if they would actually survive it.

"I'll explain later," I repeated. "I promise."

My eyes caught a glimpse of bright-white hair.

Thank God.

Keir and Emery both let out sigh of relief when they caught sight of him.

Finally, we could get the plan started.

I waved Tobias over as well and gave Ian the signal to start corralling people.

Tobias held the same expression he always had, but there was a tenseness that followed his every step.

"I hold no grudge," I said and reached out to him. "Tell me my instinct to trust you is the right one."

He looked at my hand before clasping it between both of his own.

"You were once a part of my clan as well," he said. "I would never seek to harm you in any way."

His voice was sincere, but I held his gaze a moment longer to be sure.

"They killed them," I said.

"I know," he said with a nod. "You were lucky to get out of there alive. I'm sorry I wasn't there to help."

I shook my head and clasped my hand over his.

"It was for the best," I said before removing my hand from his and walking toward the center of the room. I had to push a few people out of the way, but as soon as they saw who was following behind me, they quickly cleared the area.

Ian cleared his throat.

It's now or never.

"We have received some disturbing news from the Order," he announced, looking every single clan head in the eyes. "They thought they could steal from us. Harm us. Manipulate us. But no more."

"The Order has been killing clan heads for their blood," I told everyone. I made sure to look each vampire in their eyes as I spoke, just as Ian had. They needed to understand this. They needed to know that this was a real threat. We could not just lie here and take it anymore.

"They've been doing it since my parents were part of the Order and even before then. They mix the blood together inject it into their hunters, and pray for super powered child." I paused, looking over to Jase before continuing. His face didn't shift, but his teammates shot him looks. Realization was quick to dawn on their features followed by horror. "There have been some that were able to reproduce, but many have died. There are only a handful left. Starting with your next contract, the Order will attempt to bind you with magic and force you to give them blood."

Whispers broke out across the room.

"They are no longer hiding in the shadows," Keir said from her position in the corner of the room. "They thought they could work under the guise that they are protecting the humans, but they no longer care. They shorten our blood supply until we have no choice but to sign with them. Then after that they will cut you open and bleed you out for as long as you are tied to them."

The fear was palpable in the room. The point wasn't to fearmonger, but they needed to know. Many of the clan heads had been in their positions for over a millennium and had grown complacent.

We needed to break the cycle.

"So what do you suggest we do?" one of the older clan heads asked.

"We can't go against them," another said. "We need blood."

There were chorused agreements throughout the room.

"We are already running out of blood. It's crazy to think we can fight them!"

"But we cannot enslave ourselves to their will!" another said. "They start with blood and then what? What about our heirs? They don't want *us*, they want our blood. We have never been anything more than animals to them. They won't think twice about taking this further. Come on, we know the Order!"

Fighting broke out among the clan heads.

Ian and I stood back and listened to their concerns. Many were small clans and worried for their clan's blood supply, but they still didn't like the idea of being controlled by the Order.

Their worries were all valid. After all, for the longest time we didn't know of any other way. That's how good the Order had been at pushing out their narrative.

I motioned to Tobias, who stepped forward. When the arguing got louder, I clapped my hands. Heads snapped to look at me, some of them openly snarling.

"We will work out a plan with each of you and your clans," I said. "We start with whoever has the closest contract end date. Tobias has helped curate a blood system for his clan, and while it is less than ideal, it will serve our purposes."

Many looked toward each other, disbelief obvious on their faces.

"Do you really think the Order will just let us go like that?"

It was Xin who asked. Her brows were pulled together, a frown on her lips.

"No I don't," I admitted and turned back toward my group. "Luckily we have some insiders, though there is another option we have yet to exhaust," I said and paused. "The rebels."

Chaos. Absolute chaos descended on the group.

Screaming, shouting, cursing, all of it hurled at me.

"Not only do you want us to go against the Order, but you want us to join the very people who have killed so many of us?!"

"Who gave you the audacity to even suggest something this stupid?"

Their reaction was understandable given that the last experience they had with the rebels was the sound device as they tried to kill a clan head. But if there was one thing Krista taught me, it was that the rebels were not at all what we expected them to be.

They, like us, hated the Order and everything they stood for. And it would be what the Order least expected, so it would be the perfect plan.

I let them have their moment. Let them scream about it. Then, as they started to come down, a few looked to me for an explanation.

"They can act as a buffer," I said. "They hate the Order as much as we do. We can use them to distract the Order while we get our bearings. None of this is ideal, but the other option is to continue to bend to the Order's will."

"We don't know what they have planned," Ian added on. "That's even more dangerous. Like was mentioned before, they start at taking our blood, but when will they stop and what happens when they have an army of turned vampires?"

"So your plan is to run?" another person called out. "If we run now, we will always have to run."

"We cannot fight them and win," I said. "We can, with the help of the Underground and the rebels, reduce their size. Once they realize we will not bend, they may move on to other targets."

There were murmurs across the group.

"And if we choose to fight?" another asked.

"You cannot expect all clans to follow you," Keir said from the sidelines. "We are doing this to take care of our people. They come first."

"And just because we are preserving our clan does not mean that we cannot push back in other ways," I said. "It's not that we are asking you to not fight back at all, the rebels, Underground, and enforcers will help with that, but those in charge need to stay safe and away from the Order. We cannot lose you to them."

When there was no more fighting, I let out a sigh of relief. Without Victor here things were much easier. There was no one instigating. Everyone here wanted the best for their clan.

Though I would miss his bloodthirstiness when it came to going up against the Order. We would need it.

"If we are all in agreement, we have some planning to do," Ian said and looked over the group. "Raise your hand if your contract expires in the next six months."

Over half the group raised their hand.

"Next three months?"

About a quarter lowered their hands.

"Well shit," Keir whispered while coming to stand by my side. "We have some work to do."

I nodded and gave her a strained smile.

"Ready to get your hands dirty?" I asked.

She looped her arm around my waist and placed a light kiss to my forehead.

"For you? Anything."

CHAPTER 23

SILVIA

SIX MONTHS LATER.

Something changed in me when I was forced to watch as the Order took Keir's blood while I was writhing in a pain so unimaginable that it made my immortal brain shut down.

I didn't know if it was the way that the hunters glowered at me as I reached for her, or the way that the council smirked at me. . . but I changed in that moment forever.

I once loved my fellow hunters.

I would visit the Academy as they trained. Talk to everyone and help them out when needed. I loved my team and would protect them with my life. There was a kinship between all those who entered the Order. We were all forced here against our will because we were all in horrifying circumstances and there was no way out.

But when I found out that *they* were the reason for those circumstances, everything changed.

The captain who had stood by my side as I watched the hunters clean up the limbs of my family and scrub their blood from the walls was no longer a man who only wanted to help his friends' kid. He sat there looking over the tragedy he created with a mock gentleness as he pulled me so deep into the Order's grasp that the only way to get out was my own death.

The witches who had been favored by the Order and worked by my side through it all turned into silent bystanders as they cursed me and bound me to them permanently. They were as much of a problem as the people who ordered them because after all this, they never left the Order's side.

Except for one.

The night was still young by the time we'd taken the over the small base of hunters. One of the smaller clans had contracted them out for the night, citing fear of the rebels.

The Order fell for it, every single time.

Just like Raphael had once alluded to, *I made them see what I wanted them to see.*

I made them watch as rebels burned down compound after compound and stole blood, leaving their clan heads to run to the Order and beg for help. It was the perfect pitiful circumstance that the Order couldn't resist.

They would bleed them for money, but there was one downfall about the hunter contracts. They were not bound by magic.

This time the Order sent out their hunters. They were all gathered around the perimeter, newer recruits by the look of it. They were too jumpy and they reeked of fear.

Perfect.

It took all but ten minutes to slice their throats. There was not even so much as a rustle as we stormed in and took out one after the other. Just like every other hunter, they held a blind loyalty to the Order.

It was easy to see my actions as some sort of gift I was

giving them. A freedom from the Order's shackles. . . though that didn't mean I didn't wish it was any different.

We got all the newer ones before moving on to the leader. We'd singled him out as soon as we entered the compound, but it was from afar. When I finally got up close to see him, I paused.

He'd been sitting at the edge of the compound's walls with crossed arms and a cold stare. He didn't even move as we killed his teammates. He was a witch, I could smell his burning scent in the air, but it was his face that caused my heart to squeeze in my chest. He was the same witch who'd been by my side for years. The same one who cursed me and watched while they drained Keir of blood every month.

And the same one who gave us enough to start this plan.

"Did you do something to piss them off?" I asked, wiping my bloodied dagger on my all-black uniform.

"Did you?" he asked, his eyes trailing down my form. "Since when do clan heads get their hands dirty?"

I shrugged and leaned against the exterior wall, joining him in looking out toward the forest. If I squinted, I could make out the lights of the next city over just above the tree-tops. The night was cool, and a storm was quietly rolling toward us. The clean scent of the oncoming rain mixed with his, and it brought back a wave of nostalgia.

My people, including Emery, were waiting behind the wall for my signal. I could hear them shifting as their nerves got the better of them.

"Touché," I said with a smirk. "I guess old habits die hard."

Half-truth.

Yes, I wanted to be out where the action was, but I also was the one who knew the hunters the best. I'd spent months upon months training the vampires in the Order's combat style for this very moment.

"I wondered how you did it," he said. "They know it's you."

"But there is no evidence," I noted.

"Because you kill them all," he spat, a rare form of anger coming from him. "You are killing hunters, Silvia."

In a flash, I pushed him to kneel in front of me and placed a dagger at his neck.

"Everyone gets a chance," I said with a bitter smile. "And do you know what most of them say when I offer a chance to join?"

I cocked my head to the side. His face remained cold and unfeeling.

"Probably something along the lines of *go to hell*," he muttered.

"Correct," I said. "So what do you say? Will you be our first hunter witch to join us?"

He swallowed thickly, and a bead of sweet fell down his neck. "Jade refuses to leave," he whispered. "I have tried to get her to go on missions, in hopes that we may see you, that this moment would come, but she—"

He cleared his throat but was unable to continue.

"Jase."

The vampire was by my side in a second.

"Are there more of you?" I asked Cain.

He nodded.

"Though it has been hard for the witches to get on missions," he said. "It took me no less than nine tries to get on this mission. If I didn't get on this one, I would've had to stop because suspicions are already rising. If I go back alone, I'm dead."

I pulled my dagger back. "Get a list of names from him," I ordered Jase. "See what the enforcers can do to get them out. Maybe after this one they will realize how serious we are."

"Understood," he said and helped Cain to his feet. "Let's

go. We have less than twenty minutes before the alarm sounds, and we still need to scatter the bodies."

Jase pushed him past me, and as Cain's eyes met mine, I was overcome with a flurry of emotions ranging from violent relief to grief.

"Welcome to Carpe Noctem, Cain," I said through the lump in my throat.

"Happy to be here," he murmured as Jase helped him over the wall.

I stood a moment in my silence trying to bottle up the emotions that were threatening to overtake me.

How many times have I been on these missions? How many times have I killed a hunter and hated myself for it afterward?

It was so much easier to push everything down and just focus on the anger. It was the only thing keeping me going at times. . . But having Cain *here* in *my* clan, it was more than I could handle.

I heard Emery approach and worked quickly to steel myself. I couldn't let her know that it affected me the way it had.

"Keir is waiting for you at home," she said in a soft tone. She didn't reach out to touch me, but the shift in her tone was similar to another person's touch.

She was comforting me.

I nodded and followed my team back to our compound with a heavy heart.

It took three months to clear the compound and build on top of it. Nothing was as extravagant as it used to be, and we allowed the families in charge to choose whatever style fit them as long as it was within the allotted budget for each unit.

It was all for show after all. To the Order, it looked like we were seriously rebuilding everything and trying to start anew. There were only a few who knew better.

Keir, Gil, and I remained in the main house while others, including Emery, branched out into their own places.

Those who'd been on the mission had all piled into one car on the way back and stopped off at the hunter housing before continuing on.

It was the largest building we had and currently had enough space for thirty of them, but we were quickly running out of space.

"How many have you taken?" Cain asked as Jase opened the door for him and motioned for him to get out. He stared up at the building with a cool facade, but I could see the thoughts whirring behind his eyes.

"Enough that we will need to start construction on a new building soon," I said. "And that's just in our compound. There are others in other clans across the country."

Cain turned to look back at me, and I tensed when he threw his arms around me and held me to him.

I would be lying if I said that I didn't feel a rush of warmth from his hug, or that it didn't cause the cracks in my heart to widen further.

I'd missed Cain so much more than I'd let myself realize.

And just for the moment, I allowed myself to drop the mask of clan head and hug him back.

"I didn't mean to leave you there," I whispered. "If I could've gotten you both out of there, I would have."

He hugged me tighter. "I should've let Jade tell you what we were working on," he said. "I just never would've guessed that it would be you in that position. I'm sorry, Silv."

"Me too," I whispered, then pulled away with a forced

240

smile. "I would walk you to your room, but I should probably clean up."

He pulled away and looked down at my stained uniform with a grimace.

"Can I see you again?" he asked.

"We'll be back soon to plan the next attack," Emery said for me. "But if we don't get the clan head back soon her girlfriend will throw a fit."

Cain gave me a lingering look before he got out of the car. I sighed and relaxed back into the seat, focusing on what was ahead.

I couldn't wait to shower and get all this disgusting blood off me.

When we got to the main house, Emery and I both jumped out of the car. The others who went on the mission with us stayed behind to unload and sanitize all the weapons.

The house was two stories with six rooms. Much smaller than what we had before, but it was better for everyone to be close. That was the goal with all these houses. We needed to be close in case the Order got a whiff of what we were doing and decided to pay a visit.

I would be damned if we lost more lives because of them.

"How long until the Waita clan gets here?" I asked.

They were the next ones to ask the Order for help. It was like clockwork. There would be a clan every few days at our doorstep, and we would move not long after that. It had been like that for months.

Destroy some buildings. Kill some hunters. Negotiate with clans. And over and over again until we could slowly start to remove the clans from their space once and for all.

"Five hours," she said. "And we need to get more vampire cadavers. Waita and Levesque clan both cremate their dead, so there is no way to scatter them like we did with the rest."

I let out a huff of annoyance. "Ian may have some," I murmured.

"Vance is already on his way with theirs," she said. "We need more."

I was about to respond, but the sight of a disheveled Keir waiting for me in the open doorway to the house cause me to pause.

Her hair was sticking up all around her head, and the T-shirt she wore was off her shoulder. She let me walk toward her, but as soon as I was in front of her, her hands were on me.

"I was so worried," she murmured and trailed kisses down my neck. "You were supposed to be back *three* hours ago."

"Stop," I whined. "I have blood on me."

"Like that'll stop me," Keir said as she nibbled on my skin.

"Gross," Emery groaned. "Five hours. Dressed, presentable, and in the main hall."

Keir already had started to pull me into the house before I could respond to Emery.

"Ah, fuck," Keir whined. "More."

I let out a small chuckle as I leaned back down to pull her clit into my mouth and give it a long, hard suck.

We had less than thirty minutes to shower—*again*—and get ready for the meeting, but it was hard to tear ourselves away from each other.

Things had gotten. . . *easier* since I realized just how much I didn't want to live without her.

I didn't try to act like I hated her anymore. It didn't make the past disappear, but I'd learned quickly that if I stayed in the past for too long, I would be consumed by it.

And I didn't want to live my life that way anymore.

I wanted to enjoy the time I had with Keir. I wanted to enjoy my life.

And right now all I wanted to do was taste Keir until she couldn't take it anymore.

The morning light started to slowly shine into our room, giving me the perfect view of Keir as she writhed under me.

I had propped the pillows up underneath her so I could get a good look at her face as I settled between her legs. Her body was slick with sweat, and her breasts rose and fell with the quick breaths she took.

I pushed two fingers inside her, moaning as she clenched around me.

"More like this?" I teased and added a third finger inside of her before turning to nibble on her inner thigh.

"*Yes*," she moaned and spread her legs even wider for me.

"Or more like this?" I asked and used my other hand to rub hard, fast horizontal strokes against her clit.

She let out a startled moan as her back bowed. She was so wet as I fucked her that the sounds of my fingers sliding into her sounded around the empty room.

"God, listen to that," I groaned. "Do you hear how wet you are? I was only gone for a few hours. This cunt couldn't have missed me that much, could it?"

My own pussy was pulsating with need even though I'd gotten three orgasms from her already. Wetness was trailing down my legs, and if I wasn't so distracted by the way she was squeezing me I may have reached between my legs to finish myself off as well.

She let out a strangled whine just as her orgasm started to rise in her.

"Fuck— I'm coming," she whined.

"I know," I cooed. "Come for me, Keir. Show me just how much you missed me pounding into this greedy pussy of yo—"

I was cut off by her cry. I removed my fingers only to hold her hips in place while I continued to rub her clit. She was so over stimulated at that point that I doubted it would take long until—

"Wait— Ah, fuck, slow down or I—"

She was cut off by another orgasm. This time I dove forward with every intention of licking up her orgasm.

As soon as she was able to, she pulled me up to her and switched our positions.

"The clan will be here soon—"

I was cut off by her mouth covering mine. I enjoyed the way her tongue plunged into my mouth like she owned me. She was just at my mercy, but as soon as she was able to, she was here showing me exactly who I belonged to.

I didn't even register that she was digging around on the bed beside us until the feeling of a cold, wet toy pushed against my clit. I disconnected from her to look down at the toy between my legs. A simple wand with a bulbous head, one that we'd used not too long ago.

"We can make it," she said. "You ready?"

I nodded and fisted my hands in the covers. "Highest setting," I ordered.

She smiled and turned it on without hesitation. My back bowed as it came to life, and just like I'd ordered, it was on the highest setting. I was already so strung out from eating her out that heat immediately started to coil in my belly.

She leaned forward to take my nipple into her mouth.

One of my hands flew to the back of her neck when she tried to pull away. She let out a chuckle and pushed the toy harder into me. I was frozen as it overtook my body.

Heat burst from my center and tingled all the way down to my toes as my orgasm hit me. My pussy was clenching around nothing, but the toy brought wave after wave of orgasm so powerful that not a sound left my lips.

"All talk, huh?" she asked with a chuckle. "Now when it's your turn you lose the will to speak?"

"Turn it off," I forced out.

"No," she said and leaned down to kiss me, but just as I tried to meet her halfway, she pulled back with a smirk. "They're coming, Silvia. Be quick."

"Fuck you," I growled and opened my legs wider. She moved the toy to just a slightly different angle, and it knocked the breath from my lungs.

"When the clan leaves, I'm all yours," she whispered.

Just as the second orgasm began to rise, I heard the sounds of a car pulling up the driveway. Keir covered my mouth with hers as I cried out, muffling the sound.

It was over faster than I liked it to be, but we were in a rush.

"I'm going to make you pay for that," I growled as I pushed us off the bed and made my way toward the bathroom.

"Maybe you should bring your knife out again," she teased from behind me. "Put it to my throat while you fuck me."

I couldn't help but let out a laugh.

We weren't in the ideal situation, but for now. . . it was enough. And there were better ones on the horizon.

CHAPTER 24
SILVIA
SIX MONTHS LATER

The smell of the explosive was tickling my nose as I sat in the newest captain's office at the Order headquarters.

It was a deadly reminder that if this did not go well, I too may no longer exist on this earth in a matter of moments. But it didn't scare me.

I'd been waiting for this moment, daydreaming about it since I was forced to watch as the person I love had been cut open by them over and over again while they called my curse.

It was like a fun game to them, watching me writhe in pain while Keir pleaded.

But no more.

I didn't recognize the man sitting in the captain's old seat. Every time we visited the Order for blood donation, an enforcer would meet us directly in the lobby and bring us up to meet the council. The new captain was much younger and held himself as if he had not a care in the world. His hair was in waves around his face, and he wore a full suit. His eyes were narrowed in my direction, and there was a slight frown on his face.

I'd heard things about him from the hunters we saved. He was cruel. He loved to punish the new hunters if he even so much as sensed their displeasure with the Order. He would torture them until they were singing the Order's praises.

Our mission had been one to save the clan, but after he came, it quickly turned into saving both clans and hunters alike.

My eyes shifted toward the vampire next to him. *Chase.*

I didn't know what to think about Chase. On one hand, he'd gotten his teammate's brother killed. On the other, he'd stayed silent when he obviously knew that his teammates were trying to find out the truth of the Order.

But there was always one question that needed to be answered.

How long had he known?

He'd been visiting his rebel aunt for years but told no one about it, and the day that they went off to find her still remained a mystery to us all.

His hair had grown slightly, but he remained the same old Chase. He smirked down at me and crossed his arms over his chest. He always acted like he knew something I didn't, and each time it got on my nerves.

"I don't think you understand how this works," the man in Captain Moore's seat spoke.

I blinked and looked back at him. "I'm sorry," I said in mock politeness, "who are you again?"

His jaw twitched, and he let out a huff.

"I am the new captain," he said. "You may call me Captain Manning."

"Well, *Manning*," I repeated with obvious distaste, "I actually know exactly how this works. My clan is under no obligation to sign with you and actually"—I paused and leaned forward, looking at the calendar on his desk—"as of six days ago the contract that I did sign no longer binds me to the Order. Me being here is simply so you don't think I've run off."

We'd tested it, to see if they would come after me and force me to renew. When there was no sign of them after the second day, we began our plans.

The small tick of the clock on the bomb called me back to myself.

"Again," Chase said. When I raised an eyebrow, he just smiled. "Run off *again*, you mean."

I gave him a smile, making sure to bare my teeth.

"I was merely taking a break to consider my options," I said and moved to stand, but Captain Manning beat me to it.

"You know it won't end like this, right?" he said. "We cannot have vampires running around killing humans for supply."

I cocked my head to the side.

"Who said anything about murdering humans?" I asked.

He stood straight. "You have a clan of over three hundred. How else are y—"

"Three hundred?" I scoffed. "Those were our numbers over a year ago. We are closer to two thousand now. And don't you worry about blood supply. We will maintain the rules set forth by the Order, we just won't contract with you."

"They'll get her blood one way or another," Chase said. "After all, there is only a handful of born vampires in the royal bloodline that are still alive given the. . . *rebels'* recent attacks."

I smiled at him.

"I don't think they will," I said. "But they are welcome to try. Though given the ratio of experienced hunters to new recruits, I think we are better off. I guess that's what happens when you experiment on them."

I turned to leave but paused when my hand brushed across the cool metal knob.

"Tell the council that if they ever come to take Keir again, they will have to pry her from my cold, dead fingers," I whispered.

Chase let out a snort. "You know what, let me walk you out," he said and was by my side in an instant. He lowered his voice to a whisper. "Come on, Silvia. The clock is ticking."

My entire body was doused in cold water, and it took all my control to act as though I wasn't panicking at our entire plan being unraveled.

He was silent as he covered my hand with his and pushed the door open. He didn't speak as our shoes squeaked against the polished floors.

The all-white hallways were stained by the hunters' all-black uniforms as they walked throughout. Each of them eyed me with suspicion that was hardly concealed, but when they looked toward Chase, they visibly flinched.

It was hard to realize that I was once one of them. That I'd given the Order my everything, and in turn all they showed me was just how little they truly thought of me.

Chase pushed me into the elevator with him, and as soon as the doors closed, he pushed the emergency button, halting the elevator. I gritted my teeth and cursed internally.

He turned to lift the ceiling in the corner and paused when he realized there was no camera.

"Isaac took it long ago," I mumbled.

Chase shot me a wide smile. "How is Isaac?" he asked. "Surprised you got all of them in one go."

I shrugged. "Wouldn't know," I said.

"Keep that up and we go down with them," he threatened and fixed the ceiling quickly before turning toward me.

"What do you want?" I growled.

"Take me with you," he said. "During the explosion."

His words shocked me to my core. "You killed one of us," I spat.

"I didn't mean to!" he said, his voice rising in pitch. The desperation in it was something completely out of character, and I had no idea what to think of it. "I tried everything to save him—*them*—but I couldn't. I almost died, Silvia, please, you know what it's like. Please just let me join."

I gave him a long look. "I don't believe you've changed," I said with a voice lacking emotion.

I wanted to believe it so bad. I wanted to think that he wouldn't have hurt them like that, like he wasn't this big bad villain... but it was too hard.

"How do I prove it?" he asked. "Give me anything to prove it to you."

I paused, thinking it through. "You can't," I said simply. "It's too late."

"I'll send out thirty hunters," he said. "Please, if you won't accept me then at least the hunters."

I leaned forward and pressed the button. There was silence between us as we rode down.

"Send them on the next one," I whispered as we came to a stop. "They hesitate, we kill them."

When the elevators opened for the last time, I'd thought I might be overcome with grief, but instead I felt nothing. It was easy to leave Chase in the elevator, just as it was easy to walk through the lobby and look at all the hunters who would soon be running for their lives.

I didn't feel sad that I was leaving the place that shackled me. I didn't feel anger that they'd threatened me. And worst of all, I didn't feel any relief that it was all over.

I almost wished they would've started something public, but they didn't. The hunters all watched as I exited and got into the SUV that waited for me without so much as a second glance.

"You're late," Keir said as we pulled away. She looked back at me from the passenger seat with a tense look.

The car jerked forward as we raced down the street, quickly trying to put distance between us and the Order.

"Chase tried to convince me to bring him" I grumbled. "Wanted to trade hunters."

"And what did you say?" Cain asked from beside me. I gave him a small smile.

"I asked him to prove it in the next one," I said.

"Sneaky," Emery sang from the driver's seat. From the rearview mirror I could see a ghost of a smile on her face. "You're lucky they didn't take you in for questioning."

I let out a sigh and turned to Cain. It was a risk bringing him here, but he insisted.

"Ready?" I asked and dropped my gaze to his lap where he was clutching a device with white knuckles. If we did nothing, in the next five minutes the bomb would go off, but he held the switch in his hands to cause it to blow even sooner, or even stop it if he desired. "You don't have to do this you know."

"Jade is on a mission," he said. When his eyes met mine, I could see the small glimpse of hope hidden inside them. "So now is the only time we can do this."

"We have to move quick," Emery said. "As soon as you press that button, we need to give the clan the signal to set the fire and move out."

Cain took a deep breath and exhaled shakily. Then, without another word, he hit the large button in the center of the device.

One.

Two.

Three.

251

Four.

Fiv—

The sound of the explosion bursting through the Order was deafening even from miles away.

The car jerked to the side as Emery turned a sharp corner. Keir was already on the phone with our people who'd remained at the compound, and she told them to start the final move.

I reached over to Cain and took the device from him. He gave me a panicked look as I pressed the button again, setting off the second blast the enforcers had hidden just a week prior and up a few floors.

This one would get the council right where it hurt. Right in the only armory in the main building.

"Our burden to bear," I said and leaned back in my seat.

It wasn't the ideal way to end things, and I was honest when I told the others I wouldn't wage a war with the Order, but at least now it would be months until they could come after us, and by that time, we would be long gone.

Keir turned back to look at me with a careful smile.

"It won't be long now until we are at our new home," she said.

"We'll dump the car in thirty up north," Emery added on. "Then we'll follow the route laid out before switching again and heading there. We'll be home by dawn tomorrow."

I nodded.

Home.

We were going home.

CHAPTER 25
SILVIA

The Waita clan was located in southern Oregon right near the rocky coast.

It was a smaller compound that spread only a mile or so and housed two hundred people, and it was steadily growing as they carried out our plans.

Vampires from clans all around had heard of the "rebel" attacks and started fleeing to the strongest clans in the area, Waita being one of them.

We were surprised when they had reached out to us at all. Apparently Keir had a falling out with them before I'd taken over, but that was all in the past now. The Order had become far more aggressive in its tactics after the bombing of their headquarters and started to accelerate their plans to take all the clan head blood that they could.

And that's why the Order had finally started to send more hunters ahead of time to the clans we were targeting. It made it all the harder to try and get them out. Each day we had to smuggle vampire families out, but there was no way that we could move them without the hunters getting suspicious.

There were also a suspicious number of silver emblems around.

Even though we'd moved the compound to another country entirely, we still had a lot of work to do before we could distance ourselves from these clans. I thought after all we'd been through that telling these clans to fuck off would've been easier, but it was too easy to remember what it felt like to be in their shoes.

So we flew in, prepped for days, and now for hopefully one of the last times, we could get a clan out safely. Keir had wanted to come on this trip, but I insisted she stayed. I regretted it as soon as I spent more than a few hours away from her, but inside I knew that this was the best choice.

We'd come to an agreement between us. Unless necessary, only one of us could go on the raids.

It would be painful, and one would be stuck worrying until the other came back, but as always. . . our clan came first.

"Forty-two total enforcers," Knox's voice said in my earpiece. It was on the lowest setting. His voice could barely be heard over my racing pulse. "One witch and over thirty-three vampires."

"Clan head blood?" I asked and held on to the branch above my head before leaning out and peering down at the compound.

The coast was to my left. The crashing of the waves drowned out the footsteps of the hunters and made it that much more dangerous. Surrounding the compound were hills with tall, lush trees that provided enough cover to have a bird's-eye view of the compound.

They were walking in groups of four around the compound while some were stationed at the corners.

"Unsure," came Jase's voice. He was somewhere on the

perimeter acting as Knox's backup. "Though there are a few I recognize—*Knox, what the*—?"

"*Chase!*" Knox growled. "You fucking mon—"

His voice cut off with a high-pitched screech.

My eyes shifted through the compound but I couldn't see where Knox was.

"Location. Report. Everyone." My team was already faster than I could give signal for.

They were behind me in the trees, waiting as still as stone, but as soon as they heard Knox's voice cut off, they were moving forward in an instant. They filled the trees beside me within less time than it took to take a breath while the excess on the ground started to inch closer to the compound. Those we had hiding out inside started to sound off in my ear.

"Dining room, check."

"West wing main house, check."

"East wing main house, check."

"Medical bay, check."

"Main entrance, check."

So on and so forth the team inside relayed their location. Everyone except for Knox.

"Jase," I growled. "Where is he?"

"Lost sight," he reported. "Searching now."

"Who has eyes on Knox?" Emery asked as she came to stand on the same branch I was. She'd been a staple in these raids. I expected her to fall off at one point and focus on those in the medical bay like she had when I first came to the clan, but she remained by my side while the other two stayed at the compound.

Her presence was comforting. No matter what emotions ran through me, she was there to offset them.

There was a silence that passed through the group. It was enough to set every alarm bell off in my head.

"We should go in," Emery whispered to me.

"Wait," I commanded. My voice may not have shown my worry, but inside I was a mess.

Another second passed. The wind picked up, making it almost impossible to hear anything that was happening down at the compound.

"Silvia—"

"South wall," one of our scouts said through the earpiece. "Talking to a hunter with buzzed hair. Looks heated but no physical confrontation yet."

Chase. Damn it.

"Man your positions," I said and motioned for Emery to drop with me.

We dropped to the damp ground below us with a soft thud.

"I'm not sure we can trust him," Emery said behind me.

I straightened then shook out my legs and rolled my arms.

"Never said we should," I mumbled and cracked my neck. I patted down my sides making sure *both* my daggers were there.

We snuck along the boundary of the compound, carefully avoiding hunters with the help of our team in our ears.

My entire body was on high alert as we slipped through the side entrance and followed the maze of houses. There were too many vampires here to be safe. We had almost the same amount of people, ex-hunters, vampire and human alike. . . but if the Order had played their cards right.

These people may be much stronger than we could ever be.

Voices could be heard as we got closer to their reported location, and as soon as I smelled just the slightest bit of fear, I bolted.

Emery cursed and reached out to grab my wrist, but I was a hair too fast.

Quicker than I had time to think it through, I threw myself

between Knox and Chase. The golden stake-like dagger that Keir had gifted me was in my hand and pushed against Chase's neck. Jase was behind both Knox and me, but I paid no mind to him.

Magic was heavy in the air and burned my nose.

"Back off," I growled. "You weren't even supposed to be here."

"Silvia, please," he begged. "I've brought everyone I said. I can prove it to you."

He held his hands up in a form of surrender. His eyebrows were pushed together and his face looked just as vulnerable as it did that day in the elevator.

It had been weeks since our last encounter, but it looked like it had been years. His skin had sunken in, grayed, and the whites of his eyes had started to turn black.

He was starving.

Knox's hand clasped my shoulder.

"It was my fault," he murmured. "I saw him and I just. . . *reacted.*"

I swallowed my growl and straightened my stance.

"Are you okay?" I whispered to Knox.

"Fine," he whispered. "Just need some space."

I nodded and turned to motion for Jase to take him. The vampire was quick to pull at the witch's wrist and at least a few feet away from Chase.

"Knox," Chase called in a pained voice. "Please let me—"

"No," I growled. "You tell me right now what your plan is. You said *thirty* and you were not a part of that equation."

I never thought I'd say it, but I was tired of people falling to their knees. Chase went down with a thud.

"Please, I mean well," he said. His voice then took a strange sort of crazed tone. "I even brought you. . . a *present.*"

"Down!"

But it was too late. An ear-piercing explosion sounded to my left, and I was knocked against the compound wall so hard I could hear my bones crack. Air rushed out of my lungs, and the world around me went white.

By the time the pain began to dull and my vision cleared, hands were already grabbing at me, but none of them were my teammates'.

These were hands burning with magic, ones that I hadn't felt in years.

I was pulled against the small body, her voice breaking through the cloudiness of my hearing.

"Where is he?!"

Jade's blurry face came into view. Her once-colorful hair had been dyed a jet black. Her large eyes, which had at one point seemed so innocent, were panicked. Her expression was one of terror mixed with a flash of anger.

One witch.

We were idiots not to seek her out before we entered the compound.

My uniform had been burned in places and my skin charred. The area stank of a heavy magic, and it made each breath of air I took burn on its way down.

"Where is he, Silvia?!" she screeched and smacked the side of my face. "Where is Cain?!"

It was the thing I needed to pull myself out of my haze and lunge forward.

I was vaguely aware of the fighting happening close to us, but even then, it was only a few people while voices streamed through my earpiece.

I ignored them all and uttered one command.

"Kill them all."

Jade's face twisted underneath me, and her hands were already beginning to glow. I grasped her throat hard enough to block all airways. I was tempted to claw it straight out, but the more human part of my brain was begging me not to.

"*Cain,*" she forced out breathlessly.

"Traitor," I growled and tried to finish the deed. . . but I couldn't. My hand wouldn't move.

Kill them all.

She was pleading with me the entire time I squeezed her throat. Even though the words didn't come out, I could read her lips. *Cain. Where is he. Cain. Please.*

Her eyes drifted shut, and her body went slack.

Slowly, I released her neck. A battle was raging all around me, but I couldn't tear my gaze from Jade's contorted face. Her heart was hammering in her chest, and her breaths were deep. There was a low hum of magic coming from her that was slowly dissipating as her body sank further and further into unconsciousness.

Kill her.

My dagger was but a few feet away. I stood on shaky feet and grabbed it before pulling Jade up by her hair and forcing it to her neck.

Do it.

A bead of blood bloomed from the small prick of a cut I made and fell down her throat before soaking into her turtleneck.

"Do it," I growled to myself.

"Silvia," Emery's gruff voice called from behind. Her breathing was labored, and I could smell her blood. She was injured, but not enough that it would be life-threatening. Her body had already started to heal itself judging by the sound of her bones setting behind me.

"No hesitation," I growled. My throat began to close, and something like tears stung my eyes.

Emery's hand clasped around mine and pulled the dagger away.

"Let go," she whispered. "Come. The others are waiting. *Keir* is waiting."

The thought of Keir's arms enveloping me in warmth filled my mind, and I wanted nothing more than to fall to the ground right then and there.

I let her body fall to the ground and put my dagger back in its holster.

Emery was there hoisting her up over her shoulder without a word.

"Leave her," I ordered.

"Not a chance," she said and pushed me toward where the rest of our team was waiting.

It was a short walk before I found the rest of the team. Some of them were injured, but I quickly noticed that the blood coating most of them was not their own.

Jase had forced Chase to his knees and pulled his hair back while Knox had blue ropes of magic around his body. There were a handful of hunters off to the side, each chaperoned by one of our own.

"There are a few who surrendered," Jase said and motioned to the hunters. "What should we do about them?"

"They can come," I said while looking at Chase. "You really had me believing we could trust you."

"They knew what you were up to," he said. "There was no escaping. Just kill me already."

I looked him over. There were signs of abuse on him, which made it hard to believe that *everything* was fake. But I doubted they would go as far as to send one of their only made vampires here without a plan.

Did they truly think that he would come back?

"Hard to believe the Order would let you go so easily," I

noted. "Did they get bored of you or something?"

He scowled but said nothing. I looked toward the other hunters. I noticed the one on the right was a vampire with a silver emblem on his chest.

"Were you a part of the experiments?" I asked him.

His entire body froze.

One of my men kicked him in the back. "Speak."

"Yes," he rushed out.

"What was your mission?" I asked.

He hesitated and looked toward Chase. "Our goal was to have one of the made vampires kill you, with the help of the witch," he said slowly. "In hopes vampire law would kick in."

"They only sent forty," I noted.

He swallowed thickly. "It's almost all we have left," he said. "We've been sourcing Order members from across the country, but you've been killing us all off. The higher-ups are angry."

"Their last resort," Emery muttered. "A bit lackluster."

I made noise of agreement. "Kill him," I ordered.

The vampire didn't have time to plead for his life before a sword was lodged in his throat.

I turned toward Jase and Knox. "Take him as prisoner," I ordered. "If they are running low, now is our chance."

"Coward," Chase spat as he was hauled up.

I let out a bitter laugh. "If there is one thing I am not, it's a coward," I hissed. "Knox, he's yours when we get the information."

Knox gave me a rare smile before turning to leave with the team.

"We're close," Emery said. "I can feel it."

I could too, but there was something else on the horizon as well. We'd gotten this far through the death of the hunters *and* our own. This game was far from over, but I knew exactly the next steps to get us to checkmate.

Hunter Rules

rule 76 sec 2

The punishment for treason is
death.

CHAPTER 26
KEIR

T brushed my lips against Silvia's forehead as she clung to me.

Then each eye.

Her nose.

And then finally her lips.

She was shaking in my hold. It had happened every day since their last raid. It'd be at random moments, but only when we were alone. It would start quietly. There would be a hush that fell over us. Sometimes I would be right next to her and she would pause. Other times I'd be across the room, and the sudden pause in her breathing would be enough to jerk me out of whatever I was doing.

It scared the living hell out of me, and I hated seeing her like this. So every time it happened, no matter how much she protested, I would pull her into my arms and start gently kissing her.

Today we were prepping for something that had been a long time coming. We were in the hallway of the main corridor of our new house in the compound. Life went on around us, but even so, we paused right in the middle. The staff and various people in the clan went about their business outside the walls. It was serene, the new compound. Located near Calgary, our compound now spanned a far larger area than I could've ever imagine. We made it a haven for all the clans we accepted, and the hunters. It was the happiest I'd seen everyone, but inside the walls—while everyone enjoyed their lives —their clan head was breaking.

"I know," I whispered against her lips. "I *know*."

Her arms circled my waist, and she let out a shuddering breath as she leaned into me. She buried her head in the crook of my neck and waited a few heartbeats before she spoke.

"I don't want to do this, Keir," she whispered. "I am so tired. *Scared*."

I wrapped my arms around her and pushed her head farther into my neck. Her breath wafted across the scars her bites had left, but I ignored the heat it sent through me.

"Scared of what you'll find out, or of what you'll have to do when it's done?" I asked in a whisper.

She let out a small whimper that tore at my chest.

The entire clan saw Silvia at her strongest. Since the day of the ceremony, she hadn't let her mask rest for even a moment.

But it was different when we were alone. She let me see the true her. Just like I did to her. No matter what, we were in this together. We understood each other in a way no one else would.

Both of us, born to wear different masks, joined together by our misguided hate, and turned into something more. While we had different ways of hiding ourselves, hers angry and mine playful, inside we were the same.

Scared and woefully unprepared for what it meant to save a clan.

I found comfort in the thought that she and I weren't so different after all.

"The latter," she murmured. "She tried to kill me, Keir. My hands are tied."

I ran my fingers through her hair, trying not to pull too hard at her curly mane.

"Not necessarily," I said. "We didn't know her plan. There are ways around this. Let Ian help."

Since the merging of all our clans into one, we had given each clan head a responsibility to help us run the overwhelming amount of people in the clan. Ian was in charge of clan and vampire law. Something he volunteered to take on, even when we offered to buy him a compound and branch off.

It had been surprising how many clan heads didn't want their jobs, especially in the wake of an outright war with the Order.

Xin had taken the offer and set up a compound near Montreal. She worked across the border with Tobias often after he took over Victor's clan and promptly renamed it *the Underground* against all of our advice.

Apparently the name meant a lot to him.

"He's probably in there already," she murmured.

"They can wait," I said and planted a kiss atop her head. "They can wait as long as we need."

She let out a sigh.

"I love you," I whispered. She melted into me but did not say it back.

It hurt at first, but her soft kiss to the scars on my neck meant the world to me. And it was enough.

She pulled away with a small frown. "Let's go." She turned, but I pulled her back for another breathtaking kiss.

"For good luck."

"Too many people saw," Ian whispered from his place next to Silvia. "There is not much we can do, but if we do want to make an exception, it has to be public."

All three of us were staring at the cells in front of us. The small jail we had built in the basement of the compound wasn't something I thought we'd use, and it was getting extremely cramped with all the people in here.

We were against the wall directly across from the cells while the three enforcers, Gil, Emery, *and* Cain stood off to the side, waiting to hear what would happen to their loved ones.

Well. . . Gil and Emery were just here because in part they were nosy. Emery was a sort of ambassador for the clan, working to help the clans that came to us for refuge. She should know how we liked to punish, if at all.

Gil had given over most duties of the clan head's right hand to me while keeping special attention over the people we hired. If both Chase and Jade were to be saved, he would be the one to assign their responsibilities in the clan.

"I doubt we can make Chase do anything," Silvia mumbled. Chase was lying lazily on the bed we provided with his arms behind his head and a smirk on his face. I knew he was crazy before all this, but you'd think that he'd have a bit more sense given his experience with Silvia and the Order.

But no, he acted like this was all a game.

Jade, on the other hand, was a mess in her bunk. Whatever hardness she'd developed over the years had slowly been broken down. Her cheeks were tearstained and her eyes red, but she still somehow had enough energy to glare at us.

"What would be public enough?" I asked.

Ian rubbed the five o'clock shadow on his face and let out a hum.

"Your father enjoyed public lashings, if I'm not mistaken," he murmured. "Other clans may have them bow in front of their leader and ask for mercy, though that usually ends in a beheading."

Jade blanched while Chase just let out a bitter laugh.

"Silvia," Cain said in a pained voice.

She didn't look to him. Instead she took a step forward and crossed her arms.

"There are two things I require from the both of you," she said, speaking with a confidence that was nowhere to be seen a few moments ago. It made my chest clench. "Intel. The other is the public acknowledgment that you have come to accept me as your clan leader."

"Anything," Jade rushed out at the same time Chase let out another laugh.

"I have nothing to give you," Chase said. "And I doubt the witch does either. You think we were important to the Order? After they got Keir's blood, everything you knew went out the door. A handful of turned vampires turned to hundreds that *you* quickly started to massacre." He shook his head. "I lost my place in the latter months ago. You may have more than halved our numbers, but there are others who are far more important than I am."

I couldn't see Silvia's smile from where I was standing, but by Jade's flinch I could tell it must be pretty horrific.

"So you realize you're dispensable," she said. "Though I'm curious, why do you want to die so badly? Or is it that you hope *he*"—Silvia jutted her thumb behind her toward Knox, who watched over them with a somber expression—"would get sick of negotiating and just get revenge? Maybe you feel so bad about getting his brother killed that you hoped as soon as you attacked he would kill you."

"Reaching," Chase said with a huff.

"Maybe," Silvia continued. "Maybe you were never starving because of the Order. . . maybe you were starving yourself in hopes of getting killed when you joined the raid. You know, I never understood why the act, but maybe now I get it. Maybe you really didn't want to escape back then in the elevator, maybe you wanted me to bring you to Knox so he could get his revenge, and when that didn't work you did the only thing you could think of. Sold us out to the Order and hoped to die in the crossfire."

We were met with silence until it was broken by Chase's teeth grinding together.

"He did tell the truth about one thing though," Jade whispered. Silvia's gaze snapped to her. "They are hoarding the strongest trained vampires. I was there when he reported your moves to the Order *and* volunteered to go. They all knew he was no longer useful and were okay to use him as fodder, if only for a chance to bring you down. Though he severely undersold your numbers."

"Shut it," Chase snapped at the witch.

The sharp scent of magic rose in the air before two red bursts hit the bars that separated us and the prisoners. The magical barrier we had in place flashed before disappearing back into the ether. Silvia didn't even flinch.

"Play nice," Cain growled.

"He said you only took about ten to fifteen people on your raids," Jade continued. "He originally said he wanted twenty hunters. The Order doubled it."

Silvia nodded but didn't speak for a full minute.

"Why did you hide your aunt?" she asked.

Chase crossed his arms over his chest and cast his gaze to the floor. "I didn't want her to end up like my parents," he mumbled.

His admission stunned the crowd, and when no one spoke, he continued.

"She raised me while they were gone on missions," he said. "There were times where my parents would be gone for weeks, and then before they died, it was three months before I saw them again. She was everything to me, and if the Order knew about her. . . she wouldn't be the only one tortured for information."

"You could have told us," Isaac said. His sudden interjection caused my heart to race. I had almost forgotten he was there because he was so silent.

"I regret that I didn't," he admitted and looked his ex-leader in the eyes. "They ambushed us, the Order. They dragged us to an unknown location and injected me with blood while the witches held me down. By the time the pain had ended. . . it was already done. If I'd known we were so close to being next I wouldn't have gone, I swear."

The agony was clear on his face. Misguided as he may have been, I could understand him to some extent.

"My parents. . ." Silvia trailed off, her eyes shifting to Jade. I could feel the millions of questions just begging to be let out, but Silvia just settled on one. "What do you know about their rebellion?"

Chase's gaze fell to the floor while Jade picked at her nails.

"I only can piece together what I heard in passing," she said. "I may not have been that important, but because I was the one to help with the contract magic, I was taken around as a shadow to more meetings than I probably should've been."

"Just tell me whatever you think is important," Silvia said her voice turning soft.

"For all the enforcer's parents," she mumbled. "I don't know the details, but from what I gathered, they knew about the plan to start up the blood experiments again. After all, they were the ones killing clan heads and taking the blood, right? They had to have known what was going on."

"That didn't stop them from complying in the first place," Chase muttered. "They didn't blink twice when they filled our veins with vampire blood."

"I find it hard to believe that their parents would *willingly* hand them over to the Order for experiments," Jade hissed at Chase.

There was a moment of shared silence between the ex-hunters. I knew what they were thinking because I'd thought the same of my father.

A child would always try to believe in their parents. To them, they were idols who could do no wrong, people who would love and protect them no matter what. But when children grew up, they realized they too were just people. Many of them flawed as well.

So maybe, just maybe, they did hand over their children willingly at first, but when it became too much to bear they pulled back.

"Did they say anything about Jane?" Silvia asked in a whisper.

Jade shook her head. Chase cleared his throat.

"Just that it was a loss," he said. "I heard them murmuring about her and the other enforcers when I was undergoing my change, but I was too out of it to gain anything useful." He paused for a moment then added, "Sorry."

Silvia nodded then stood abruptly. "They will join the final raid," Silvia declared and turned to Ian. "That should work right? We can have a few people at their side, and once the clan sees them kill for us, they should accept them, right?"

Ian's pursed his lips before nodding slowly.

"It's a risk though," he said. "And not something I have ever seen done."

She nodded. "That's okay. We can try," she said, then looked to Knox. "You okay with that?"

Knox gave a short nod.

"Though I would like a moment," he said. "Alone. Completely."

Silvia looked over to Jade with her eyebrows pushed together.

"Cain, you're in charge of her," she said then added after a moment, "Jase, you follow them. Sorry, Cain."

"I understand," Cain said. There was a small bit of hope lighting his face.

Cain worked to pull Jade from her cell while Knox, Silvia, and I stayed.

"Get information about the current state of the headquarters," Silvia said to Knox as he stepped in front of the cell. "And the location of the armory. I think I know where it is, but I'm not sure."

Knox nodded. Silvia held out her hand for me. I took it eagerly and followed her out of the dungeon and back to the corridor of the main house.

"The other armories?" I ask with a raised brow.

She sent me a devilish smirk.

"Going out with a bang."

CHAPTER 27

SILVIA

S
moke surrounded us on all sides.

Just like Chase had promised, all the armories had been stocked full. It was quick work with over three hundred of our team members each targeting different locations. There were only six of them, but each held far more than we could imagine. It'd taken just under an hour for us to steal every single weapon and set them ablaze. We'd lost count of the hunter deaths, but only ten had surrendered.

The wind was strong from where we stood, and it threatened to deafen us. But even atop the second tallest building in the area was not far enough to drown out all of the sirens around the city.

Keir was to my left, Emery to my right. This was the one time I couldn't keep Keir away. The weight of her hand in mine was just what I needed to keep me tethered to this earth, and every single plan that we'd put in place started to come together.

Everything rode on this.

My eyes lingered on the tall black building that was now

defaced with random splatters of paint and a bright yellow banner that called the Order cowards.

The outside world had fallen into a panic over the last few months. Humans were scared mostly, some relieved, to see that all the clans were being "annihilated." The vampires who were not privy to what was happening had started to push the Order. Claiming that they were incompetent and had been focusing too long on the humans instead of protecting those they contracted out.

The rebels had helped us behind the scenes spread word of the Order's incompetence, and before we knew it, we'd turned them into the number one enemy.

The world had fallen into a chaos, and I couldn't help but revel in every single part of it.

"I bet they ran," Emery murmured. "As soon as they heard, they bolted."

I rolled my eyes and shoved her lightly. "We would have seen them."

"Or," Keir added with a smile, "they have tunnels."

Emery let out a snort. "Tunnels, really?"

Keir's smile only widened as she looked toward Emery. "You have any better ideas?" she asked.

I hushed them as my earpiece crackled.

"Team one is in place," Isaac said in a whisper.

I took a step forward, toward the edge of the building, and peered down and to the left to see Isaac and his team in the shadows of the building right across from the Order.

There were no hunters out today. All of them were either killed or now remained inside, protecting the valuables.

"Team two as well," Knox called. "Jade is accounted for."

They were on the ground as well, though I did not have eyes on them from our position.

"Team three is in place, and the target is locked," Jase said.

They were on a rooftop not far from us. They had a total of six people. Three for lookouts, three with small missile-like weapons that were small enough to hold in their hands yet powerful enough to take down a ship.

Courtesy of the Order.

"Team four is in place," Cain said. "Chase is accounted for."

They were surrounding the perimeter and also out of sight.

"Five, six, and seven?" I asked.

Three distinct voices came through. All of them were previously a part of the Order and had surrendered to us.

It was almost surprising how many of the people the Order caged hated them enough to join us in their downfall. Well. . . I guess I shouldn't be too surprised really. I'd been there as well. The Order shackled every one of us, stripped us of our will to fight, and turned us into unfeeling monsters with only one job.

It was just a matter of time before we turned it back to them.

Every moment had led up to this. Every punishment. Every death. Every cent they stole from us.

My mother, my father, Jane, and every other person who'd died because of the Order would be getting their revenge today.

I took a deep breath and squeezed Keir's hand.

"Are you ready?" I asked. "We have but three seconds to watch the show before we run."

"More than ready," Keir said and pulled my hand to her lips. "I'll be right behind you the entire time."

Emery cleared her throat.

"And I'll be behind her," she said. "If you even care, that is."

I let out a light laugh. "Always."

I took a deep breath and straightened my shoulders. For the last time I took in the Order. The black-paned windows reflected the world around it, but even as I squinted, I couldn't make out my reflection. Everything became warped, much like what the Order did to us on the inside.

"Counting down," I warned.

Each team sounded off and then slowly, I counted back from ten. My nerves were alight with an excitement I hadn't felt in a long time. There was fear there too, but it was overshadowed. Our team had this. There was nothing to fear.

"Three, two," I paused and took a deep breath. "*One.*"

There was a hollow-sounding thud before three high-pitched sounds echoed through the air. I could only describe them as something similar to a scream, though it was so haunting and deadly that I imagined it was what a banshee would sound like if they existed.

The missiles flew through the Order's dark windows. One on the second to last floor, another three floors below, and the last one on the two floors below that. All high enough to give the hunters who couldn't go above the thirtieth floor a chance to make a break for it, but a sure way to ensure that none of the council or higher-ups would escape.

Our teams were below, ready to corral the hunters as they fled and give them their final chance to escape.

I imagined the faces of those bastards on the council as their building burned. I imagined them screaming and panicking as they tried to run. It was enough to finally get some relief.

This would never undo the harm that they did to us. To me. To the hunters. To *Keir*. But it was enough to end *this* battle.

But as always, just as this battle ended, somewhere another began. Just because we cut off one of the Order's heads, doesn't mean the others would die as well, or that this one wouldn't grow back. There were buildings all over the country, and we wouldn't stop until we burned down every single one of them.

I would make sure of that with my last dying breathe.

It was in that moment, as I watched the burning building and held Keir's hand, that I realized maybe everything that had happened was meant to be.

I may not be the perfect clan leader, neither was Keir. . . but we did *this* together. If I had never taken that contract, if I had never killed her father, if I had never fallen for her. . . none of this would have happened.

As soon as the building started to crumble, it was our cue. We turned and ran out of there as fast as possible. We helped our teams as best as we could, but as soon as sirens sounded, we rounded up everyone into vans and made our way back home.

Later, I would look back on this moment and realize as we all drove in a tense silence that this would be the first battle of many we'd win. There would be many that we'd lose as well. Hunters who'd found a home with us would turn, others would perish in battle. But we always stayed strong.

We persevered no matter what, and this one win would be the start of it all. During that time, I felt that maybe this was the end, but that was far from the truth.

Regardless, I let the team enjoy. I let them rejoice and celebrated with them.

Because together, no matter what, we would make it out alive.

And we wouldn't just survive. . . we would *live*.

EPILOGUE

I would've thought that, after years of running a clan, I'd enjoy a crowd.

It was quite the opposite actually. I hated being the center of attention when I didn't have to be. I preferred standing on the sidelines, or lurking in the shadows, as opposed to being right in the center of everyone's attention.

But I guess that was what I'd do for love.

For the first time since I took over, Carpe Noctem would be holding an event.

And not just any event.

The banquet hall fell to a silence as Keir and I made our entrance. It was filled to the brim with people dressed in their finest clothes. Keir, Ian, Tobias, and everyone other clan head that had joined our clan since the start of the war against the Order. A few of the rest of the clan were invited as well, including Emery, Gil, Jade, Cain, and the enforcers.

All of them were toward the front of the banquet hall on either side of the long black aisle runner. The hall was dark, only lit by red candles that hung above us and at the end of the aisle.

The candles at the end of the aisle were on long black stems that were arranged in a semicircle. The wax had trailed down the stems and to the floor, perfecting the dark vampiric theme.

Tonight would be the night that Keir and I solidified our relationship. At least in royal vampire terms.

Over the years, there had been no question of our love together. Everyone knew, and we knew. That was what was important. There was no need for the outside to recognize what we were to each other because just being *together* was enough for us.

But sometimes, it was nice to celebrate something. Especially when I'd spent so long fighting it.

I snuck a peek toward Keir, and my breath caught in my throat when I saw her wide smile as she looked out at everyone. She'd worn a bodysuit not much different from the one I'd worn when I took over the throne. Her hair was slightly longer than it had been for most of the time that I'd known her and now went to the ends of her ears. She'd done slight waves in it, her bloodred diamond earrings peeking out whenever she turned her head.

When her gaze met mine, all the nervousness I was feeling disappeared.

This was why I was making the exception. She came to me one day with an idea. She'd been so hesitant to bring it up. Something I never thought I'd see with Keir. She'd always been brazen and spoken her mind around me, no matter the circumstance.

I watched as she deliberated in silence for days, and when she tried to bring it up, she would quickly close her mouth and retreat back into herself.

On the fourth day, I forced her to tell me.

A wedding.

"Are you ready?" she whispered and grabbed my hand.

I nodded with a smile. A genuine one. It didn't matter that in moments I would be drinking her blood in front of everyone, or that they would have to watch as we vowed our eternity together.

All that mattered was her.

I gripped her hand with one of mine and used the other to smooth down my dress. It was made of a flowy black material hemmed with lace. Matched with my red cloak that I'd only worn once before.

We walked together down the aisle. Heads bowed as we passed, and we sent small smiles in return. Each person murmured their blessings for our union as was customary.

The wax from the candles above had fallen over the black runner beneath our feet and lightly stung as we stepped on it.

Gil and Jase moved to meet us at the end, Gil with a golden cup in his hand. It was encrusted with rubies and sparkled in the dim light. The golden dagger that hadn't left my side since it had been gifted to me was in Jase's outstretched hands. They both bowed their heads when we reached them.

Keir took the cup and I took the dagger.

Unlike human ceremonies, the vampire one would be quick. Though afterward, there was no saying how long the celebration would last. Vampires would party through the night, celebrating the new couple until they were dizzy and intoxicated on blood.

Keir held out her hand for me.

"I, Keir, offer my blood to thee as a sign of my love and devotion," she murmured. Her eyes were lit with excitement. "I give thee my life, my flesh, my soul, so that we may become one."

I dragged the dagger along her palm. Blood fell quickly and began to fill the cup. I reached out with my free hand to help her hold it. Her eyes never left mine, not until her wound healed, and I handed her the dagger.

When I handed her my palm a wave of warmth ran through me. She looked as if I was offering her the best gift in the world.

This was not the first time that we'd shared blood, but it was the most important.

"I, Silvia, accept thy love and devotion and in return offer my blood to thee as a sign of my love and devotion," I repeated. She dragged the dagger down my palm, blood quickly filled my hand and fell into the cup. "I give thee my life, my flesh, my soul, so that we may become one only, never to be separated for the rest of eternity."

I took the cup as soon as my wound healed and kept her gaze as I drank half the contents. Keir's blood exploded across my taste buds and warmed my body. My own blood was mixed in there and left a spicy aftertaste on my tongue.

When I handed it to her, she threw it back, taking it in almost one gulp. When she was done she gave me a wicked smile, our blood staining her lips.

I couldn't help but return it.

The audience dropped to their knees, acknowledging the union, before springing up and clapping. I sought out Gil and Jase first. They were both clapping with small smiles on their faces. Gil's arm brushed across Jase's, who in turn leaned into the smaller man. Their relationship had been a surprise, and even though they hadn't made it public yet, I was ecstatic that they'd found something in each other.

Cain and Jade were next, the smaller girl was looking at us with tears in her eyes while Cain gave her an almost exasperated look but continued to clap.

Isaac, Knox, and Chase were next. I never thought of us as that close before, but seeing them here warmed my heart in a way I didn't expect.

I singled Emery out and gave her a smile. She met it whole-heartedly with one of her own. Even through it all she remained by our side. Not just as someone of power in the clan, but as a *friend*.

And then of course, Tobias was there, raising a glass full of blood he definitely was not supposed to have yet. Next to him were both Xin and Ian who were looking at us with soft smiles.

Even after everything, it was amazing the type of community we'd been able to build here. Through all the battles and running, we managed to stay strong and together.

In the end, it had been worth it.

I turned to Keir, my smile so big by then that my cheeks started to hurt. She leaned down and left a burning kiss to my lips before pulling away just enough so our eyes met.

"I love you, Silvia," she whispered.

Without missing a beat I said, "And I love you, Keir. Truly and more than life itself."

She gave me a devilish smirk. Her eyes lit up the same as they always did when I told her I loved her.

The memory of the first time I ever spoke the words was burned into my mind. It had been after the fall of the Order's headquarters. Everyone was celebrating, and of course Keir and I had snuck away for some privacy. I hadn't expected all the emotions I'd been carrying for the two years prior to come crashing down on me, but they had and the words were out before I could stop them.

I swear she didn't stop kissing me for days after.

"Keep it up and we will be ending this party soon," she threatened.

I gave her a pointed look and heat rose in my body. "Maybe that's the point."

She shook her head with a laugh and turned to the crowd. "Now we celebrate!"

There were cheers all around, and the crowd dispersed, looking for blood and food.

Keir stole another kiss before pushing us back down the aisle.

"Be good, little hunter," she whispered in my ear. Her breath wafted across my face and neck, causing a shiver to run down my spine. "I'm not done with you yet. If you were sick of me before, you will *loathe* me after this."

"I could never," I whispered back and pulled her back in for a kiss.

It'd been a long grueling journey to get to where we were now. Blood was spilled, clans had fallen, somedays it felt like this war would never end. . . but that didn't mean that we still couldn't find our own little happiness in the darkness of the world around us.

And for me that was Keir, and if the look on her face told me anything, I was that for her too.

ACKNOWLEDGMENTS

Keir and Silvia's story is finally over...

It has been years since I first started crafting this story and I cannot believe it is finally over.

I also cannot believe the love you have shown for this series. I tend to thank the readers a lot in my acknowledgement, and this one isn't any different.

Thank you so much to every one who gave the Blood Bound series a chance!

I also want to give a special shoutout to my partner and my writing friends who have sat through me complaining nonstop about editing this book.

Without you, I would have given up a while ago.

ABOUT THE AUTHOR

Elle is a California native who has lived in Los Angeles for most of her life. From the very start she has been in love with all things fantasy and reading. As soon as Elle found out that writing books was someone's career, she started writing stories. While the first ones were about scorned love and missed opportunities of lunchtime love, she has grown to love all things spicy and paranormal!

For more books like this visit ellemaebooks.com.

For updates on my release schedule and behind the scenes look follow my Instagram @ellemaebooks

Sign-up to my newsletter here https://view.flodesk.com/pages/615e296bf88d548e68f5c7bc for a free short!

For free shorts and NSFW art check out my Patreon! https://www.patreon.com/ellemaebooks

Printed in Great Britain
by Amazon

25509884R00170